SEP

W9-AHX-625

DISCARD

Date: 9/28/21

MYS CRAWFORD
Crawford, J. A.,
Jove Brand is near death /

PALM BEACH COUNTY
LIBRARY SYSTEM
3650 SUMMIT BLVD.
WEST PALM BEACH, FL 33406

JOVE
BRAND
IS NEAR
DEATH

JOVE BRAND IS NEAR DEATH

J. A. CRAWFORD

CamCat
Books

CamCat Publishing, LLC
Brentwood, Tennessee 37027
camcatpublishing.com

This is a work of fiction. Names, characters, places, and incidents are either products of the author's imagination or are used fictitiously.

© 2021 by J. A. Crawford

All rights reserved. Printed in the United States of America. No part of this book may be used or reproduced in any manner whatsoever without written permission except in the case of brief quotations embodied in critical articles and reviews. For information, address CamCat Publishing, 101 Creekside Crossing, Suite 280, Brentwood, TN 37027.

Hardcover ISBN 9780744301700
Paperback ISBN 9780744301786
Large-Print Paperback ISBN 9780744302370
eBook ISBN 9780744302691
Audiobook ISBN 9780744302936

Library of Congress Control Number: 2021933097

Cover and book design by Maryann Appel

5   3   1   2   4

To all the folks who ever knocked me around.

Thanks, I needed that.

And to my wife, who, when I was down for the count,

convinced me to go just one more round.

Introducing
Ken Allen

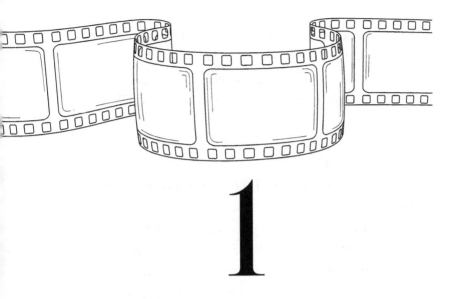

1

I WAS WAITING IN THE WINGS, STARING OUT AT A LIVE studio audience with seven million viewers behind them, and like everything that had ever happened to me worth mentioning, it was because of *Near Death*.

I looked good for my age, trim in my salmon blazer over a blue button-down and brushed-watercolor tie. Vintage Ken Allen, on the bare fringe of pop culture I occupied. For all intents and purposes, I was born in this outfit and had no doubt I would be buried in it. At least the jacket hid the wet patches under my arms.

"We might not even need you."

The executive producer was hoping for the best, but you didn't keep *Beautiful Downtown Burbank* running every Friday night for thirty years without preparing for the worst. Which was why they dug me up. If there was one thing I was good at, it was taking the hit. If the scene needed saving, I would make the perfect sacrifice.

"Keep an eye on the monitors. Come back when the house band wraps up."

It wasn't the most tactful way of telling me to get lost, but the guy had a lot on his mind.

"Just happy to be here," I told him. I'd been living a lie for eighteen years, why not keep it going?

I turned away from the stage that didn't want me and wandered around behind the scenes, following the pre-show progress on the countless monitors mounted in the halls and cramped dressing rooms, both dreading and praying they would need me.

On the far side of an open dressing-room door, a drop-dead gorgeous woman was doing her own makeup. I didn't mean to stare, but it was hard not to, with her making those getting-ready faces that, for whatever reason, I had always found hotter than anything a woman did after getting ready. She was glamorous in an evening gown that had Brand Beauty written all over it.

She caught me reflecting. "Yeah?"

"Sorry. Just killing time until someone tells me to go home."

"What are you here for? Like, who are you?"

I wasn't offended. All those fuses were blown long ago. I wasn't surprised either. *Beautiful Downtown Burbank* was known for its young cast.

"I'm nobody," I said. "But once upon a time, I was Jove Brand."

"No you weren't." She looked up to think, ticking off the timeline on her fingers. "First it was the mean guy— so hot— then the prissy guy, before Sir Collin."

"I was between the prissy guy and Sir Collin."

She didn't reply, but her face said it all. Claiming you were Jove Brand was too big of a lie. You'd be better off pretending you were an astronaut or had invented touch screens. I took my phone off airplane mode and typed *Ken Allen Near Death*. It knew what I wanted when I got to the *N* in *Near Death*.

The first image result was me, eighteen years ago, pointing a pistol at the camera. I was trying for tough but came off looking confused about how this lemon tasted.

Pretend Brand Beauty—though I suppose they were all pretend—snatched my phone and swiped through the sequence of images that all too accurately told my life story. She stopped on the one of me holding up a container of Kick-A-Noodles.

"Nice."

"A week's worth of sodium in one little can." It was one of the ten or so responses I had ready for one-time exchanges. Meet a hundred thousand people sometime and you'll develop a list too.

Brand Beauty handed my phone back with an appraising tilt of the head, trying to decide if she liked what she saw. She stroked the front of my salmon blazer. "This isn't from props."

"I brought my own."

"You got the look, kid," she said, giving my cheek a squeeze.

My blessing and my curse. "You can't get by on looks alone."

I stepped aside to let her pass. She turned back, just out of arm's reach. That was when I caught the act. Until then her performance had been flawless.

"I'm just screwing with you, Ken. Everyone is so hyped you made it. *Near Death* is such a piece of shit. I love it."

I didn't step on her exit. That girl was going places. I hoped they would be good ones. On the monitors, the cold open was crashing hard. The tension in the air said it all—Jove Brand was in the building, and the audience was restless for his entrance.

I reminded myself to breathe on the path back to stage right. Jove Brand almost ran me over, but I stepped aside in time. He walked onstage ready for action, the king of his jungle.

Bone dry under glaring, thousand-degree spotlights and 14 million eyeballs, Collin Prestor—sorry, *Sir* Collin Prestor—made a tuxedo look like casual wear. There was acting and there was acting and then there was being able to control when you sweat. Whether it came with British blood or was the product of a Shakespearean theater pedigree I would never know. Lawndale, California, wasn't exactly London, England.

The audience went wild. The world's most famous fictional superspy stood before them. Women wanted him. Men wanted to be him. And Jove Brand was about to announce his chosen successor to the waiting world.

That successor now stepped from the shadows to stand beside me in the wings, waiting for his grand entrance. Niles Endsworth would be the next Jove Brand. He bore the same label as his predecessor, but of modern vintage, with a body sculpted by a strict regimen designed to produce a physique like a special effect. I couldn't fault Niles. He was just giving today's audience what they demanded in a hero.

Despite everything Niles had on his mind, I rated a second glance. He had been expecting the Ken Allen of eighteen years past, an image imprisoned in cinematic infamy. The kid was a good actor. He was almost able to mask his disappointment.

When his cue came, Niles snapped to the present and rushed to join his predecessor on stage. The merest sheen of perspiration betrayed the junior man's anxiety. His calculated display won the audience over. They'd be freaking out too, if they had been chosen to be the next Jove Brand. But the next Jove Brand would also have the nerve to mask it.

The two Brands, old and new, discussed the perks of playing an icon of fiction. You wore tailored clothes while driving luxury vehicles to exclusive locales. You could kill anyone who annoyed you. You always got the girl, who either conveniently died or disappeared between escapades. They played their roles to the hilt, master and apprentice. The production assistants could have ditched their cue cards and snagged a sandwich for all the good they were doing.

The problem was no one laughed. The part of Jove Brand had never been cast based on comedic chops. Fault for the only farcical portrayal of the character landed squarely on me and no one was looking to repeat that mistake. Sir Collin and Niles were gifted the perfunctory chuckles any incredibly attractive person with half a sense of humor scores, but the audience rapidly cooled as the initial rush of watching two Jove Brands together faded.

Beautiful Downtown Burbank's executive producer white-knuckled his headset, waving me toward the stage like it was a live grenade in need of a warm body. *This is what you're here for, isn't it?*

Yes, yes it was.

A life lesson: Go at whatever you're dreading full tilt. Sprint right into it. The worst thing that could happen was the entire world got to witness the train wreck for time eternal. That your epic failure would become an object lesson studied—literally—in college courses. That you became a walking punch line.

It really wasn't so bad.

I exploded onto the stage with a butterfly twist, transitioning into a flurry of fancy kicks, battling through a horde of unseen foes toward Sir Collin and Niles. I kept the phantom attacks wide and slow to ensure the audience could follow along. This was all on me. I'd choreographed the sequence myself, drawing from an arsenal of techniques made instinctual through decades of dogged repetition. If you had enough tenacity, you could fool people into believing it was talent.

I hit my mark an arm's length from the two Brands. Right on the bull's-eye. My surprise appearance had shocked the audience into complete silence. A small section of the crowd hooted, then the hoots built to applause and my heart started up again. Some of them were ringers but the rest sounded like my demographic— hipsters in the know.

I stretched the moment, resting my hands on my thighs as if I had come a long way. Pretending to catch my breath let me avoid eye contact not only with the audience but also with the two men who were arguably my contemporaries.

Sir Collin and Niles turned to face the interloper who had fought his way into their conversation. The consummate pro, Sir Collin held his expression through the cheers, freezing the scene for as long as it had legs. Meanwhile, my stomach explored heretofore unknown depths. When the crowd quieted, the time had come for me to deliver my first line.

"Sorry, my good men," I panted. "Bike broke down. Asian imports, you know?"

It was a good thing I was supposed to sound breathless. My American-*cum*-British accent was atrocious. I could have done better, but who wanted that?

It didn't get a huge laugh, but the audience members in on the joke lost their minds. No one wrote for the audience anymore, anyway. They wrote for the internet, for the bloggers, the tweeters, and the streamers. They let the fans explain the references in postmortem. There was nothing like free labor, and no one worked as hard as someone made to feel smart.

"How *did* you get in here?" Sir Collin asked. Stressing the *did*, not the *you*, kept the question at the appropriate level of condescending. Considering the audience's reaction to my appearance, it was the right choice.

"Who is he?" Niles asked.

Sir Collin moved to block the younger man's view. "No one worth remembering. Now, as I was saying, a gentleman shoots only once, and never first."

I stepped out from behind Sir Collin to add, "But he chops as many throats as required."

Don't ask me why, but that's when I ad-libbed. Not a line, not on live television—I'm not a monster. I offered an unplanned hand to Niles, who furtively extended his own in return. As we were about to touch, I turned my shake into a knife-hand aimed at his Adam's apple. Niles hopped back, genuinely shocked. I threw him a wink and a nod, my eyes a little crazy.

The big screens facing the audience had been playing a *Near Death* highlight montage from the moment I crashed the sketch. Now that everyone was in on the joke that was Ken Allen, the entire studio erupted in laughter at my action and Niles's reaction. It was a dizzying level of hot onstage. I reminded myself to not lock my knees.

Sir Collin moved between us again, precise in rhythm and position. The stage was his native turf, the sacred ground he retreated to when he wasn't playing a super-spy. He was fighting for Niles's attention now.

"He always looks his foe in the eyes."

The strain in Sir Collin's voice projected concern his successor was learning all the wrong lessons.

"Then gouges them!" I interrupted, darting my fingers at Niles like a striking snake. I mimed a second, goofier gouge as Sir Collin put an arm around my shoulders. He turned our backs to Niles for a confidential moment as we switched cameras, me and Sir Collin and the millions watching at home.

"Ken, old boy, I'm trying to impart some wisdom on the lad," Sir Collin said. "You understand, don't you?"

Trust me, I did. Sir Collin had starred in six Jove Brand movies over fifteen years, each more successful than the last. If anyone could speak with authority on how to play Brand, it was him. He was so authentic, so genuine, it made me want to leave. But that wasn't the scene.

I hoped my attempt at a wide-eyed, thoughtful nod conveyed understanding. "Oooh. Sorry about that, Sir Collin." I forgot to use my crappy British accent, but breaking character fortuitously worked for the scene. The audience roared at every beat. Opening monologues were tough pitches to hit, and the writers had knocked this one out of the park.

"There's a good man." Sir Collin gave me a pat I liked a little too much before turning to again address Niles. "Now, when a lady demurs—"

"Chop gently, but firmly," I interrupted again, "right where—"

Sir Collin silenced me with a no-look elbow—a short, tight shot, measured to be effective but not punitive. His gentlemen's strike sent me airborne. I managed a full rotation from a dead stance and hit the stage flat with a resounding thud. Not trusting myself to appear unconscious, I buried my face in the crook of my arm.

The crowd cheered while Sir Collin adjusted his cuffs. "And there you have it."

He assured the audience they had a great show lined up, though when he announced the musical guest, it was apparent Sir Collin had no idea who they were. When they cut to commercials, I hopped up as the stagehands broke down the set for the next sketch.

The executive producer flagged me down with one arm while pumping his fist with the other. He wasn't in the best shape and the effort turned his face red. "You killed it. Don't go anywhere. Prestor is a dud. We might work in a callback."

I froze, trying to process this as the producer stomped off to put out the next fire. He said two things I hadn't heard in a long time: that I'd done a good job and that I should hang around. I snapped back to reality and headed toward the green room. Niles Endsworth was there, sipping a sparkling water. Hydrating, but not overhydrating. You never knew when you were going to have to take your shirt off.

I shot Niles a friendly, wide-eyed nod as if to say *Crazy, huh?* but I don't think he saw me. He looked like he was beginning to grasp what it meant to be Jove Brand, his eyes flicking back and forth like he was watching different versions of his future unfold on the monitors.

I could relate.

"Hey! Ken! Ken Allen!"

I knew who it was without having to look. Layne Lackey, owner and operator of JoveBrandFan.com, the number-one place for everything Jove Brand on the web. Layne Lackey, equal parts savior and devil.

"Ken, it's Layne Lackey. From JoveBrandFan.com, the number-one—"

"Layne! How're ya!?" I spread my arms for a hug and Layne took a step back. There was nothing like overenthusiasm when it came to setting someone on their heels. "You afraid of doorways?"

"Pass excludes the green room," Layne replied, dangling his lanyard. "Can I get a shot of you and Niles Endsworth for the site?"

A glance back told me Niles would rather drink from the tap than perform fan service right then and there.

"Producers need Niles for promo crap." I stepped to block Layne's line of fire. Niles slipped past us as if he were late for something. Become an actor and never get work. Become a star and never stop acting.

"You were great, Ken." Layne always used your name, like he had to constantly confirm to himself he was really talking to you.

"We'll let trending decide." I guided Layne away from the backstage chaos of live television. "That and my convention take. I have an appearance in Fresno coming up."

"Already plugged it on the site," Layne said. "The platinum pistol is going to be there too. Well, one of the five originals."

"Double billing." I was able to keep most of the salt out of my tone. "Sounds like they're starting up again."

"I'll catch the replay," Layne said, adjusting the settings on too much camera. "I'm going to run Niles down and ask if he's ever thought about doing conventions."

I didn't wish him luck.

The Brand Beauty was on the monitors in a sketch where she brazenly threw herself at Sir Collin, who was more interested in the strapping bartender. He killed it but got few laughs. Sir Collin was simply too understated for the American audience.

I winced at the screen. Watching other people bomb struck my most tender places. It was an empathy thing. I sought solace in

Sir Collin's dressing room, telling myself it was out of everyone's way, but that was just me telling myself. The truth was, I wanted to sit in his chair.

I wasn't bitter. Sir Collin deserved everything he'd earned. His Brand movies really were better than the early ones, though the lens of nostalgia kept the fans from acknowledging it. His performances helped restore the series to the juggernaut it had been in the sixties and seventies. I wanted to be Sir Collin the way I had once wanted to play guitar in Nirvana. The ability was simply beyond me. It was a pipe dream—only it wasn't. I had been Jove Brand, once.

But *Near Death* was indeed a piece of shit.

"Harsh lights, wouldn't you say?"

Sir Collin's voice was purely chummy, but it launched me out of his chair.

"Sorry, Sir Collin." When in doubt, it was best to come clean. "Guess you caught me."

Sir Collin waved my apology off as he came over to stand with me at the dressing table. "Of all the moments we spend in the light, these are the ones I dread the most. Having to face myself, every flaw exposed."

He was right. His age showed in the bulb-bordered mirror. Jove Brand was not a young man, but he could never be an old one. Four walls and two generations away, the musical guest kicked in as if on cue. If anyone deserved accompaniment, it was Sir Collin.

"You saved me out there. Thanks, old boy."

"I don't have range, but I know my role," I replied.

"I didn't want to do this, you know," Sir Collin said. "Every time such an offer is tendered, I tell myself it's more money for the troupe, to put on the shows we want. Being Jove Brand has given my fellows a life on the stage."

I'd read as much but took it for PR until that moment. "Same here. But I did want to be a great Jove Brand. Problem was, I did my best."

Sir Collin laughed as he rested his hands on my shoulders. "Without your film, I would not be here, and the fifty men and women I support would have been forced to abandon their dreams. Tonight, you again displayed a true player's spirit, putting the show before the man."

It was the nicest thing anyone had said to me in eighteen years. I lost my voice. I couldn't even look at Sir Collin.

"Now if you'll excuse me, I'm off to sneak a drag or two before my next sketch," Sir Collin said. I managed a nod as he gave me a last squeeze and left me in reflection.

Going purely on appearance, I was the spitting image of Jove Brand as described in the books. The passionless killer. The distant lover. Tall and pale, with light blond hair and ice-blue eyes. A face and body reminiscent of renaissance sculpture. But sculpture didn't come to life, which also accurately described my acting.

I looked more the part now. Eighteen years ago I was eighteen years too young, but casting had been tight. *Near Death*'s entire pre-production took place on a flight from Kiev to Hong Kong. Had the internet of today existed then, my tender age would have caused the same uproar it did with Niles Endsworth now. A combination of professional discipline and CGI smoothing had sustained Sir Collin for a spell, but his time had come. Soon he would meet his fate—most likely during a pre-credit sequence—and the alias of Jove Brand, Royal Gamesman, would be passed to Niles.

The executive producer burst into the dressing room, breaking my self-indulgent reverie.

"I didn't do it, I swear," I said.

"Where the hell is Sir Collin?"

The executive producer bent over to rest his hands on his knees. The dash to the dressing room had left him about a burpee away from a heart attack. I checked the monitors. The *Beautiful Downtown Burbank* regulars were dying on stage as they fumbled through a cut sketch.

"He left like five minutes ago," I said to his back.

I trailed after him, hunting for one of the most recognizable faces in the world. The EP was coordinating the show and the search simultaneously through his headset. "Go to break while we set up the house band. I don't care. Wait—the national anthem. It makes everyone clap."

We checked the coatroom, then the coke room, but found no sign of Sir Collin. The EP leaned against the wall to stay on his feet. "A-listers," he wheezed.

He was worried about the show, but I was worried about Sir Collin. Stage royalty didn't miss their mark. Sir Collin did not require an understudy. Sir Collin was his own stand-in. Then I remembered.

"He went to smoke."

The EP almost bowled me over reversing course, but when we hit the stairs up to the roof I overtook him, ascending the flights in bounds, ignoring the handrail as I regulated my breath. While I came off as having Asperger's in reflective close-up, I owned interval cardio. I hip-checked the door, expecting resistance, but it blasted open. Instinct forged by thirty years on the mat sent my forearm up to block the backswing.

The bare bulb above the doorway cut into the night sky. Sir Collin was on his knees at the edge of the light, clutching at his collar. The asthmatic EP had me thinking heart attack.

Then I saw the bloody pits where Sir Collin's eyes should have been.

"I got you," I said, reaching for where he was groping.

It wasn't his collar he was looking to open. It was his airway. Sir Collin's Adam's apple was crushed, his throat swollen past his jawline. I tore his shirt open, spraying buttons everywhere. He was turning blue. His state triggered uncomfortable flashbacks. It was happening all over again, and all over again I was helpless to stop it. I forced him onto his back and rifled through his pockets, praying he was a cigar smoker.

The EP finally caught up. When he saw Sir Collin, he coughed up a string of curses.

My heart plunged when I found a case of custom gold-banded cigarettes. "You got a knife?"

Sir Collin was gulping air like a fish out of water. The EP wasn't doing much better. I jumped to my feet and patted him down.

"Call 911. Do you carry a knife?"

"Why . . . why . . ."

Near Death and everything it cost flashed before my eyes.

"This isn't the first time I've run into this. We need to cut his airway open."

The rooftop was an island fifteen stories high. I scanned the area, hoping for a tool box, but didn't spot so much as a door stop. The neighboring building had a broken window, but the glass shards were out of reach. I dodged knocking heads with the EP and yelled down the stairs for medical.

All the while Sir Collin was drowning on dry land, kicking and clawing at the gravel. I tilted his head in an attempt to open his airway to no avail. There was nothing else left but to talk to him. I took my lines straight from cliché.

"Hold on. Stay with me, Sir Collin."

His lips were moving, mouthing the same windless word over and over, but I couldn't make out what word. I wish I could say Sir Collin went peacefully, but he fought until the end, groping and scratching, gasping and pleading.

Sir Collin Prestor died in my arms on that rooftop, his eyes gouged out and his throat crushed.

Just like the villain at the end of *Near Death*.

2

THE COPS SHOWED NO MERCY TO CRAFT SERVICE. Anything edible bore a partial set of prints, minimum. I'd idled in a state of low-level hunger my entire adult life, but right then my stomach was howling out for fatty protein. Loud enough for my interviewer to hear.

"That you, Allen?"

State Special Crimes Investigator Ava Stern was a top-cop casting dream, built like a fitness model and overflowing with New York attitude. Methodically disheveled in no-makeup makeup, she balanced competence with apathy. Everyone in This Town was playing a part. Such was the nature of the place. Play a part long enough and eventually you became it.

"Yeah," I apologized.

"It goes one of two ways. You either lose your appetite or find it—" Stern paused to make eye contact "—when it comes to murder."

Sir Collin Prestor, celebrated star of the stage and screen, had been murdered. No matter how many times I repeated the thought, I couldn't absorb it.

"Let's run through it again," Special Investigator Stern said. "And remember, you aren't under arrest."

"I know," I said, then retold the events beginning from my encounter with Sir Collin in the dressing room. The next time through Stern backed me up to start from my performance onstage. Then she put the interview on shuffle, skipping ahead, doubling back, repeating herself. I was theorizing Stern had ADHD when it dawned on me: She was trying to trip me up. It didn't bother me because I didn't do it. I had nothing to hide. I liked Sir Collin. I wanted to help catch his killer.

That's how stupid I was.

I only left out one detail. The one that made me look guilty: Sir Collin was killed exactly how the Big Bad went out in *Near Death*. As crazy as it sounded, it couldn't be a coincidence. A coincidence was two guys with the same name getting hit by the same type of car. It was not getting your eyes carved out and throat crushed before dying in the arms of the guy who did it in a movie eighteen years earlier.

"Okay," Stern said. She rubbed her forehead to show she was thinking, but not hard enough to actually stretch her skin. You didn't spend all that time moisturizing to go around pulling on your face. "You going anywhere?"

For an airheaded instant I thought Stern was asking me out. Then I realized as the last person to see Sir Collin alive, I was the prime suspect. There had been plenty of time for me to do the deed while the EP was crawling up the stairs.

Stay calm, Ken, I thought. While you do have blood on your hands, you do not have eyeball juice, or whatever it was called. "I'm in Fresno next weekend for a con."

"Fresno is fine," Stern replied. "But stay in the state. You're a witness."

Stern played it well, leaning close and employing a confidential tone to let me know we were on the same side. I wondered if she always wanted to be a cop or had fallen short in a quest for the big screen. She could have passed for thirty, but in This Town a woman had to look twenty-two.

I faced the rising sun with an empty stomach and blood on my clothes. At least until forensics showed up to seize everything I was wearing. Props sent over some replacements. The EP knew better than to talk to me. Instead he threw me half-suspicious, half-apologetic glances while no doubt calculating the ratings bump *Beautiful Downtown Burbank* would get off airing Sir Collin Prestor's final performance.

I made it to my car without being detained and dug the hand sanitizer out of my gear bag. It was terrible for your skin but I didn't skimp. There's no evidence, I told myself, because you didn't do it. I tried not to think about all the based-on-true stories where innocent people died in prison. If they came after me, I didn't have the fame, influence, or wealth to defend myself. No one stopped me when I started the engine. No one jumped on my hood as I drove off.

I was home in fifteen minutes and in the shower for an hour, scrubbing every trace of Sir Collin away. Everything in me wanted to go hide under the covers, but that tactic never got me anywhere.

So I made my smoothie a double, running the net carbs twice to be sure, and drank it in the car on the way to my scheduled session. My clients often kept me waiting, but the other way around was professional suicide. Trainers were a dime a dozen in This Town, though my schtick rated two bits: Fight with Jove Brand himself.

For the first time in three years the gate guard called up to confirm access. Word had gotten out. The first cancellation would get the ball rolling. If they didn't catch Sir Collin's killer and fast, I was headed from the D-list to the blacklist. I parked in the sub-level garage between the rest of the help's vehicles and the riding mowers. My guest code still worked, so that was something.

Of all the things they possessed worth envy, REDACTED's private gym was at the top of my list. There was enough mat to sponsor a gymnastics team, a bag for every practical purpose, and a buffet of functional resistance equipment. The space had good air flow without a hint of chlorine from the pool next door. Opposite of said pool were float and cryo tanks. It was my dream gym, down to the choice of towels. This was no coincidence. I had designed it at REDACTED's request.

I moved through a stretch sequence also of my creation, getting loose without breaking a sweat. If you wanted to keep this gig, you could never appear to be working harder than a client. These were people who lived in a state of constant, brutal comparison. Framing yourself as competition was filling out your own pink slip.

The dark cloud that had occupied the airspace above my head for eighteen years thundered to life. Would Sir Collin's death spark renewed interest in the darkest chapter of Jove Brand lore? There was no digging into *Near Death*, I told myself. Its skeletons were buried a continent away, eighteen years deep. And, if I had any say, it was going to stay that way.

I unfocused, slipping into meditative space as techniques flowed on autopilot, chaining in combinations internalized by a lifetime of study. It didn't keep me from replaying Sir Collin's last breaths over and over.

What had he been trying to say?

REDACTED broke my trance. "Wow, show me that one."

"Sure. I was warming it up for you," I lied.

I ran REDACTED through the motions a step at a time. REDACTED had studied dance alongside acting, so it was easier. In actuality, that's what screen fighting was—a sequence of movements performed in time with one or more partners. The more steps you could string together without stopping, the better. If Ginger Rogers were alive today, she'd be a huge action star.

"After the spin, you want the audience to know it's really you," I explained. "When you snap your head around, that's your expression moment."

I played camera while REDACTED went through the sequence again.

"Slower. Perfect. Now instead of intense, try confidently amused."

REDACTED nailed it this time, smirking as they stuck the landing.

"That's it," I said, punching my opposite palm. "That's your hero shot."

REDACTED gave me an innocent, big-eyed smile known the world over. They followed it with their signature pout when I said, "Okay, let's do some work."

REDACTED was leaning up for filming, so I put them through intervals, hitting the muscle groups evenly to maintain proportion and symmetry. Then we spent an hour on the mat. REDACTED liked a little contact—on me, not them—but I didn't mind getting hit. Hope sprung I was going to get away clean, but during the cooldown they started asking questions.

"So you were you really with him when he died?"

It was such a This Town way of asking: half-challenge and half-disbelief. I had spent the entire workout formulating my answer, rehearsing a blend of frightened and earnest.

"I'm not sure what I can say, with the cops and network. I don't want to get sued."

If there was anything a famous person could relate to, it was a lawsuit. My guess how REDACTED would reply was right on the money.

"Oh, I'm not going to tell anyone, Ken. This is just for me."

Baloney. REDACTED would be relaying every word, with their own embellishments, to their nutritionist within the hour. I was walking a tightrope. If I didn't give them what they wanted, I would be fired. If I did, word would get out I couldn't keep my mouth shut. I was good at my job, but I wasn't special. This Town was bursting with boutique services. There were a thousand stuntmen who would have gladly thrown me off a roof to take my place. It was time for PR rule number one: Get ahead of the story.

"I can't. I might be a suspect."

REDACTED ate it up. "Oh my God, juicy. I'm going to text you my ghostwriter's number. Like right now. Trust me, there's stuff you're going to forget you'll wish you remembered later."

I had no doubt said ghostwriter would be sending their drafts REDACTED's way. "Oh wow, that's awesome, thanks! Time for your post-workout."

REDACTED ran off to meet with their nutritionist-slash-dealer and I was out the door unscathed, my workday done. Expanding my client base would only cost me money. The more exclusive I was, the more I banked. When I started private sessions, I made the mistake of charging too little. Missy Cazale, who always had been and always would be smarter than me, straightened me out. Her advice earned me a living. Chalk up another addition to the tally of things I could never pay her back for, starting with *Near Death*.

Sitting in traffic on the drive home lulled me into a trance. My thoughts drifted on their own accord. What would Sir Collin's death mean for the Jove Brand franchise? Eighteen years ago, the three of us had saved it: Missy, me, and above all, Kit. Two of us were still paying the price. Kit paid with his life.

I cranked the AC and slapped myself awake. Always keep it as cold as you could stand it. Maintaining your core temperature burned calories. It also helped me keep alert. Eight hours had passed since Sir Collin died in my arms. By now there were sure to be cameras on my condo.

To my shock Layne Lackey wasn't parked on my curb. Instead there were two broadcast vans, engines idling and dishes deployed. I timed the garage door opener to allow me to drift inside without braking. Too fast looked guilty, too slow could be interpreted as an invitation. I didn't want to appear to be fishing for an interview, because I sure as hell wasn't.

I made sure no one slipped under the overhead door before checking the other doors and windows. I needed to straighten up. The vultures were going to break in the first chance they got. Didn't want people thinking Ken Allen was born in a barn. I intended to sit down for five minutes.

A pounding at the door woke me up six hours later. I didn't even get up to pee. Considering my age and the amount of water I drank, that was saying something.

The peephole put Special Investigator Ava Stern in perspective, making her appear both close and far away. My first instinct was to let her knock. If she had a warrant, she would have kicked in the door by now. But the vans parked on the street were recording, so I let her in before the press could report I was refusing to talk to the police.

Stern nodded toward the vans as she closed the door. "You're drawing flies."

"They do love this crap. Gotta hit the bathroom. Lock the door, would you?"

I turned my back on her and headed down the hallway. She would poke around, but there was nothing to find, which was maybe worth a few points in the *Ken Allen Is Not the Killer* column. My bladder was halfway empty when I caught the cracked door in the mirror.

"Want to check before I flush?" I asked.

"That and the toilet tank," Stern replied.

"You won't find any gear. I don't use it or move it."

"I could care less, Allen."

It was a believable enough lie. This Town ran on illegal performance enhancers and thermogenics. In the general sense Stern didn't care, but in the specific one a drug charge would give the cops cause to shake my condo through a sifter. Should they find evidence of murder during said search . . . well what a happy accident that would be.

I didn't bother with a shirt. Stern couldn't suspect a concealed weapon if there was nowhere to conceal one. "Water, coffee, low-carb smoothie?"

"Gluten free?"

"You roll this place, you won't find a gluten."

"Then sure," Stern said.

I slammed sixteen ounces of water before starting on our smoothies, gathering everything I needed slow and easy with both hands in view at all times. Stern stood on the far side of the half-wall countertop, which didn't quite hide her holster. In any other place she would have been tall, but here she was average height.

Funny thing about This Town: Its giants lacked stature. Talent could be measured by the formula of success over inches. The farther a guy was from six feet while still being on top, the more impressive his résumé would be. That was for men. For women, it was years over twenty-five instead of inches under seventy-two.

Stern was around my age and three fingers under my height. She didn't have kids. Not with those lustrous locks—all hers, no extensions—which were a red that didn't work on camera. Her eyebrows and skin tone confirmed it was her natural color. The faint lines around her eyes and corners of her mouth were signs she hadn't had much work done. And no one would have chosen a nose with so much character. It would have pigeonholed you right from the start.

My first impression was Stern displayed the right amount of effort: enough to care without looking like an experiment in cybernetics. To be fair, this was coming from a guy who was about to have back-to-back liquid meals. Still, the subject merited further study.

Stern wrapped up her evaluation the same time I got done with mine, me pretending to be focused on blending the smoothies and her pretending to give a hoot. I wasn't about to speak first. I didn't have anything to say and had also spent enough time in Asia to know not to break the silence. She took me setting her smoothie on the half-wall as a sign.

"I have some questions." Stern watched my reaction as she took her first drink. "There's no sugar in this?"

"I know what I'm doing."

"The EP says he didn't pass anyone coming down the stairs," Stern said.

"That's not a question."

"Did anyone pass you on the stairs?"

I shook my head.

"You sure?"

"I would have noticed."

"Yeah, it's a tight squeeze." Stern took another drink. She looked at the glass this time, like I was playing some kind of smoothie prank on her. "Heard you vaulted right up them."

"Sir Collin disappeared during a live broadcast. I was worried about him."

"Worried? Why?" Stern leaned in slightly, interested for the first time.

"Sir Collin was a theater guy. If he missed the call, something was wrong."

"You and him close?"

"The only conversation we ever had was minutes before in his dressing room." I stared Stern straight in the eyes and told the truth. "I liked Sir Collin. I didn't kill him."

"I didn't say you did," Stern replied. She was into the smoothie, despite herself, and stopped for more. "I spent my sack time learning all about Ken Allen."

"Always nice when a beautiful woman thinks about you in bed." The words rushed out before I could stop them. Who knows where they came from? Too many movies, maybe. Or maybe I hoped Stern would interpret my frivolity as a sign of innocence. Either way, she didn't budge an inch.

"I wanted to know, why you? For Brand, I mean."

"Try JoveBrandFan.com," I suggested.

"I did."

"Then you know I wasn't the first pick."

"Yeah, the first choice overdosed," Stern said, "making you the only guy in Hong Kong who fit Brand's description."

Stern left out that my also-ran died in the Ukraine, while I was in China. Still, it left me defensive. "Rumor has it same thing happened with Niles Endsworth. Sir Collin's first successor committed suicide. Revealing Niles Endsworth on live television was damage control."

"If Layne Lackey is to be believed."

Taking a drink slowed my reply, but I had to get the mixture down before the oil in it separated. "As much as I hate to admit it, Lackey knows what he's doing. If he wasn't obsessed with Jove Brand he could be a real journalist."

"Being a big-time martial arts expert must have helped your chances, way back when."

"Placing third in forms didn't exactly make me Chuck Norris."

"Third is something, for a white guy in Hong Kong." Stern tilted her glass to toast me. "And you kept it up. Ken Allen, Sensei to the Stars."

I chugged the remainder of my smoothie. "My clients get to say Jove Brand trains them. I get to keep in fighting shape for a living."

"That's the thing, isn't it?" Stern commented. "There's stage fighting and there's real fighting. JoveBrandFan.com says you're legit. Beat up an MMA pro in a bar three years back."

There was no point in denying it. That was the thing about fighting: Tell people you're good and you're full of yourself. Tell people you're not and you're humble-bragging.

"It was a juice bar, and I wasn't charged with anything. Also, he ended up in prison over what he did to that barista."

"It helped that someone put the video online. You rolled right over him."

I went to the sink to rinse out my glass. "Do something long enough, you get good at it."

"How good?"

I scoped Stern's casual but loaded stance, the state of her hands, forearms, and elbows. The fit of her slacks. The way her sidearm was holstered and its oversized trigger guard. Everything matched what I had guessed about her background.

"Good enough to know you do Krav Maga."

Stern skipped a beat, her mouth open. It was the first genuine expression I got out of her.

"That's pretty good."

The compliment bounced right off me. Stern set down her empty tumbler and turned toward the living room. I washed her glass right away to keep from having to scrub it later. When I joined her, she was studying my shelves.

"Movie buff," Stern said. She was leaning forward a little, her jacket concealing whether her hand was on her service weapon.

"No more than anyone else in This Town."

"Lots of noir."

I couldn't help but laugh. "You think I've been taking murder lessons?"

"You wouldn't be the first." Stern kept her left side—the side opposite her weapon—toward me. She traced the disk cases with the same hand, keeping it high in the event she had to clear or brace.

"All the other Brand films, but no *Near Death*."

"If you saw it, you'd know why." I sat down because there were no good places to stand. Stay on her left and I was blocking the door. Join her and I was inside her safety zone.

"I started it in the car," Stern said. "Don't tell me how it ends."

"You're watching it because you already know how it ends." I kept my hands in my lap. Not behind my head or on the back of the couch or anywhere else where I could produce an Uzi.

"I got it spoiled for me last night," Stern admitted. "Kind of grisly for my tastes."

"Mine too, but *Near Death* was filmed right before the wirework revolution. The more graphic stuff was in back then. Tight-shot limb breaks, all that jazz. Kit Calabria asked me to come up with a finish with two beats. One move, space for a one-liner, then another move." I shrugged with my palms up. "I was young."

"Kit Calabria was the producer?"

What the hell was wrong with me? Why was I putting Kit on Stern's radar? "And writer and director. His family owns the film rights to Jove Brand."

"Didn't he die before *Near Death* was released?" Stern wasn't writing anything down, which told me this wasn't news to her.

"His plane crashed, right after he delivered the reels." The thing about old lies was that after a while, they felt like the truth. Sounded like it, too.

"But that final sequence was your idea?"

"Guilty," I confessed. There was no point denying it. Along with the leading role in *Near Death*, I was also credited as fight choreographer. "But the sequence isn't realistic. You know as well as I do there are more efficient techniques."

"Yeah," Stern replied. She was checking for dust, noting what I'd recently watched. She stopped to read the back of the latest

Niles Endsworth action vehicle. I really should have cleaned. "The killer must have wanted to make a statement."

"There are also less messy ways," I said, holding up my hands.

Stern looked past my hands at the rest of me. "Sir Collin rough you up? In his confusion, I mean."

I should have put a shirt on after all. "I had a private session this morning. My client likes to play rough."

Stern nodded absently as she looked around the room. "You into memorabilia?"

"I do the convention circuit. Comic books, pop-culture shows. Take photos, sign stuff."

"There money in that, for a guy at your level?"

"I don't do it for the accolades. Anyway, people like to give you presents. If the fans found out you were selling or throwing stuff out, they'd revolt. It sort of piles up."

"All Jove Brand related?"

"What else would it be? Model White Stags, replica Quarrelers, custom action figures. Some guy gave me a disturbingly photorealistic painting of me and Missy Cazale, sans clothing. You'd think he would have emphasized Missy, but I'm definitely the focus of the composition."

For the first time in a while, Stern stopped to study me. "How about gloves?"

I didn't like where this was going. "Gloves?"

"That's one of those things, isn't it? Tropes or whatever. Like how Jove Brand always puts on gloves before the big chase scene."

"If you did motorcycle stunts you'd wear gloves too," I replied.

"Anyone ever give you gloves?"

I searched my memory before answering. This was one of those moments you saw on true-crime shows. The suspect said no, he'd never worn gloves in his life, then later it's revealed he had an extensive mitten collection. "In six years? I don't know, maybe. I'd have to check."

"I could help you look," Stern suggested. Her phone went off and kept me from making the horrible decision of accepting her offer. "Duty calls. Thanks for your time, Allen."

Stern's fixation on handwear was wrinkling my brain. "You want a keto coffee for the road? I'm about to make one for myself."

Stern wanted to say no but remembered the smoothie. "What kind of butter?"

"Scottish grass fed."

"How can I refuse?"

Stern followed me to the kitchen. I was careful not to make any sudden movements while I ground the beans, pressed the brew, then blended the butter, vanilla, and cinnamon into it. I didn't sweat losing a travel mug. I had the feeling this wasn't the last time I was going to see her.

During the whole process, Stern took more than one glance toward the side door, concerned she had triggered my flight response.

"You found gloves," I said.

"In the alley next to the studio. Chamois lined with cashmere."

Jove Brand's handwear of choice. I went to take a sip of coffee, but my hand was shaking a little, so I set the cup back down.

"No getting prints off the insides of those." Stern took a sip, her hand steady, and gave an appreciative nod. "That's good coffee. Have fun in Fresno. Don't leave the state, Mr. Allen."

3

I SPENT THE NEXT WEEK SNEAKING IN AND OUT OF my own condo while ignoring my phone. Layne Lackey won the harassment award, calling or texting every two hours.

Three years ago I'd experienced a brief resurgence of fame when the cell-phone video of my not-really-a-fight was posted online, but it was nothing compared to the attention I was getting now.

No one outright called me a murderer, but they drew an outline a kindergartner could have colored in. I was the last person to talk to Sir Collin Prestor and the first person at the murder scene. None of the dozen witnesses who came up the stairway leading to the single door to the roof passed anyone coming down. The only notable event in my murky, violent past was failing at the role Sir Collin restored to worldwide acclaim.

Then it leaked how Sir Collin was killed.

No one knew for sure who broke the seal, though my guess was *Beautiful Downtown Burbank*'s executive producer. After the first trickle, the reports poured in. In true This Town fashion, new information was presented in a series of dramatic reveals. First, no murder weapon was found. Next, an unnamed source stated no murder weapon would be found because Sir Collin's murderer had used their bare hands. Then half a dozen people came forward anonymously to confirm the nature of Sir Collin's fatal injuries.

The internet did the rest. Highlights of *Near Death* started trending on all platforms. The video clip of me as Jove Brand finishing off General Moon-Tzu got twenty-one hits a second for ninety-six hours.

A micro-expression expert, whatever that was, broke down every second of Sir Collin and me on *Beautiful Downtown Burbank*'s stage frame-by-frame. That squint, right there, was the moment Ken Allen broke, they informed the host. When the corner of Ken Allen's mouth turned down, he became a murderer. Ken Allen foreshadowed his intentions when he threatened Niles Endsworth's eyes and throat on stage in front of millions, mere moments before the murder. Look at his sweat flow. Ken Allen was a man on the edge, and Sir Collin unwittingly pushed him off.

Then the memes started, crafted from stills and GIFs ripped from *Near Death*. Montages of all the throat chops. Hard loops of gouging into chopping with blinking text displaying catchy phrases like *Franchise Killer*. Skillful photoshops of Sir Collin's face pasted over General Moon-Tzu's. A recut of *Near Death*'s chase scene with the words *What's next for Ken Allen* captioned over it.

My Wikipedia entry was edited every ten minutes. My profession kept getting changed to fugitive. Someone inserted a fake fight record of 1–0, with my lone win being over Sir Collin Prestor by fatality. A pro-wrestling fan listed my signature move as the "Eye-Gouge Throat Chop." After the moderators locked it, my entry reverted to what Layne Lackey had written years back.

Ken Allen is an American actor and martial arts expert, best known for playing Jove Brand in the foreign-only release Near Death.[1][2] Chosen for the famous role based on his strong resemblance to the character as well as his physical ability, Allen was an unknown at the time of his casting. A cultural oddity, Allen's sole film credit to date is the lead role in one of the largest movie franchises of all time. He is also known as the Sensei to the Stars.[citation needed]

While all that was true, it made my landing the part of Jove Brand come off as a Cinderella story. A triumph after a grueling audition process, instead of what actually happened. The truth was, I was the only warm body in Hong Kong who fit the bill. Kit Calabria was desperate.

His first choice was dead of an overdose and no other actor would touch the role for fear of being blacklisted by the studios. Kit had thirty days to wrap production or lose the franchise his father had helmed for thirty years.

Plain and simple, *Near Death* was an act of triage, an emergency procedure to stabilize the patient long enough to get them expert treatment. Kit and I kept the franchise alive. We did what we had to do and paid the price in full. His estranged sister, Dina, and Sir Collin restored it to health.

Thanks to the social-media justice system, I lost two of five clients with no chance of replacing them. Reddit compiled a complete timeline that proved I definitely did it, along with a psychological profile cementing my motives. The conspiracy crazies pointed to my time in Hong Kong as evidence I was a foreign agent tasked with eliminating Sir Collin Prestor to tank the franchise so the Chinese film industry could take it over.

I needed a lawyer but couldn't afford one. Every media outlet you could think of wanted an interview. The offers for an exclusive were rapidly rising, but I knew better than to take the bait. Appearing on camera was profiting off Sir Collin's death. It also looked bad, which was a distant second to my sheer disgust.

As much as I wanted to, I couldn't afford to skip the convention in Fresno.

I cleaned my condo like it was going on the market before performing a walkthrough worthy of a Brand film. Everything worth anything went in the attic. A ladder wouldn't fit in the only closet with attic access. If you couldn't do a muscle-up, you weren't getting in there, and guys who sat in a van for a living couldn't do a muscle-up. I took four-corner photos of each room, powdered every knob and pull. I passed a sleepless night staring at the ceiling. My condo wasn't much, but it was all I had. It was going to hurt, coming home to find it in ruins.

I left for Fresno before sunrise on Friday. It would get me to the convention center early, but if I waited any longer, commuter traffic would make me late. My level of celebrity didn't merit a second pass if my booth was empty on the first. I couldn't afford to miss a single fan. Convention appearances barely covered my health insurance, much less legal coverage.

I didn't really have fans, not in the traditional sense.

My presence was a curiosity, a quirky detail in the story of what you did last weekend. The tenth photo in the Facebook album labeled *Conventions 2016*. People hated hipsters, but they paid my bills—may the god none of them believed in bless them. Who knew a guy could scrape by on irony?

Four hours of driving and I didn't so much as turn on the radio. Instead I spent the whole time devising a plan to prove my innocence. The results weren't encouraging. There were things that made me appear less guilty, like trying to save Sir Collin. But that could also be explained as a guy who lost his temper in the heat of the moment trying to save his own skin after waking to what he had done.

Despite my tough talking at Stern, everything I knew about the criminal justice system came straight from the screen, including the expression *the criminal justice system*. Now I was on my way to being one of those stories ripped from the headlines.

Three broadcast vans trailed me north, and why not? They could write off the mileage, and what if they hit the jackpot and I made for Tijuana? I dreaded what was waiting for me at the convention center. My appearance schedule was posted at JoveBrandFan.com.

My badge got me access to guest parking. No way the show-runners would pull me. Conventions were all about attendance. They were our modern sideshows, except instead of the Wolf-boy and the Bearded Lady, there was the Guy Who Was in That One Thing and The Lady from the Magazine You Found in the Woods. If a peek at the One Jove Brand Who Murdered Another Jove Brand got warm bodies through door, so be it.

After a check to make sure there was nothing in my car I minded losing, I shouldered my merch and headed for my table. Everyone was setting up, which gave them an excuse not to make eye contact. Though I had broken bread with most of the other guests, my loaf had gone moldy.

Yuen was already at our table when I got there. My former co-star was now my convention partner. Like me, Yuen was cast solely on appearance. Slap a goatee and top bun on Bruce Lee and you'd have the villain of *Near Death*. My once archenemy was now my closest friend. Shared experience has that kind of power.

When Yuen saw me, he raised his hands in surrender. "Don't kill me, man. I'm just a poor boy from Kowloon making my way in the world."

The hoarseness of Yuen's voice undercut his wide-eyed innocence. It wasn't the result of aging. He'd had a musical lilt once, before he met me.

"Shut up," I told him, tossing my bags on table.

Yuen kept his hands up. "Better not make you mad. I got four kids. Maybe more. Your sister, she got any good-looking dark-haired sons?"

I sorted the eight by tens into piles. "I don't have a sister, you know that."

"Damn man. Your mom, she really takes care of herself."

I laughed against my will, which made Yuen grin, which made me laugh more. With a mug like his, you couldn't blame him, no matter how much he deserved it.

"The cops give you a work release?"

"Time off for good behavior," I replied. As I lifted the table skirt to cache my bags, Yuen put a hand on my shoulder. My eyes were drawn to the ragged scar below his Adam's apple—a line leading to a puncture reminiscent of a sunflower. Eighteen years and I still couldn't look at him without feeling a fresh stab of guilt.

Yuen bent down to meet my eyes. "I know you're innocent."

"Yeah?" was all the reply I could manage. The tension inside me felt like a bolt wrenched past stripping. It had steadily tightened from the night Sir Collin was killed, ratcheting a helplessness I hadn't experienced since *Near Death* hit the internet. That someone believed I wasn't a killer brought overwhelming relief.

Yuen gave a dismissive wave. "The shit people say to you at these things and you haven't killed any of them."

"The weekend is yet to begin," I grumbled.

We hung the banner together. While Yuen hooked up the TV/ DVD combo, I gave the spread a last once-over.

"There's a print missing."

"Is there?" Yuen ducked down to check under the table. "Guess I forgot a stack at home."

It was a touching but futile gesture. The missing print was a still taken from a scene that was currently getting over seventy thousand hits an hour. And Yuen didn't do these shows for fun. He really did have four kids.

"Put them out," I said.

Yuen grinned from ear to ear as he uncovered a box. "I ordered a triple run. These are going to flip like flapjacks."

The print in question was landscape style. I'm on the left as Jove Brand, in my salmon blazer sans tie—a casualty of the zipline fight. The red slash across my forehead and down my cheek is a souvenir of General Moon Tzu's bladed hemline. My tattered shirt provided a clear view of my sculpted midsection.

Yuen as General Moon-Tzu was on the right, resplendent in his silver Mandarin robe. He was dramatically exhaling as the edge of my left hand caught him square on the Adam's apple. Blood bloomed from his eye sockets like twin poppies. The composition wasn't bad and we looked great. Static and silent, the shot could pass for a real Jove Brand film. It was *Near Death*, summarized in a single photo.

With my primary ensemble currently bagged in police lockup, I was forced to rely on my backup costume. You never knew when you were going to get someone on your clothes. I got into wardrobe, buttoning up the baby-blue shirt and knotting that awful tie before slipping on my signature salmon jacket. My Brand skin on, I shook my muscles out as if I were bracing for a punch.

The rank odor of microwaved fish invaded my space. Yuen was already cracking the Tupperware. I watched him shovel down shrimp and inhale sticky rice. "How you can eat so much and never break one thirty-five?"

"I burn it off dancing like no one is watching," Yuen replied.

Yuen made sure the volume was muted before hitting play. Neither of us possessed the level of masochism it took to listen to *Near Death* on a loop for three days. It was cringe-worthy imagining what Kit Calabria went through in a Hong Kong editing booth, scrambling to transmute a lead balloon into a golden parachute.

Near Death opened with the passing of my predecessor. The Brand before me had filmed his exit during the production of *A Beautiful Disaster*, his final film. What was another twenty million on top of the most expensive—adjusted for inflation— Brand film to date? Tacking that polished sequence on the front of *Near Death* was like having Yo-Yo Ma open for a high-school marching band. Those ten minutes cost more than the ninety that followed them.

The film proper opens with my trial sequence. Every new Brand has one in their debut, an action set piece that ends with a journeyman agent being promoted to Royal Gamesman and adopting the alias of Jove Brand. In *Near Death*, my trial sequence consisted solely of me doing endless kata while a stuntman ran out of the shadows and into one of my feet every ten seconds.

Tender, head of WARDEN—Brand's secret section—in his one-scene appearance, watched the somehow-already-edited sequence on his product-placed laptop. Pausing the video on a close-up of my screaming face, he said, "He'll have to do."

Truer words were never spoken.

In *Near Death*, Jove Brand and Tender didn't ever appear in the same shot, one of many unique occurrences in the nineteen-film series. We weren't even in the same country. According to JoveBrandFan.com, Walter Morris was watching a rugby game on that laptop.

It had been fifteen years since Sir Collin's debut and a Brand film with a trial sequence. Fan expectations on the next one were sky-high, considering the fight sequences in *Raid the Roof*, Niles Endsworth's indie breakout role. With a shoestring budget in a country an ocean from OSHA, Niles did all his own stunts, including the parkour. The scene where the fire escape collapsed was real. Niles's right pinky was now permanently crooked from grabbing the window ledge that saved his life. But *Raid the Roof* came out of nowhere, and Niles Endsworth with it, absent online fanfare. His Brand's trial sequence would air in the clickbait era, which meant it would be the first to face the speculators, the leakers, and the trolls.

I pitied the poor bastard.

Security cracked the doors and the tide was unleashed. Even way in the back, we could hear the rumbling wave of excitement. We didn't expect to see action for a few hours. Our table sat in a distant corner, past the vendors, feature booths, and actual stars.

The bulk of our traffic usually came on Sunday, when the weekend-pass holders explored every nook and cranny in search of things to do.

It wasn't five minutes before we got our first customers—two college-aged guys dressed to the nines in full white tie, one of Jove Brand's signature costumes. JoveBrandFan.com was correct in reporting that when you signed on to play Jove Brand, you were barred from wearing white tie in any other film. This wasn't an issue for me. I was in white tie for maybe thirty seconds, and only then because the infamous Brand rights contract demanded it. It was a rental that barely fit. You could make out about four inches of cuff in one shot. Kit had to film me from the waist up to keep my socks from showing.

"You're here. Sweet," the left fan said. He gave our table a polite browse before saying, "We just want a picture."

"Buy one or take one—it's twenty bucks," Yuen replied. It was only natural he played the bad cop.

"But buy something and we'll sign it," I added.

Of course, they had to run to the ATM. A gaggle of college girls immediately replaced them, each dressed in a shimmering evening gown.

"How much for all of us?" the bravest one asked while the others stole glances. I hoped I had resting innocent-face.

"Four people eighty bucks," Yuen said, quadrupling our profit without skipping a beat. He never developed a tolerance for our fan base. In his eyes, treating us like a sideshow attraction made them the rubes. Yuen tucked the money away and started around the table, but the girls stopped him.

"Just Ken. Is that okay?"

"You're the boss," Yuen shrugged. "You want me to take it?"

"I know my angles," the pack leader replied, shaking out her hair.

The girls huddled around me, each of them striking a kung-faux pose. It took six attempts to satisfy the pack leader. They didn't try to talk to me at all, except one girl, who thanked me over her shoulder as an afterthought. The white-tie guys had been waiting their turn.

"Just you," the left one said to me. "Can you do like, a double chop?"

Yuen caught my expression and answered for me. "No problem."

This was a first. I arranged a guy on each side, slightly behind me. Looking intensely at the one on my left, I extended my flattened hand across his neck. To keep them in frame, the right one got more of a forearm. Yuen counted down from three. On one, both guys rolled their eyes back and lolled out their tongues.

They were thrilled with the result.

The next customer came before I was back behind the table. I froze when I saw him. He was dressed like Sir Collin in *A Gentleman's Play*—full riding gear, cheeks bloodied from his first kill.

"Chop me, dude," he said, handing Yuen two twenties. Not-Sir-Collin must have seen the other guys pay.

I tried to make it light, rolling my eyes while bringing the edge of my hand down on his neck, Captain Kirk-style.

"No, like, across the front," Not-Sir-Collin explained, miming as if he were sawing his own head off.

"Fuck off," Yuen replied with a tight grin.

The guy fumed for a minute, checked his phone, then split.

A couple came looking for a threesome. I put them side by side and chopped them both with the same arm. Yuen cleaned out his

Tupperware so we'd have a place to stash the cash. I pulled out my phone and went straight to trending. Nothing. Then I searched by keyword.

The photos were under *#FranchiseKiller*.

Layne Lackey called while I still had my phone in hand. He followed up immediately with a text.

I'm here. Need to meet. ASAP. 911.

A line was forming. Yuen and I shared a glance.

"Proceeds go to the Ken Allen Defense Fund," he said, wiggling his eyebrows.

The last eighteen years had prepared me for this. *Near Death* turned me into a living, breathing inside joke. Now the whole world was lining up to deliver the punch line. I could let that beat me down, or I could roll with it, but I couldn't avoid it.

The time had come to show my chops.

I chopped Jove Brand in white tie and I chopped Jove Brand in his striped racing suit. I chopped my way through Brand Beauties of every color and gender. I chopped Sir Collin and I chopped General Moon Tzu. I even chopped some nutjob cosplaying as the Black Knight, though I had to admit: his black bodysuit and motorcycle helmet—tinted visor and all—were spot-on. Unlike the bulk of his peers, the Black Knight spent as much time making sure he looked good in the costume as he must have sewing it together.

But most of all I chopped myself. Ken Allen after Ken Allen came to die, in their baby-blue shirts and salmon jackets. In true mirror-match fashion, we traded chops or crossed arms like dueling swordsmen. I dove in head first, full of enthusiasm, smiling and thanking every last "fan." I would convince the world I didn't kill Sir Collin, if I had to do it one person at a time.

The morning surge petered out into the dead zone before people got off work. Friday was usually our slow day, but here it was, only half over, and we had made more than four thousand dollars. We had also created enough buzz that attendees were detouring our way to see what the hubbub was all about. Most people passed by whispering, but one group lingered. There were four of them, three men and one woman, dressed in pseudo-tactical gear and sporting masks.

Real-life superheroes. In essence, a trumped-up citizens' patrol. It wasn't a new idea. New York had the Guardian Angels back in the seventies. They turned their backs to our table and started streaming, the leader pointing over his shoulder now and then.

"You know these guys?" I asked Yuen.

"Nope." He dug out his program to do some research. "They call themselves Street Justice. Have a scheduled self-defense demo on stage C. Says here they have ten black belts between the four of them."

"Well sure. They need them to hang all those holsters." Most of the loops on their tactical gear were empty. These jokers were a prime example why pepper spray and Tasers weren't allowed inside. Still, they didn't pat you down in Fresno.

"Tomorrow we're charging fifty," Yuen said. He took out expenses before handing me a wad of ATM-fresh bills. It was better to keep the cash in your pocket at these things.

"My half is bigger," I said.

"My donation to the Ken Allen Defense Fund."

I evened the sheaves out. "And here's my contribution to the Children of Yuen Hung College Fund. If they throw me in prison, this side gig is going away."

Yuen tried to wave me off. "You can sign stuff from prison. Plus, when you die behind bars, *Near Death* memorabilia is going to shoot through the roof. I'm looking forward to my fat book deal."

Yuen had to refuse three times, but on the fourth pass I got him to take the weight off me.

"You lead, Ken," he said. "I'll try not to step on your toes."

It was our little inside joke. My two qualifications for the part of Jove Brand were the looks and the moves. Every absurd, over-the-top fight scene in *Near Death* was hatched in my immature, tasteless mind. The closest thing Yuen had to any training was being a salsa dancer on a cruise ship.

It showed when we fought in *Near Death*. Mostly Yuen stood there, pretending to get hit while I strung together ludicrous combinations of punches and kicks. Layne Lackey counted once. Moon-Tzu takes fifty-seven hits to Brand's nine. I sold each of those nine hard, spinning through the air and crashing into walls in response to Yuen's suspiciously graceful blows.

"I thought for sure the networks would have film crews here," I said.

"That's because you aren't savvy, baby," Yuen replied. "The showrunners lock them out, then sell them their house footage for six figures easy."

"Tell me we didn't sign a waiver."

Yuen grinned. "All part of the rental agreement, my naive sidekick."

"Wonderful." I checked my phone, fingers crossed #FranciseKiller. wasn't trending, and found a dozen missed calls and texts, all from Layne Lackey. The last read: *VIP cafe. I know what happened. I have proof.*

When I showed it to Yuen, he said, "He's full of it. Layne is going to the Hell of Fruitless Gossip."

"That a real place?"

Yuen rested a hand on his chin. "Rumor has it."

No one stopped me on my journey to the lounge reserved for convention guests, though some troll lurking in the crowd shouted, "Killer Brand!" when he saw me. The Black Knight was coming out of the lounge as I approached. He was in character, striding through the crowd like he expected it to part for him, which it did. Layne sure got to him fast. No such thing as too much content for JoveBrandFan.com. And the Black Knight was Layne's type.

I jogged to catch the door before it closed. The room was empty, except for Layne Lackey, who was crumpled against the far wall with a hand down his pants. I was halfway to him when I processed what I was seeing.

Layne Lackey's throat had been crushed. His discolored neck was rapidly swelling.

"Hold on!" I yelled at Lackey. The closest thing to a knife on the complimentary refreshment table was a bagel slicer. I didn't think to bring one. Let one guy with a collapsed airway die, shame on you. Let a second, shame on me.

Layne wasn't looking good. I dialed 911 and put my phone on speaker to free up my hands. I fought to force air into Layne's lungs while informing the operator a person was choking to death and needed immediate medical attention,

It was an exercise in futility. The killer was getting better at flattening windpipes. From the way Layne Lackey was folded against the wall, I was guessing they used a stomp. Probably started off with a shot to the groin, considering the way Layne was cradling his junk. But if you were kicked in the throat, wouldn't your hand go there instead?

"You crotch something?" I asked, but Layne was past answering.

With a sigh of resignation, I shoved my hand down Layne's pants. There was a flash drive nestled behind his privates and I would go to my grave knowing Layne Lackey kept everything Bic-smooth. I was looking for a place to boil my hand when I realized the killer had walked right past me.

"Help's on the way," I told Layne's lifeless body. Maybe the paramedics could revive him. If Layne Lackey beat the odds and lived, he could clear my name.

Or I could catch the killer myself.

The lounge door burst open before I was halfway across the room. A wiry guy, maybe twenty-five years old, rolled over the threshold. A heavier man executed a tactical entrance behind him, clearing the room with an imaginary rifle. A third man blocked the door. Air rifle played spokesman.

"Face Street Justice!"

I walked forward, palms out. "The killer is dressed as the Black Knight. Let's get him."

"On the ground, citizen's arrest!" Air rifle commanded. He was wearing a hockey goalie mask with a silver skull enameled on it. If it wasn't for the muffled lisp, he might have been intimidating.

"Y-yeah!" said wiry guy. He had gone full tactical ninja, from split-toed boots to a hooded facemask.

I didn't break stride. "I don't have time for a playdate."

They were more posing than taking up any kind of stance. Every second they held me up, the Black Knight got farther away.

Tactical Ninja was closest. I didn't want to hit him in the head—I wasn't looking to alter the kid's future. I just needed him out of my way. I flicked my fingers in his eyeline and took out his leg. He was wearing hard knee pads but had nothing shielding his thighs. My shin connected an inch above his knee, chopping down like an axe right on the sweet spot. He issued an involuntary yelp as he tumbled over.

I stepped through and blasted a thrust kick into Air rifle's hip-thigh junction. It was a tough spot to guard. The force sent him into the door frame. Before he could recover, I swept out both his feet with a switch low kick. He hit the tile hard and stayed there.

The guy blocking the door was dressed like a steampunk wizard. He swung a cane, topped with a brass globe security should have never let through the door, at my skull. I tracked the arc of his swing and didn't bother to block it. The cane bounced off the door frame and back into his head as I floated a right hand into his solar plexus, fast and light. It took a second, but he went down, melting slowly into a crouch. Been there, felt that.

The final Street Justice member, a young woman, was stationed outside the door. She was armored everywhere but her midriff and pointing a chunky black object at me. I ducked out of the line of fire and swept my arm in a tight arc. When our forearms connected, I jerked down hard. She snapped forward a step and involuntarily tossed what she was holding.

I blurted an apology as I sprinted away. Pointing toward the remains of her digital camera, I said, "Tag me in that."

I wove through the crowd, hunting for a black motorcycle helmet. Friday was the slow day, but there were still ten thousand people in the convention center. The Black Knight wasn't a featured guest, which meant he would have to exit through the main entrance.

I followed the far wall around. It was the long way, distance-wise, but it was also the least congested. Paramedics were coming from the opposite direction. I pointed them toward the VIP lounge without breaking stride.

I hit the food court full tilt, sending hot dogs and nachos into orbit. "Killer Brand!" the troll shouted again, stretching the two words into a sentence. The gate guards were more confused than concerned. I didn't bother asking or explaining as I blasted the door open with my shoulder. The lot was packed with people and cars. I jumped on top of a table advertising the best cellular network in Fresno and checked the lot a section at a time.

I heard the Black Knight before I saw him, his tires peeling out as his motorcycle issued a pitched roar. He was still in costume. It was the perfect getaway outfit, helmet and all. I recognized his ride right away. Any fan would. It was a Triumph Bonneville.

The same model Jove Brand used.

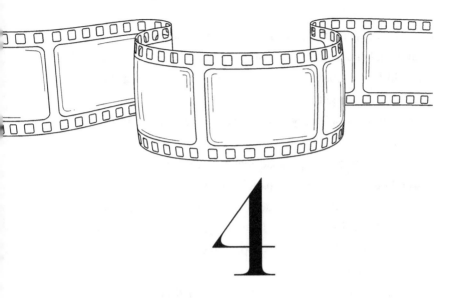

4

I HAD BEEN MAKING A FIST FOR SO LONG IT HURT TO stop. The flash drive was still buried in it, no worse for wear despite the places it had been and things it had seen. Layne Lackey thought it was more important than his own neck and I was going to find out why before Stern slapped on the cuffs. If Layne had the evidence proving my innocence he claimed he had, maybe he knew who the killer was, and what the hell I had been dragged into.

There was no reason to go back inside. Everything I needed was in my pockets. Ditching my jacket—the big salmon beacon it was—brought relief, like I was shedding my skin. There was no going back now. I owned two of the three originals and hadn't seen the last one in eighteen years.

I thought about calling Yuen but was concerned that contacting him would make him an accessory. I exited the lot with no direction. My old beater couldn't play MP3s, much less read a flash drive. Was it better to get some distance from the convention center, or stop at the closest library? Having never been a wanted man before, I was at a loss.

A big-box store up ahead made up my mind. I turned in and parked on the far side of a panel van. The automatic doors didn't care I was in a hurry. I made for the display models and shoved Layne's flash drive into the fanciest laptop. A prompt asking if I wanted to run ALBION.EXE appeared on the screen.

Yes, I clicked.

The screen went black, then the WARDEN crest came to life, antlers and all. It was no shock Layne Lackey had a flair for the dramatic. He had designed JoveBrandFan.com as if visitors were agents accessing the WARDEN database. The same code or HTML or whatever websites were made of was installed on the flash drive. Having been to JoveBrandFan.com more times than I cared to admit, I knew how the interface worked: mousing over each letter in WARDEN made an option expand. *W* opened the Watchlist, *A* the Armory, and so on. I chose *D* for Dossiers out of habit. This is where Layne Lackey would pile the freshest dirt he had dug up on me. A pop-up flared to life.

Warning. Access for Gamesman only. Please confirm.

The same "terms and conditions" rigmarole present on the JoveBrandFan site popped up, giving the choice of *Aye* or *Nay*. I clicked *Aye*.

A list of file folders appeared, each styled to look like a WARDEN dossier. Some were stamped complete, like the Sir Collin Prestor dossier, and some were not, including the one on

Ken Allen. Each person featured was linked to the Jove Brand series, either in front of or behind the camera. There was a Kit Calabria dossier. A vibration erupted in my inner ear and spread throughout my body. How much had Layne uncovered about Kit?

When I clicked the dossier on Kit, it triggered another warning box.

Please confirm your identity, Gamesman.

I stared at the cursor blinking in the dialogue box. Should I type Layne Lackey? Jove Brand? Ken Allen? After seven seconds of wondering, a pop-up appeared, blinking red.

SELF-DESTRUCTING

I waved an employee over, a high-school kid who needed a shampoo.

10 . . . 9 . . .

"Help."

8 . . . 7 . . .

"Uh, you can't use that here," he replied, looking around for a higher power. "Dude, is that you?"

6 . . . 5 . . .

I followed his finger to find my face on every screen in the store. The footage from *Beautiful Downtown Burbank* was playing silently with FORMER BRAND FLEES SECOND MURDER SCENE under it.

4 . . . 3 . . .

I yanked the flash drive and made for my car. I couldn't have the police looking at its contents before I found out how many skeletons Layne was storing on it. Particularly any skeletons tied to *Near Death*. Plus if the cops plugged the drive in now, the last seconds would tick out. Knowing Layne Lackey, it would literally self-destruct.

I used my phone to locate the nearest shipping service. Being the subject of a manhunt was not pleasant. My pulse throbbed in my neck. Every traffic light on the way was red. If I sent the flash drive to myself, a van vulture was going to snatch it out of my mailbox.

What did files about *Near Death* have to do with Sir Collin's murder? It was the only movie Kit touched, and my only connection to Jove Brand, and we both had dossiers on Lackey's flash drive.

I burst into the shipping store like I was crossing a finish line. I surrounded the flash drive and a note scribbled on a shipping label in an excessive amount of bubble wrap. The cushy bundle my life depended on went into the smallest, toughest box money could buy. Big packages didn't fit in mailboxes. People stole big packages. Overnight rate was the fastest I could get it to a Ms. June Wedding. Having played a part in *Near Death,* June had a dossier as well.

My mission accomplished, I called Special Investigator Stern and asked what she was doing for dinner.

WHEN FORCED TO eat out, breakfast was the best low-carb option. An omelet wasn't my first choice for a last meal, but prime suspects couldn't be choosers. Prison food would not match my macros. Well, I had always wanted to try intermittent fasting. When life gave you lemons it was time to break out the monk-fruit extract.

I dined al fresco, taking my time, savoring the fresh air and sunshine. A gentleman would have waited for Stern to order but I had serious doubts she'd let me finish. No one pointed me out and screamed "Murderer!" in the two hours it took her to get there. Maybe I wasn't such a hot commodity.

Stern pulled up in an unmarked, flanked by a pair of state patrol cars. She didn't approach with her weapon drawn, so that was something. I set down my fork and put my elbows on the table.

Stern pointed at the nearest wall. "Place your palms flat with your legs wide."

Once I assumed the position, Stern searched me. I wasn't one to kiss and tell, so let's just say Stern would have found Layne Lackey's flash drive. She braced an arm against my back to keep me from turning toward her. "You pay?"

My mouth had gone bone dry so I nodded too many times instead of talking.

"Put your hands behind your back."

In a demonstration of skill, I complied without face-planting into the wall. "I'm turning myself in, doesn't that earn me any credit?"

"Not fleeing the scene would have earned more," Stern replied.

As Stern cuffed me, she read my rights without inflection, letting the sentences run together to gloss over my essential liberties. She didn't tell me I was under arrest, she just arrested me. She didn't mention any charges. Art clearly did not imitate life.

"Let's go, Allen," she said, opening the back door of the unmarked. I lowered myself in and maneuvered for a position that didn't strain my shoulders. There wasn't one. The flurry of activity had helped me escape the dread, but it was catching right up.

Stern cranked up the AC before pulling out of the lot, the two of us all alone. The oversized rear-view mirror gave me a look at her face. I assumed the opposite was also true.

"I don't get you, Allen."

"What's to get?"

"Lackey has been ruffling your feathers for years, why now?"

"You're inquiring as to my motive?" I shuffled to the edge of the seat in search of relief. "Good, because there isn't one. I didn't kill Sir Collin and I didn't kill Layne Lackey."

"The Collin Prestor thing is also a mystery," Stern admitted. "Whatever he said to you in his dressing room must have really honked you off."

"Oh, come on."

"Now Lackey. You know what I'm thinking? I'm thinking there was a new factor. Maybe he dug something up and put the squeeze on you."

"Like what?" Layne Lackey's last text message popped into my head. *I know what happened. I have proof.* Couldn't have Layne done me a favor and typed *I know you didn't do it?*

"Who knows?" Stern said. "Maybe you've been at this a while. Maybe Lackey did what we're doing right now, comparing unsolved murders to your convention schedule. Looking at cold cases with crushed throats."

"You've got to be kidding me."

"We'll see what the eggheads turn up. They already found out those gloves are vintage. That's the kind of gift the giver would remember. And these convention centers have cameras everywhere."

"Good," I said. "The sooner you review the footage the better."

"In a hurry to be punished, Allen?"

"In a hurry to be cleared. I hope there were a hundred cameras in that lounge."

Stern stared at me for so long I got nervous she was going to run us off the road. I tried lying on my side. It didn't help.

"Sit up, Allen. For safety."

I ignored her, turning on my back instead. After what felt like an hour, Stern asked, "What's on your mind, Allen?"

"That it's time to get a lawyer."

Stern sighed. "And here I thought we were developing a rapport."

Stern booked me at the nearest state police station, where I formally requested a lawyer be provided for me. Good thing public defenders were free. Then again, you got what you paid for.

I had a cell all to myself, which was good because I could touch opposite walls both ways. Still, there was plenty of room to knock out a body weight routine. I tried to sleep, but every little noise snapped me awake. Would a hacker be able to get into Layne Lackey's flash drive? Where did one enlist a trustworthy hacker? Did the murders have something to do with *Near Death*, or was I only a convenient patsy?

Near Death was not a labor of love. It was a necessary evil, a Hail Mary to save the Jove Brand franchise. Nineteen films spanning fifty years, the product of the most successful independent production studio in film history. All because Kit Calabria's father, Big Don, sat down at the card table with Jove Brand's creator.

They didn't make writers like Bowman Fletcher anymore. He was the product of an entire generation going to war. When Fletcher wrote about killing, he didn't have to imagine what it was like. He just had to remember.

No one knows who Bowman Fletcher really was but it's believed he was a spy himself. That deep divers like Layne Lackey never uncovered his origins adds credence to the theory. Layne postulated the Jove Brand stories were a form of therapy: Technicolor tales designed to make sense of the senseless. Never glorifying, but forever justifying.

But Bowman Fletcher only wrote when the darkness came for him. The rest of the time he manically blew through money, usually at the card table. "Jove Brand knew the odds. He also knew they didn't apply to him," Fletcher began in *The Gamesman Afoot,* the first Brand novel. It was carved on his tombstone.

Big Don Calabria was a giant in his own right. A smuggler during the Second World War, he plundered Axis ships to unload war spoils on the private market, often selling them back to their original owners. When the cards were dealt, neither he nor Fletcher would back down. The stakes rose every round, until Fletcher had wagered away the Caribbean estate bought with the proceeds of his best-selling novels. Fletcher wanted his private paradise back and he only had one thing left to wager with:

The film rights to Jove Brand.

Four sevens versus a royal flush. The odds of those two hands occurring at the same time were so astronomically small, they might as well be impossible. Recounting the tale on JoveBrandFan. com, Layne Lackey suggested that should anyone face a notorious pirate at the card table, it would perhaps be best to have a third party shuffle the deck. Those in attendance recalled that Big Don Calabria didn't look surprised when the cards were turned over.

Big Don had cleaned Fletcher out. The two of them locked eyes, the pirate's dark pools and the soldier's icy orbs. How many bodies had they stacked between them? In the end, Fletcher decided that particular gamble wasn't worth it.

The next day, Calabria met Fletcher in the estate he now owned. Fletcher had drawn up the rights contract on the same typewriter that had birthed Jove Brand. It was already signed. Big Don, eager to seal the deal, added his own name. He didn't bother reading the details, which was where Bowman Fletcher got his revenge. His weapons were words, and the lawyers have been using that contract as ammunition for a half century.

Having gotten what he wanted, the former pirate gave Bowman Fletcher his house back. Big Don needed the author at his desk, churning out future volumes to one day become Calabria productions. It wasn't until Big Don got that contract in front of his lawyers that he learned his treasure was not bought, but forever borrowed.

The chief provision of the infamous Brand rights contract was the expiration clause. If a Jove Brand film wasn't released every three years, the rights reverted to the author, or the author's estate in the event of his death.

Thus began a race the Calabria family had run nineteen times, often crossing the finish line by a hair. No one was looking to help them. The big studios were too busy praying the Calabrias would drop the baton so they could scoop it up.

Every Brand film had been independently funded, often from nebulous sources the Calabrias never disclosed. Once released in a limited run, the distributors accepted defeat and Jove Brand was seen on screens worldwide. Each film was expected to top the last in a series of increasingly costly spectacles to satisfy audience expectations.

It all came to a head with *A Beautiful Disaster*.

The growing volume of my lawyer laying into Stern on their walk to my cell brought me back to reality.

"You went fishing and came up with a bare hook is what happened, Special Investigator. You have twenty hours to charge my client. Unless you wish to release him now."

Stern opened my cell door and stomped off without replying.

"No hello?" I called after her.

"Why would you do that? Don't do that."

"What?"

"Speak to the police, ever," my lawyer said as she handed over her card.

"Mercie Goodday?"

"I was conceived at Woodstock. Pleased to meet you, Mr. Allen."

None of the years Mercie Goodday had on me showed. She looked like a pixie got trapped in a library. Her features were small and sharp with a chin that came to a point. Her long auburn hair was seeded with white strands. Her suit was both professional and comfortable. Mercie wore minimal makeup and no jewelry.

"Guess I got lucky," I said.

"You did not. June Wedding sent me."

Too fast. It had been less than eight hours since I mailed June the flash drive.

"She's quite the lady," I replied.

"Yes she is."

"How bad is it?"

"Not," Mercie answered. "The case is being built. Thus far, all the evidence is circumstantial. The police are searching your car and home now."

"They won't find anything," I said. "I didn't kill anyone."

"That doesn't make it permissible to speak with law enforcement."

"I'll try to stop." I got up off my cot. Being confined had me stretching every ten minutes. "How long will I be here?"

"They won't charge you, not yet. I'll get you released, hopefully today."

My breath of relief was a half-decibel under a lion's roar.

"From now on, no more interactions with the police, no matter what they look like. Refer them to me," Mercie said. She leaned in to whisper the next part. "June would like to speak with you."

"And I would like to speak with her," I whispered back.

"We will discuss your case as it develops. Any questions, Mr. Allen?"

"Can I get food delivered?"

Mercie was too professional to roll her eyes. "I'm going to get to work on this. Don't discuss your situation with anyone but me. That includes the police."

"That's the third time you've said that."

"Then consider yourself charmed," Mercie replied. She left without saying good-bye.

I SLEPT AWAY the rest of my time in jail. Mercie escorted me out of the station to ensure my trap stayed shut, then drove me to the impound where my thoroughly rifled vehicle awaited.

"You were right, they didn't find anything," she told me.

"How do you know?"

"If they had, we'd be going to arraignment."

Mercie handed me a GPS and a giant-sized coffee. "June's address is already programmed. See her at your earliest convenience."

"I'm on my way now," I said, opening the car door.

"If I could make one more suggestion, Mr. Allen? Try running away from danger instead of toward it."

"It's not on purpose," I protested.

Mercie didn't look like she believed me.

The sky lightened on the journey north. The GPS reported a six-hour drive. I was itching for a shower but wanted answers more than I wanted to be clean. When I couldn't ignore my stomach anymore, I stopped for another omelet. The waitress refused to accept that I didn't want potatoes, toast, or a fruit cup. That's how far I was from This Town.

Six hours and again no radio. I was lost inside my head, trying to make sense of what had happened to my life. Why was Layne interested in *Near Death,* and what had he uncovered? If you were going to dig into the movie's troubled production, you had to start with what caused the trouble in the first place.

Bryce Crisp was the second Jove Brand, guiding the series through the eighties and nineties as he transformed the character from assassin to knight-errant. The first Brand was a taker. Bryce Crisp was a giver. Bryce's Brand always left the ladies in better shape than he found them. Even the title songs changed, from boisterous lyrics over blaring horns to smooth ballads delivered via saxophone.

A Beautiful Disaster was supposed to be Bryce's big send-off, everything expected of a Jove Brand film turned up to eleven, with action set pieces on land, sea, and air. Two problems arose. The first was Calabria Films didn't have the special effects resources the big studios did. *A Beautiful Disaster* didn't compare well with the aliens invading Earth on the next screen over.

The second was Bryce himself. The audience had always overlooked his weak action chops. Crisp's Brand got by on gadgets and charm, but he qualified for social security when filming *A Beautiful Disaster*. No amount of hair dye could conceal he was a senior citizen. Any scene requiring more than a brisk walk was handled by a stuntman. Big Don even used the old first-person fight cam trick, the viewer looking out of Brand's eyes as the bad guys sent punches and kicks his way.

Even worse were the love scenes. Brand Beauties were the it-girls of their time. Audiences weren't up for watching Bryce Crisp lock lips with an actress who could have been his granddaughter. Bryce himself appeared uncomfortable with the proposition and displayed more of a fatherly attitude in lieu of his famous charm.

A Beautiful Disaster was the first Brand bomb, falling well short of making back its enormous budget. Critics declared the end of the Brand era, writing the genre itself was dated and Brand a product of a demographic now out of touch. Jove Brand had become a parody of himself. In fact, the Brand parody movie released the year after was a huge hit, launching its own comedy series.

The coffers were bare and the world was against the Calabrias as the three-year countdown to the next release started ticking.

No one followed me up the coast. Somewhere in the chain of custody, I had lost my tail. Even the flash drive was headed to a different address than I was. The woman calling herself June Wedding lived a private, migratory life. My destination was a little town out of a fairy tale. Even the trees were on theme, curling and swept. She had a lonely cottage clinging to the edge of a cliff, its stones bound together by ivy.

I pulled my car into the garage next to a Tacoma with a half million miles on it, conscious of my rankness. When summoned by Hollywood royalty, one should not stink up the place.

She greeted me with a warm smile and lingering hug. She might have forgiven me for *Near Death*, which made one of us. But it was easier to forgive when you didn't know the whole story. She pulled away and took my cheeks between her palms. "Thanks for coming, Ken."

The stab of guilt stuck deep. "Anything for you, Missy."

FRESH CLOTHES WERE waiting for me when I got out of the shower. Simple, comfortable garments in muted colors that cost more than anything in my closet, the result of ethical sourcing and labor.

"Does my lawyer know June Wedding's secret identity?"

"She's an old friend," Missy said. She handed me a mug as warm as her smile. Here I was, enjoying a cup of tea with *the* Missy Cazale.

Four Oscars, five Golden Globes, seven Tony Awards, and who knew how many Emmys. Missy could have an Emmy whenever she wanted one. She was the greatest actress of her generation. Some would argue of any generation, including me. Her credits were a murderer's row of best pictures and modern classics.

But they started with *Near Death*.

That's right, Missy Cazale was my Brand Beauty. Missy was the only real actor in *Near Death* and even she could not elevate it out of schlock-dom. But Missy didn't do a Brand film for the money or the fame.

She did it for love.

When Kit Calabria saw Missy onstage it was love at first sight. They were in Ashland for the Shakespeare festival. She was playing Miranda, and he was a young man with a vision. The only son of the legendary Big Don Calabria wanted to be a filmmaker.

The two were immediately inseparable, drifting in the shimmering bubble of delicate, perfect love most of us burst one way or another. Usually by being stupid and taking what we had for granted. They would have done anything for each other, which was how Missy ended up starring opposite a talentless schlub in *Near Death*.

One of the many clauses detailed in Bowman Fletcher's byzantine rights contract was that each film feature a feminine role exemplifying "the finest British breeding." I won't beat around the bush: Fletcher was all the things ending in -*ist*. The Jove Brand novels would be incredibly offensive to modern audiences. The non-white and never British women were chattel, easy to bed and not long for the grave. The masterminds were always white or educated in Europe, with brutish henchmen drawn from a menagerie of offensive stereotypes.

When *Near Death's* first lead overdosed in a Ukrainian hotel room, the rest of the cast scattered like high schoolers hearing the sirens at their first kegger. To satisfy the parameters of the contract and thus retain the rights, Kit needed a young, white, passably English actress. Available immediately. In the middle of Hong Kong. Who was willing to work for free.

Eighteen years later, Missy Cazale still glowed. In photographs, there were other women who blew her out of the water, but on screen no one compared. She was even better in person.

"Is it bad?" she asked, looking over the cup she had cradled in both hands. The total focus of her attention was electric.

"It shouldn't be. They won't be able to prove anything because I didn't do it."

Missy's laugh sent ripples across the surface of her tea. "I know that, Ken. You wouldn't kill anyone. Do you remember when the stunt with Yuen went wrong?"

I winced like I had bit through a popsicle. "How could I forget?"

"You were so mortified," Missy drank while she thought. "It was clear you didn't enjoy hurting people. Which I found so strange, considering what you brought to the movie."

I never knew what to do with praise. When people said good things about me I wished they would shut up. In the search to change topics, I noticed her watch.

"Is that mine? From *Near Death?*"

Missy glanced down at it. I'd never seen her sheepish. "Kit gave it to me, right before he left to deliver the master print. He promised it was better than a ring, but an hour after his plane took off the battery . . ."

Missy couldn't manage the word *died*. We drank tea while she figured out how to say what she wanted to say. "I want to talk about something, but it's going to sound crazy."

"Sir Collin Prestor died in my arms. Layne Lackey was killed by a guy dressed up as a Brand villain, who got away because I had to fight a group of superheroes. My definition of crazy has evolved lately."

"Those are fair points," Missy nodded. She stopped to get us refills. Keeping her back to me helped her get it out. "Layne Lackey kept trying to meet with me. He even sent a certified letter."

Missy nodded at an envelope on the counter. I could feel her watching me read it.

Dear Ms. Cazale,

In the course of my duties as webmaster and content creator of JoveBrandFan.com, the premier Jove Brand fan site (visited by more than one hundred-thousand unique users every day), I have uncovered a scandal guaranteed to rock the foundations of the entertainment industry. As I live under constant threat of security breach, I only feel comfortable discussing my discovery in person. If my theory is correct, your past and future will change forever.

Sincerely,
Layne Lackey, Esq.

P. S. This concerns your star-crossed love with Kit Calabria.

I read the letter twice before giving the envelope a once-over. Layne had sent the letter to Missy's Ashland address, where I had sent the flash drive.

As far as bombshells went, this one was underwhelming. "I wonder how many drafts he wrote."

"He did not rival the Bard, may they both rest in peace."

I drained my teacup. Broth would have really hit the spot, but I wasn't about to put an order in. "It would have to be quite the revelation to change your past forever."

"Relatively." Missy smiled.

I didn't get it, but her smile brought mine out.

"I didn't think anything of it," Missy went on. "You know how it is with the letters. People proposing, or pitching their dream project, or sure they are the secret child you gave away."

"I can only imagine and would rather not."

Missy sighed. "I always wanted to be an actress, but I never wanted to be a star."

"Looking back, I'm glad I didn't have the talent to get what I wanted."

"You were fine," Missy said as she took our cups to the sink.

"No, I wasn't."

Missy turned around to make sure I was focused on her.

"You were hardworking, devoid of ego, and not a creep, which puts you above most of the actors I've worked with." She started digging around in the refrigerator. "Self-actualization is not a common quality among the A-list."

"Remind me to thank the internet. I get daily reminders what my problem is."

Missy lined up a selection of fresh produce and chose a knife. "When I heard the news about Layne Lackey, I started to wonder if he really had uncovered something about the Calabrias and the Jove Brand movies."

My heart rate spiked. "What do you mean?"

"I don't know." Missy started chopping away. "I haven't talked to anyone since Kit's funeral, but I'm sure it hasn't been easy for Dina, with what happened between them over *Near Death*."

Missy was brushing too close to my skeletons for comfort. "What happened to the rights?"

"They went into a trust controlled by Dina until Dean turns eighteen, which he does next week."

I perked up at the name. "Dina named her son Dean?"

"She did," Missy answered.

"Could Dean sell the film rights? Does the contract allow that?"

Missy chopped on without raising her head. "The only people that know for certain are the ones who have read the contract."

Which was a short list. The Calabrias kept the contract on lockdown. "Is the franchise in trouble?"

"No, but that hasn't stopped the offers." Missy swept the discarded roughage into her compost bin. "Some Russian billionaire tried to partner with Dina on the last film. When she refused, people had accidents. Fatal ones."

Even Layne Lackey hadn't reported on those rumors. Russian billionaires dealt with the press more definitively than their American counterparts. They also were known for the type of security breaches Layne was paranoid about.

I leaned against the cabinets and crossed my arms in an attempt to project confidence. "Who's backing the next one?"

"No one. The films are funded one hundred percent by the Calabrias these days. Dina's done an incredible job at the helm.

I wish we were still close. She could have taught me a lot when I started producing."

I turned it all over in my head while Missy portioned out the salad. Like the criminal justice system, everything I knew about being a detective came from the screen. Such as stating the obvious.

"Whatever Layne Lackey was working on, it was worth killing him over."

"And Sir Collin," Missy added, pushing a chilled bowl toward me. "Avocado oil?"

"Yes, please." When Missy lifted it after barely a drizzle, I reached over to push the bottle back down. "You might be onto something. Layne Lackey had a flash drive on him."

Missy's eyes went wide, the oil bottle forgotten. "What was on it?"

"The files were locked, but I saw a list of names. All of them were tied to *Near Death*."

If I had a spine, this would have been the time to tell her all of it. Instead, I swallowed down the temptation. Missy handed me a lid and we shook our bowls.

"Where is it?" Missy asked.

"I couldn't think of anyone else the vultures couldn't scavenge so I mailed it to your Ashland place. It should be there today."

"I'll get it. Do you know any computer people?"

"No." I crunched into the salad. It had a good balance and everything was fresh. Boiled eggs would have made it perfect, but there weren't any to be found under Missy Cazale's roof.

"Maybe Mercie does," Missy said. "Oh, did you want bread?"

"What's bread?"

We shared a laugh. It felt good to make her laugh. Despite everything she had accomplished, you'd be hard-pressed to find a candid shot of Missy Cazale giddy. She and Kit were to wed after wrapping *Near Death,* at the height of the season. But their day never came. We finished eating in silence. I got done way before her.

"I can't afford Mercie Goodday."

"I have money," Missy said, warding me off with her fork before I could reply. "I was thinking I should hire a private investigator or someone like that, but . . ."

But the studios were slavering over the Jove Brand franchise. Sir Collin's last film, *Final Bow,* topped a billion worldwide. While racking up a real-world body count. Now the bell was tolling again. If someone was willing to kill Sir Collin Prestor, no one was safe.

"There's no one you trust," I said.

"I just—I had a terrible thought," Missy replied. She turned the water all the way up to rinse out the bowls. It covered up getting herself together. "What if the murders go back farther? The actor you replaced—he died in the Ukraine, didn't he?"

But it wasn't him Missy was thinking about. Missy was thinking that they, whoever they were, might have had something to do with Kit's death. That his plane crash wasn't equipment failure or pilot error. Killing Kit would have killed the franchise, if it wasn't for me. But Kit might also still be alive, if it wasn't for me, which was a secret I intended to take to my grave. A secret that meant no matter what I did, the scales between Missy and I would never be balanced.

"Only one way to find out," I said. "The same way Layne Lackey did."

"Are you sure?" Missy asked. When she grabbed the counter, everything from her shoulders down tightened.

I could sit around with my fingers crossed in hopes the police investigation cleared me. Spend as much time in public as possible.

Hope someone else got their throat crushed, preferably while I was in a different zip code. The dossiers on Layne Lackey's flash drive might as well have been a hit list. If I followed his lead, I was almost certainly putting myself at future crime scenes. And who did I think I was? I wasn't a detective. I didn't even play one on television.

But someone was out there, hanging corpses on me. And I had to know what Layne Lackey had discovered about *Near Death*.

"My schedule has opened up recently."

"Whatever is happening, I want it exposed. They need to pay." Missy was a tremor short of desperate. A tremble shy of pleading. "Kit was murdered, Ken. Prove it. For me."

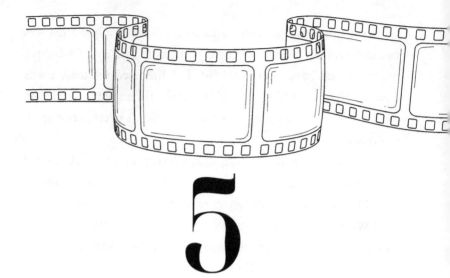

5

THE LAST FIVE YEARS, THE INTERNET HAD ROASTED
me on a daily basis for my horrendous portrayal of a spy. Pretending
to be a detective wasn't starting off much better. Sitting at Missy's
driftwood slab table, I listed the names I could remember from the
flash drive. I was going to need Missy's help with some of them.

"Can your people get me a sit-down with Bryce Crisp?" I
asked.

"Maybe. I had lunch with him once, with Kit," Missy replied.

"When?"

Missy got quiet. "When *Near Death* was in pre-production."

Near Death continued to be the common thread. "Tell Bryce
it's a matter of life and death."

"Who will you start with?"

"Ray Ford. He's the only one I'm on speaking terms with. Then the Shensei brothers, if Yuen can broker a meet."

Missy left the table to fire up the teapot. "The Hong Kong producers? What reason would you have to meet with them?"

"The Shensei brothers are the closest thing the Calabrias have ever had to a partner. They financed *Near Death* and distribute Jove Brand in China."

Missy's back was to me again. "I still don't see what they could tell you."

I was as keen to get off the subject of the Shensei brothers as Missy appeared to be. "Neither do I, but they had a dossier on Layne's flash drive. Those meets should give you time to set up the others. Schedule Dina Calabria last. When I sit down with her, I want to have as complete a picture as possible."

"Okay." Missy sucked on her lip to keep it from vibrating.

"Dina needs to know what's going on. She'll thank you, if this turns out to be anything."

Missy exhaled from her stomach, the way I taught her. "You're right."

I took a breath myself before telling Missy the next part. "The two people on this list I got close to were murdered. You had a dossier on Layne's flash drive too."

Missy's eyes flickered.

"You need to get somewhere safe, and fast," I said.

"I don't want to run, Ken. I want to help."

"There's nothing you can't do from, say, Europe."

"My Ashland place is secure," Missy countered. "I had it tightened after a break-in last year. And I need to get the flash drive anyway."

From Missy's posture, I knew to surrender. "Okay, but don't let anyone know where you are."

"I won't."

I decided not to mention I also had a dossier on the flash drive. Missy was worried enough as it was.

MISSY WENT TO the bank, withdrew too much money, and tried to give it all to me.

"I'd take maybe a quarter of this," I said. "You're paying for my lawyer."

"Detectives incur expenses. What do you charge to train someone, per month?"

I told her.

"For eight hours of instruction?"

"Closer to twenty, counting drive time."

Missy cut a stack of bills from the sheaf. "Sign me up for a year then. Paid in full now."

"A month," I countered.

"Six months."

"Three."

"Deal," Missy said. If the stack of cash were a script, she passed me the first act.

I didn't like taking her money but also had no idea what this sort of thing would cost. Living on the road added up. Missy's down payment joined my Friday take in my pocket as I headed into town to gear up.

I bought a few changes of clothes, keeping it simple: linen pants and plain short-sleeved shirts with no breast pocket. You wouldn't think a breast pocket would get caught on things but endless hours in the gym taught me otherwise. I fished my Otomix boxing shoes out of my gear bag and laced them tight. They looked ridiculous, but they also stayed on from bell to bell.

I wandered the aisles of the local stores, trying to decide what a detective would need. Going by my film collection, the essentials were a revolver, a pack of cigarettes and a fifth of rye. I ended up with a pocket notebook, a pack of pens, and a multi-tool. My last stop was a grocery store for a few bags of pecans, beef jerky, and a case of water.

Locked and loaded.

The drive north was as painless as it got. People who drove for fun, made a hobby of it, mystified me. I resented all the time wasted behind the wheel. The whole point of driving was getting to your destination. My blender and slow cooker were sorely missed. Road food leaned heavily toward carbs. A man could only eat so many omelets. There were a lot of nuts and slabs of jerky in my foreseeable future. I should have bought dental floss.

The lanes didn't clog up until I was in the Bay Area, where the roads were permanently jammed. For a center of peace, love, and happiness, the residents sure drove angry. I maintained a bored expression and ignored the honking and screaming, which only got people madder.

Ray Ford built his compound cheap back in the seventies, when it was still in a bad neighborhood. He was looking for plenty of room and neighbors who didn't mind gunfire and explosions. Forty years later, the lot alone could have fetched eight figures easy, but Ray wasn't ever selling. With the cost of moving everything to a different site, he would be lucky to break even.

Ray's lot was bordered by a twenty-foot-high fence and patrolled by a squadron of drones that somehow avoided collision with each other despite their airspeed. A graveyard of discarded sets haunted by junked vehicles turned the space between the fence and the warehouse into a labyrinth laced with tetanus. The fence was not only topped with but also woven from razor wire. Sparks snapped and popped down its length. A sign on the gate read: *Trespassers Will be Disintegrated.*

There was no buzzer or call box, so I got out of the car and waved toward the warehouse. One of the drones strafed toward me, stopping on a dime a foot short of the wire. A modulated voice sounded from it.

"Say cheese."

I automatically fell into a head shot pose, tilting towards my good side.

Auto-tuned Muzak issued from the hovering drone. I took another look around and laughed at what the locals must have thought of this place. Ray Ford's voice, sans modulation, issued from the drone.

"Ken Allen, is that you?"

"Yep," I said, sketching a salute.

"Well get in here, you old so-and-so."

The gate dragged open, crackling and squealing, as if Ray couldn't have made it slide as smooth as butter if he wanted. The drone guided me through stripped and repurposed vehicles of every type, including the remains of an Apache helicopter. My old beater blended right in. I parked in a spot by the roll-up doors. Not having any latinum or galactic standard credits, I ignored the parking meter.

The exterior door had no handle, but when I was close enough, a plate slid open to reveal a small submarine-style wheel. When I gave it a spin, the door let go with a pressurized hiss. There was no telling how much of this was functional and how much was for show.

I stepped into an airlock. The outer door closed behind me and something that wasn't steam washed over me before the inner door opened. The hallway beyond was reclaimed from a familiar spaceship. A line of green track lights flowed along the base of the wall, guiding my way toward the third door on the left. The door snapped open to disappear into the wall when I was a step away.

I was expecting a workshop but found myself in a comfortable den with wood-paneled walls and a natural stone floor. A roaring fire burned in a hearth big enough to do jumping-jacks inside. Two chairs, each with their own side table, sat in front of it. The heads of a dozen fantastical creatures were mounted on the paneling, the fictional weapon that dealt the fatal blow displayed under them. The door slid shut behind me, joining seamlessly into the wall.

Though I felt the heat, heard the crackling logs, and smelled the fragrant wood, Ray walked through the blaze without so much as a singe. He looked like the cat who ate the canary.

"Well hey there, Ken."

"Looking good, Ray."

I wasn't lying. Since losing the weight, Ray looked like a jockey in a fitted racing suit with reinforced panels on his thighs and forearms. His skin shone like polished walnut. He still kept his head and face closely shaved. These weren't style choices. Loose clothing and static electricity were serious hazards in his line of work.

In an act of retributive deterrence, the big studios blacklisted almost everyone who worked on a Jove Brand film. Missy Cazale beat the blacklist on pure talent, seasoned perhaps with a small measure of sympathy following Kit's death. Ray beat it because, as one of the best effects guys in the world, he was indispensable.

"I owe it all to you," Ray said. "I still do those workouts you showed me in Hong Kong."

"I'll send you my new ones. I didn't know what I was doing back then."

"Bodies still have two arms and legs, last time I checked. You want a coffee?"

I could tell Ray was dying to show off. "I would love one."

Ray turned back to the hearth and swung one of the stone corners open to reveal a built-in brew station. Cups were shelved in the door. He set one on a pad under a brass nozzle and the java began to flow.

"Sweeten or lighten her up?" Ray asked.

"No thanks. I blend butter into it these days. Smooths the caffeine out."

"You don't say." The gears in Ray's head were turning.

He handed me my cup and started brewing one of his own while gesturing for me to take a seat. The chair fit like a glove, the coffee was a breath away from scalding, and the faux fire toasty.

"Now what brings you here, after years of ignoring my Christmas cards?" Ray asked.

"Hey, I kept those. They're probably worth something."

Ray pafawed as if he weren't a living legend, the Magician of Make-Believe himself. If you had a tricky stunt, Ray had been the go-to guy to pull it off for forty years. If you were shooting an effects-driven film and could afford the best, you paid Ray whatever price he demanded.

"I came about Layne Lackey," I said.

"Layne Lackey?" Ray sat down. "I made the mistake of meeting with him last fall."

"How'd Layne rope you into that?"

"Little peckerwood had dug up some behind-the-scenes effects footage I didn't want public. His price was an interview."

It wasn't much of a shock to learn Layne was willing to resort to blackmail. "What did he want to talk about?"

"What didn't he? He questioned me for hours. Even tried to stay the night. Would have moved in if I let him."

If Lackey was looking for a safe haven, it was hard to beat Ray's compound. "Did he ask about any of the Jove Brand movies?"

Ray stirred his coffee with a finger. "He tried to play twenty questions with each of them. Like he didn't know what I'm about."

"A magician never reveals his secrets."

"Damn straight," Ray replied. He stopped to take a drink. "Butter, eh?"

"Grass-fed. Layne ask any questions not related to special effects?"

Ray thought about it for a minute. "I can go check the recording."

"You taped Layne's visit?"

"Wanted him to admit he was squeezing me on camera. You think Layne was pulling smoke and mirrors?"

"He wouldn't have been direct. He was onto something big and didn't want anyone knowing. It's what got him killed."

Ray set down his cup, his squint intensifying. "Layne Lackey is dead?"

"A few days ago. I was there when it happened, same as Sir Collin."

"Collin Prestor is dead?"

I looked around at the doorless, windowless room cached in a warehouse, surrounded by an electrified fence patrolled by drones. "You don't get out much, do you Ray?"

Ray stifled a laugh. "All right, point taken. Why don't you catch me up?"

I started at the beginning. Ray made for a good audience, leaning on the edge of his seat and exclaiming in all the right places. When I was done, he let out a long whistle.

"Boy, someone is setting you up but good."

My coffee was still piping hot. I hoped whatever Ray did to the mug didn't cause cancer. "I'm walking Layne's trail, but I'm also warning everyone on his list."

This time Ray didn't hold back his amusement, adding in a knee slap for good measure. "Ain't no one getting in here. Hell, you think I'm in this chair right now?"

Unable to resist, I reached out and poked a finger into his shoulder.

"Watch it, I'm ticklish."

"Let's keep that one between us," I laughed. "Now, about Layne Lackey."

"Yeah, I'll go pull his tapes," Ray said, standing up.

"I'll come with you."

"Oh no you don't. I like you Ken, but ain't no one getting a peek backstage."

As much as I wanted to see the footage for myself, I let it go. Ray wasn't the sort of person you could argue with. Five seconds after he disappeared through the hearth, I heard his voice.

"Over here. Turn your chair this way."

The chair didn't swivel before, but it did now. I turned ninety degrees to find Ray's face on a screen integrated into the paneled wall.

"The right arm on the chair opens up. Find a picture to suit you."

The lack of pronouns clued me in I was watching a recording. There was a built-in remote under the armrest. Every movie Ray had ever worked on was available for perusal. I picked *Open Season*, Bryce Crisp's debut as Jove Brand. Of the Brand films, I had watched the three transition ones the most, which technically included *Near Death*.

Open Season started with the death of the first Brand, Connor Shaw. A tricky affair. How did you kill off the beloved original and keep the audience from turning on you? Give him a noble, self-sacrificing death. Shaw's Brand went out in a hail of arrows, saving the lives of Bryce Crisp and another squire—the treacherous Huntington Smythe—when their training exercise turned deadly.

Bryce Crisp and Connor Shaw being friends helped the transition. Shaw was done with the franchise and passed the mantle to Crisp during media promotion. Neither I nor Sir Collin had that advantage. Niles Endsworth wouldn't either. With my luck they'd end up calling it the Ken Allen Curse.

The third act was starting when Ray came back, where Bryce as Brand was infiltrating the big-game preserve, only to discover the animals were actually animatronic death traps.

"Still holds up," I said.

"That's because it wasn't crapped out by a hundred underpaid kids slaving away on computers," Ray replied. "I went through my Layne Lackey footage. We talked about the different Brand gadgets I mocked up."

"He didn't ask about the production side of things?"

"Only to do with budget. How I built props, did they really work, the stuff reporters always ask."

It didn't track. Layne came here for a reason. "Did he ask about *Near Death*?"

Ray went quiet while he recalled. At least I had a movie to pass the time.

"You know, he did." Ray finally announced. "But I didn't have much to tell him. I barely touched your picture. Not enough money or time."

Among many other tropes, every Brand film had a scene where he met with Viviane Lake, who outfitted him with all the latest gadgets. Her exposition was always heavy with innuendo and double entendre. Viviane circled but never ended up in bed with Brand. Whether they should or should not was hotly debated among the fans.

I didn't get my scene with Viviane Lake. In *Near Death,* I stared into my video watch intensely—intense was one of the expressions I thought I had down, but I came off as constipated— as she explained that since this assignment was off the books, they couldn't provide support, only the location of a weapons cache I might find useful. Viviane signed off by promising me a proper fitting, should I ever get back to England, so she could find out how I measured up to my predecessors.

Ray must have noticed my disappointment. Eager to give me something, he got personal. "You know, Kit Calabria and I had it out over that movie. If he had lived, I never would have worked for him again."

This was news to me. "Why?"

Ray couldn't believe my question. "Why? Because you almost died about ten times during shooting! It was like someone was out to get you."

Ray wasn't lying. If you saw a scene in *Near Death* and wondered how we did it, the answer was we actually did it. Still, the desire to defend Kit was too strong to let it go. "We had no budget. Kit was desperate, and I thought I was invincible. We were both young."

"What you were was naive and eager to please. You ever grow out of that?"

I developed a sudden interest in my coffee. We had passed the conversational limit I had when it came to talking about myself. "Missy still has my video watch. It made it about a day past filming before breaking."

"That's how long it was supposed to last." Ray could get loud when he wanted. For example, when he was feeling attacked. He leaned in and waited for me to fire back.

"Hey, I wasn't going after you. That it really worked in the first place boggles my mind. Every other production would have pasted on the video screen in post."

Ray relaxed into his chair and mumbled out a defense. "Mostly I broke things out of storage and tuned them up. Give me five minutes to replace the battery in that watch and it would work just fine."

"Missy wouldn't survive it being taken apart. It's the closest thing to a wedding ring she ever got."

"What can you do?" Ray put his hands up. "Anyway, props and effects were all Layne wanted to talk about. Maybe he struck out."

I didn't agree. If Ray had contributed nothing, why bother giving him a dossier on the flash drive? If Layne learned something beyond *Near Death's* meager effects budget, Ray hadn't taken note. It would have helped to review Ray's tapes myself, but that wasn't going to happen.

"Well, time to get moving," I said, climbing out of my chair. When Ray shook my hand I held onto it. "Don't let anyone in. I'm serious. People are dying over whatever this is."

It was Ray's turn to hold me in place. "If that's the case, then let me outfit you."

I laughed, expecting Ray to laugh along, but he was dead serious. The Magician was offering to open up his wardrobe.

It was a step too far.

"No way. I'm not looking to kill anyone, including myself."

Against his better judgment, Ray let me go. "If you change your mind, you know where I am."

6

I DROVE AWAY FROM RAY'S COMPOUND UNTIL MY cell service returned and called the best dim sum place around. My Cantonese was rusty, but it did the job. The woman who answered the phone slammed it on the counter and yelled at someone about how his business wasn't their business.

"I can have you on the midnight cruise to Jakarta." The combination of Yuen's muted voice and ancient landline made it feel like I was calling a time traveler.

"I need you to get me in touch with Shensei Studios."

I took in the static as Yuen went back to chewing. In all the time we knew each other, we never talked about his connection to the Hong Kong film industry. But no one was cast in *Near Death* on accident, including Yuen. Kit didn't know him from Adam. Yuen had clearly gotten a push from someone else. A push that sent him from Hong Kong to California.

"I know I'm asking a big favor."

Yuen finished what he was chewing on. "The real favor might be not doing you the favor."

"That's a good one. What were my lucky numbers?"

"I'll call you back and let you know."

If Yuen struck out, I had no backup plan. If Layne was looking into *Near Death's* production, Shensei Studios was an essential piece of the puzzle. Kit had struck a deal with Shensei that included equipment, crew, and locations in exchange for distribution of the Jove Brand franchise in Asia.

Given the desperate situation, Kit had no leverage to negotiate. Shensei Studios got the lion's share of the Asian box office. That distribution deal now made the Shensei brothers half a billion dollars every three years.

In return, the new films were guaranteed to be screened, fulfilling the rights contract. American and European distributors could no longer force a default by shelving the release. It gave the Calabrias the upper hand when dividing the take in those markets.

I decided to gas up while I waited, but the gauge showed full. Ray was some host. Five minutes later, my phone rang.

"Go to the Shishi. They will let you in or they won't."

"Fifty-fifty, huh? Hope I get lucky."

"Call no man lucky until he is dead," Yuen rasped. In the background, the woman who answered the phone was going off on Yuen about abusing their all-you-can-eat policy.

"Four thousand years of philosophers, and your cookie place is ripping off the Greeks. Shameful."

The woman who answered the phone yelled something about tying up the line.

"You might want to be unlucky this time."

The phone went dead before I could reply. Fine with me. Yuen had delivered a solid closer.

Chinatown wasn't far from Ray's compound, while also being a world away. I parked in the neighboring zip code, took the BART to Union Square, and walked the rest of the way. Being in the tech capital of the world, at least a dozen people took pictures of me. I might as well have flagged my location on social media. I should have asked Ray to whip me up a disguise.

I saw Chinatown last. I heard it first, then smelled it, then felt it thrumming through my veins. It would never be a real place to me. I would always view it through the lens of a lanky teen who ran away from home, searching for something to search for. An outsider who refused to break, grudgingly passed from one master to the next, graduating against all odds to Hong Kong. My time here had been short, but it would stay with me forever.

I wove through the narrow alleys without too many bumps. It wasn't long before my entourage formed. Tall, blond, white guys stood out on the secret streets. None of my escorts bothered to pretend they were doing anything but tailing me. I didn't acknowledge them, but I didn't ignore them either. It was good I didn't need directions because no one would have provided them. Not to where I was going.

Shishi Opera House had always been and would always be in Chinatown. There were multiple performances every week, but you couldn't buy a ticket. You had to be gifted one. Sometimes the players performed to a packed house, and other times for a solo audience. Those latter nights were the ones that mattered most.

Four pairs of Fu lions glared at me as I climbed the carpeted stairs. Yuen could announce my appearance, but he couldn't secure an invitation. The doors would either open or they wouldn't. I couldn't control that. I could only control myself.

They didn't open. I stood at the threshold, displaying no cracks in my veneer. I didn't pace or turn away. The time had come to face the sin of fleeing Hong Kong, my aspirations at the bottom of the ocean with Kit's plane.

The sun burned my neck. Sweat rolled down my face and stuck the shirt to my back, but I didn't show any sign of discomfort. I would collapse first. Twenty years ago I made it three days. Like any aging man, I wondered if what I had gained made up for what I had lost.

I wasn't given the opportunity to find out. After two hours the doors opened, washing me in cool air. The quick response could only mean one thing: the Shensei brothers wanted something from me.

What exactly that was would be good to know so that I could deny them it until I got the answers I came for, but nothing came to mind. We hadn't crossed orbits since *Near Death* wrapped.

I inclined my head slightly and removed my shoes. A pair of slippers was waiting on the far side of the door. They were my size. I didn't look into the hexagram mirror as I took the right turn into the lobby.

I was no expert on Chinese culture—countless others had forgotten more than I would ever know—but I was aware of my status. I wasn't Chinese, so I would always be an outsider. The credit for my accomplishments went to my instructors. It was like sending a chimp up in a rocket. Sure, the ape had a seat, but it wasn't really steering the thing.

The lobby was small. I took the only door that stood open, neither hurrying nor lagging, instead moving with the confidence of purpose. It led into the house room.

The floor seats were in curved rows facing the stage. The balcony seats were likewise arrayed. The sole box seats, which had their own entrance, sat at a ninety-degree angle to the stage, so they could watch both the performance and the crowd. My host sat in that place of honor.

I chose the seat at the end of the row closest to the box seats, facing the stage, so my host could observe me without my observing him. I looked to the closed stage curtains in silent stillness. I didn't fidget. It would cause me to lose face, and I had precious little to begin with. As a young man, I had dreamed of being here. Now I dreaded it.

The curtain parted. I concealed any hint of surprise. The play was silent and short. A young builder struggled to erect a palace, but ceaseless storms undid his work. Desperate, the builder met with a sage, who gifted him a monkey. With the monkey distracting the storms, the builder was able to finish the magnificent palace. But the effort exhausted the builder, who collapsed before the palace's threshold. As the curtain closed, the monkey bore the builder inside the creation that had cost him his life.

The silence built, but I said nothing. It wasn't hard. I had plenty to think about.

My host finally spoke. "I am Shensei Runshaw."

It was a challenge not to react. I had expected an intermediary. Runshaw Shensei was Chinese film royalty. His father founded one of China's first production studios, committing traditional Chinese opera to film before birthing an entirely new genre: martial arts movies. What was one of the actual Shensei brothers doing in America?

"My name is Allen Ken," I said, mirroring Runshaw's family-first introduction. My reciprocation was purely for form's sake. Runshaw knew exactly who I was. Even so, staging a production for my benefit in two hours was impressive.

"You were in one of my movies in Hong Kong," Runshaw said.

"Yes. The one in partnership with Kit Calabria."

"A partnership which transferred to his sister."

Runshaw was letting me know where his bread was buttered. He wasn't about to risk the steady windfall of a Jove Brand movie every three years. I could work with that. Not answering a question could be as good as answering it.

"The killings I stand accused of may relate to that agreement. Layne Lackey was murdered after investigating the production of *Near Death*."

"Then you face the same danger." Runshaw looked to the stage. "Are you prepared to weather the storm a second time?"

So this was what they wanted. To test me. Whatever the Shensei brothers had told Layne Lackey contributed to his death. And here I show up, another lamb to the slaughter. Runshaw was looking for a lion.

I rose up out of my chair. "Only one way to find out."

The curtains opened to again reveal the golden palace. The backdrop had changed to indicate a passage into fall. Burnished leaves began to drift down from the concealed catwalks above. Unseen drums sounded a slow but building rhythm. The time had come to once again defend the builder's fatal creation.

My muscles were stiff, but stopping to prepare would be a loss of face. I jumped onto the stage, ignoring the stairs. All those box jumps were finally paying off. I landed with a stomp. The wood reverberated under my feet.

Not knowing where the challenge would emerge, I took center stage. A man dressed in a baseball cap and a windbreaker strode from the left wing, his face concealed under an ivory demon mask.

Surprise wins fights. If you took two fighters of equal skill and size, the victor would be the one who seized the unexpected. The demon closed the distance between us with rhythmic bounding spins. The final rotation that brought him into range had a kick on the end of it. It arced down over my shoulder line, scything toward the back of my neck. For all its show, the technique was a fight ender, a one-shot knockout with the potential to put me in the ground.

I spun in the opposite direction as the attack descended, dropping my shoulder low. My hair swept the stage as I brought my own kick around. As the demon's foot passed by, my heel connected dead center in the middle of his mask. He went down, his leg coiled under his limp body.

Runshaw Shensei knew who I had been, eighteen years past. Now he wanted to discover who I had become. This was my audition for the part he wanted me to play in the plot that left me framed for two murders. I saluted him, my fist and palm meeting under my bowed head.

The next demon came from above, leading with a flying knee that had twenty feet of drop behind it. His skintight black bodysuit transformed him into a floating ivory head. I hopped back, fully expecting the fall to finish him, but for a mind-boggling instant the demon's descent halted and he landed lightly. He took to the air again with a physics-defying triple kick. My hands moved by instinct, but I checked the attacks poorly while stifling a cry of pain. I would be lucky to get out of this without broken fingers.

After another feather-light landing, the demon rose into a hover, reversing from a turning kick into a spinning backfist. The surreal change of direction tipped me off. I circled hard as the demon floundered in an attempt to rotate. I grabbed him by the back of his bodysuit, yanked him horizontal and hammered the heel of my hand into his collarbone.

He gave a muffled scream as the bone snapped. His limp body was pulled back into the rafters by the elastic wires that had made his assault possible.

I regulated my breathing to conceal any signs of exertion. If this went on for more than ten minutes I wasn't going to make it. Ten minutes was an eternity in full-contact fighting. The falling leaves were cut from crepe paper. Their accumulation made the footing treacherous. I accepted the surrealism of the setting. Everything outside would occur as it occurred. All I could do was address each moment as it came.

The third demon strode onto the stage wearing tight shorts, without shirt or shoes. He inched forward, his muscles coiled like springs. My other opponents had been traditional performers. The man behind this mask was not interested in putting on a show. He was a fighter.

His first attacks were feelers, noncommittal jabs designed to test my guard. I saw the kick too late. It landed solid below my ribs, a sweet explosion of pain that brought the world to into sharp focus. I did what I could to lessen the impact, going light and letting the force push me away rather than absorbing it.

Saving my wind cost me mobility, and the fighter pressed his advantage, launching a tight combination ending with a trip attempt. That's when I knew I was dealing with *Sanshou*—a Chinese hybrid of kickboxing and wrestling.

I stepped out of the trip and put two shots into his body: right-hook left-hook. He slipped my follow-up to his jaw and went for the stomp. All my weight was on my right foot. If the kick connected, I was looking at knee surgery.

I slammed my knee into the stage and spun into a sweep. His stomp missed and my sweep hit. It wasn't enough to put him down, but he slipped on a pile of paper leaves. After that he never recovered. Each of his parries were a breath behind my strikes. He should have submitted, but face did not permit it, so I ended it with a floating punch to his liver.

The drums stopped. I stood to show my respects, first to my foe, then to the stage, and finally to my host. Runshaw had gotten what he wanted in taking my measure. Who knew if he was pleased or disappointed by the results? Inscrutable might have been an out-of-fashion descriptor but it fit him to a tee.

"Three foes, three questions," Runshaw said.

I gritted my teeth to hide a grimace. A detective who knew what they were doing would have come prepared. I had to wing it.

"What did Layne Lackey wish to discuss?"

"If we facilitated a transfer of contract for Kit Calabria."

"Did you?"

"No."

I had plenty more to ask but nothing worth my last question. Like how Layne Lackey had earned his audience with Runshaw Shensei. It would have been nice to know, but it was irrelevant. What mattered was what he'd learned when he'd had a seat at the table.

"I wish to reserve my final question for a later date."

I could tell Shensei didn't like it but he couldn't refuse. He gave the slightest incline of the head and left without another word.

I stifled a yelp of pain as I dropped from the stage. The opera-house doors closed behind me before I was down the steps. I did not look back. I was dying of thirst but didn't stop. Showing weakness was a loss of face and I was still being watched.

I bought a bottle of water waiting for the train and drained it in one pull. The impromptu play had been for my benefit. Kit discovering me at the Wushu Championships eighteen years ago hadn't been happenstance. Kit needed someone to save the day, and the Shensei brothers had guided him to me.

Now they were betting I could pull it off again. They needed the killings to end to save the franchise. It all had to do with the Brand film rights. If the Calabrias defaulted, the Shensei brothers would lose a distribution deal worth a billion and a half dollars every decade.

It was impossible to explain how much fighting took out of you to someone who had never fought. It was an all-in endeavor. You gave everything, mentally and physically, to stop another person from inflicting permanent damage to your body. Most times, that person worked as hard as you, knew as much as you, and was as motivated to escape injury. I was soaked with sweat and couldn't get enough air. If they'd let you ride on top of the train I would have.

I tossed the water bottle on the way to my car, seriously considering a hotel room. I was reaching out for my car door when lightning struck me. All my muscles seized as my joints locked. Everything that could cramp did as my body twisted into a chain of linked knots. The surge lasted somewhere between seven seconds and forever. When it stopped, all I wanted to do was lie there, which was good, because it was all I was capable of.

"Sorry about that, Mr. Allen, but safety first."

I had been hit by a lot of things but this was my first Taser. Someone was kind enough to stand over me and block the sun. My eyes wouldn't focus on account of not being able to blink. I tried to reply but my jaw was locked. I might have nodded.

"My firm has been employed to relay a message: Please cease and desist your amateur investigation."

"That," I paused, struggling to sit up, "wasn't a bad workout."

"If you'll indulge me, I'll add my own rider. You're playing fantasy ball in a big-league game. That sort of reaching gets people killed."

Something tapped me gently on the temple. I smelled the oil, felt the cool machined cylinder. It was shady, wherever my ambusher kept his gun.

My vision was coming back. I made out two men heading toward a pair of green Range Rovers. Two more men waited on the far side of their hoods. All of them wore the same outfit: blue ball caps, gray windbreakers, Dockers, and combat boots. The passengers got in before the drivers. I watched them pull away. I wasn't chasing anyone in my condition and didn't want to catch them anyway.

I sat in my car for a while, enjoying the air-conditioning while relearning how to use my arms and legs. Once I was able to work the pedals, I headed back the way I came.

Thankfully, I didn't have to get out of the car—the gate opened for me when I pulled up. The drone guide was a lifesaver. In my current condition, I would have gotten lost in my own condo. Ray was waiting for me in the den.

"Boy, you look like you got ran through a press."

I found my voice. "Changed my mind. If I'm going to play pretend, I might as well dress up."

7

I WAS TEMPTED TO HUNKER DOWN IN RAY'S COMPOUND
based on his bathtub alone. Calling it a tub really didn't do it justice.
Designed to emulate a natural grotto, it was as big as my bedroom.
The waterfall vents generated a soothing white noise. The water
was seasoned with a mineral mix that emulated how the ocean had
been before humankind had had its way with it.

Toweling off, I checked myself out in a mirror mounted on a
fieldstone wall. A footprint was materializing under my ribs. My
forearms were bruised from catching kicks and my knee swollen
from slamming into the stage. Twin bite marks from the Taser
shone on my back.

Hell of a first day.

If I lived anywhere but This Town, people would say I looked five, even ten years younger than my age. There I looked average, the product of six workouts a week and three cheat meals a year. Though I wasn't on camera, my business was fitness and with it came a certain expectation. There was more to it, if I was being honest. I had been training like this since I was able to walk. If you took that away, who was I?

I wrapped myself in a fur robe that could have used another six inches of hemline and followed the track lights back to my room, a cozy space that was largely bed. I had no idea how long I slept. Neither the sunshine nor moonlight were real. My old clothes were a lost cause. I abandoned them for a fresh set. Turns out sleuthing called for frequent wardrobe changes.

I laced my boxing shoes up tight and said, "Ready when you are."

My door slid open to let me out. I followed the trail of lights down stone stairs into an armory stocked with prop weapons from a hundred imagined worlds. Ray was standing by the half wall bordering a shooting range.

"Boy, have I got something for you," he said.

"I'm not licensed to carry a gun."

"Well, that depends on what the law defines as a gun, doesn't it, Ken?" Ray set a metal case down on the half wall. "Latch works off your fingerprints."

"You got them from my coffee mug, didn't you?"

Ray answered with a twinkle of the eye.

The case opened with a pressurized hiss. I waited for the lid to rise dramatically, as to not spoil Ray's reveal. A light set into the underside of the lid flickered to life to reveal a Quarreler.

King Arthur had Excalibur. Indiana Jones his whip, and Luke Skywalker his lightsaber. Jove Brand had the Quarreler.

The Royal Gamesman didn't wield a mere pistol with mundane bullets, oh no. The best way to describe the Quarreler would be to call it a dart gun, though that was oversimplifying. Since its debut in *The Gamesman Afoot*, the Quarreler had gone through many incarnations, each with different features.

Ray was more excited than I was. "Go ahead. She ain't loaded yet."

I withdrew the Quarreler from its foam bed, feeling its curves. It had no sharp edges, slightly bowing from the muzzle towards rear sight and trigger guard. It also had no hammer or sights. Combined with the short, sloping grip, its lines were more akin to a miniature shotgun than a pistol. I aimed it downrange, knowing enough to not point it at Ray, whether he said it was loaded or not. I had to admit, it felt good in my hand.

Damn it.

"Petite as I could make her, for concealability," Ray said. "Gotta bigger behind than I like on my ladies, but there was no getting around it."

"You actually built a functional Quarreler."

"Sure did, and she uses fléchettes, same as in the books." Ray held up a dart with a short point and a slim, steel-veined tail. "They're saboted, sort of like shotgun shells."

Ray reached into the case and took out a metal cylinder that looked like the middle part of a revolver.

"I color-coded the quivers so you'll know what you're getting at a glance. Standard are red. Yellow are shock rounds. Not much battery room in the dart but they'll put a guy down long enough for him to think about what he did. Green are explosive. Black are smoke."

"Hold on, explosives?"

"More like a concussion. Packs a decent wallop. Shock rounds are no good against body armor."

"By shock rounds you mean Tasers."

Ray snorted. "Sure, if by trebuchets you mean catapults. These little babies will make the Taser charge you took feel like licking a battery."

"But they won't kill anyone?"

"Only the reds are lethal," Ray confirmed. "Extremely lethal. They're built sort of like those Russian dolls with shells inside shells. Dumps all the energy in the target. They can't penetrate for crap, but you also aren't going to rack up collateral damage if you miss."

"Good to know." I was a little overwhelmed. I'd only shot a gun a handful of times, all of them because I had a client who didn't want to prep for a role by themselves.

"Now, she's no good outside of fifty feet," Ray cautioned. "The Quarreler isn't a traditional black powder weapon. She's a hybrid: part electric, part compressed gas."

"A plug-in gun. Is there anything we don't need to charge these days?"

"Don't worry, it's standard USB. You should only have to top her off every hundred rounds or so, which is when you'll need to change the gas cartridge anyway. If you need to recharge in a hurry, pop the entire grip off like so and slap another in. Fresh battery and canister in one package."

There were two replacement grips in the case. I dug out one of the yellow-coded quivers. "What's the capacity?"

Ray made a sour face. "Try as I might I couldn't fit more than seven fléchettes in the damn quivers. Seventeen short of what the Quarreler from the books supposedly has."

The smooth cylinder was heavier than it looked. "Cramming seven shots into this thing is pretty good, if you ask me."

"Well, since she's not a traditional firearm, I was able to keep the walls thin and use carbon fiber." Ray studied the Quarreler like he could see through it. "See, the internal pressure is different. Rounds are subsonic, and there's no percussion cap."

I did my best to pay attention, but Ray droned on about internal suppressors and gas compensators and other things I was clueless about. I tuned back in when he broke open the pistol to load the quiver. With a flick of the wrist, Ray snapped the Quarreler back together. There was a three-dimensional target not unlike a tackling dummy standing in the firing lane fifteen feet away.

I remembered enough about shooting to recall using protective gear. "Don't we need eyes and ears?"

"You must already have ear plugs in, because I just explained you won't," Ray replied.

The Quarreler issued a snap-hiss no louder than slamming a door. The fléchette hit the dummy center of mass, the veined fins spinning like a fan. Ray put the pistol down on the half wall and stepped back.

"Your turn."

I copied Ray's stance—decades of martial arts instruction had transformed me into a physical mimic on par with a professional dancer—while trying to recall the basics of shooting: when to breathe, to squeeze and not pull the trigger. I'd held babies that kicked harder than the Quarreler. The first round landed low.

"It's got a drop," I said.

Ray nodded. "Parabolic arc. Like a bow."

I worked through the rest of the standard quiver. I didn't do too bad, but I was standing in a firing range, unwinded, with no one shooting back at me. When it struck a dry chamber, the Quarreler automatically broke open and ejected the quiver.

Ray handed me a yellow cylinder. "Shock rounds next."

As I dropped the cylinder in, the Quarreler sucked it from my hand, locking it into place. "Magnets?"

Ray had a flawless poker face.

The shock rounds impacted harder than I expected, rocking the dummy as ozone filled the air. The explosive rounds made the dummy buck like a horse. The gas rounds made my eyes water and my nose run from fifteen feet away.

Ray handed me a handkerchief. "With those you can miss a little and it still works out. Good for getting guys around corners."

In my second pass, Ray used his phone to move the dummy around. Outside of thirty feet, my accuracy was dicey. I tried not to think about how much the fléchette cartridges had to cost.

After I had worked through the quivers in the case, Ray spread a stack of paperwork out on the wall.

"Best part is, if you skip the red quivers, the Quarreler is technically not a firearm," he said. "Though if she ever gets seized, I'm sure they'll amend the statutes. Keep these papers in your glove box regardless. Seeing as you aren't a felon yet, it shouldn't be a problem."

It was good news for me, because I had no intention of ever loading a red cylinder. I'd never gotten over the one death I had a hand in, nor forgotten my near misses. Not that it helped, being reminded of it every time I saw Yuen's scar.

I signed my way through the forms before tucking them into the leather pouch provided. "According to this, you're a licensed firearm instructor."

"I'm a licensed everything. Now for your other goodies."

Ray opened a case containing a dozen textured rubber spheres, also color coded, each about the size of a golf ball.

"Non-lethal grenades. Colors match the quivers. Yellow are flash-bangs, green are regurgitants, and black make smoke."

I was happy there were no red balls. I picked up a yellow one, feeling its jagged ridges.

Ray picked up a smooth black ball.

"Each has a different texture so you can find what you need without looking." He tossed the ball a good fifty feet. When it hit the concrete it bounced up a foot, then stuck where it landed. A heartbeat later it exploded into an oily smoke. "Gel-based. Needs an impact to activate the agents. Throw 'em hard as you want, they'll stop wherever they hit."

Ray broke out goggles and earmuffs for the grenades, making me throw each so I knew what to expect. It turned out a regurgitant made you puke.

"There's more," Ray said with a grin.

The next case held a smooth-banded watch with classic lines supporting a modern touch-screen face. It came with a companion Bluetooth earpiece, half a dozen pencil cameras, and the same number of quarter-sized microphones.

My thumbprint brought the touch screen to life. "This is a heck of an upgrade from my old video watch. I didn't know you were into this modern stuff."

"Bluetooth is paired to the watch, both cellular and wireless," Ray replied, ignoring my ageism. "Switch between the cameras with this button and the mics with this one. Hit this button and the mics switch over to ultrasonics. Anyone close will get a raging headache, fast."

"Why would I want to give someone a headache?"

"How the hell should I know?" Ray gestured to the Quarreler. "I couldn't get the GPS and camera fléchettes working right. Maybe next time."

"Next time." When I laughed, Ray didn't join me. "You've been waiting for something like this to happen, haven't you?"

"Damn right I have," Ray said, pulling out another case.

"Man, you must keep your case guy busy."

Ray was clearly offended. "I am my case guy."

The next case had a crazy multi-tool with a vibrating lockpick. The one after that wasn't a case. It was a suit bag and I knew what was in it.

"Oh no way."

"Oh yes way."

The zipper got stuck more than once. I usually had steady hands, but after eighteen years of sporting a salmon jacket, I was finally going classic. Jove Brand had several iconic outfits, but this was my favorite.

"The blue blazer," I said. It wasn't a solid blue but rather a weave of light blue and gray, tailored in a clubhouse cut. It looked like a summer jacket but was way heavier.

Ray ran his fingers over the fabric. "I call it mimetic chainmail. Pliable, until it takes an impact. A layer of gel is sandwiched between the outer and inner protective weaves. Good for anything a trauma plate would stop. But remember, your chest isn't protected. If you think you're walking into trouble, button up."

The blazer wasn't easy to slip on, but I managed to maneuver into it.

"Don't move," Ray said. He blasted two hooks into my body, left-right, using his hips and pivoting like I taught him. Punches that should have cracked ribs landed with all the force of a pool noodle. "The gel disperses impact energy. And the jacket tends to keep its lines, no matter what you're hiding under there. Little unintended bonus."

Inside the last case was a harness with a shoulder holster and a belt. The Quarreler hung upside down under my left arm. The quivers were mounted on the back right side of the belt, with the cylindrical ball dispensers on the back left.

With the blazer on, you couldn't tell there was anything underneath it, though I guess my shoulder-to-waist ratio helped. Still, I felt like I was wearing a radiation apron. The jacket looked good with the white short-sleeved shirt and linen pants, but my black boxing shoes stood out.

"I didn't have time to cobble up proper footwear." Ray grimaced.

"Don't sweat it. I look like one of those hipster sneaker guys."

Ray shrugged it off but I could tell it bothered him. Next time I came by, I was getting rocket boots and fireproof underwear.

Ray led me back over to the quiver case. "Let's practice reloading. Break your Quarreler open and hover the breech over a quiver."

I did so, and the quiver jumped from my belt into the Quarreler's chamber.

"Presto!" Ray said with a flourish. "Practice a bit and you'll find it's actually faster to reload one-handed. Plus, you don't have to look away from what you're doing."

I got it down in no time. When Ray grudgingly admitted he was satisfied, he asked, "So who roughed you up?"

"Who hasn't? This time it was Chinese opera guys dressed like demons followed by some private security firm."

"You're living a weird life there, Ken."

JOVE BRAND IS NEAR DEATH

"Tell me about it," I said, loading shock rounds into the Quarreler.

"These security guys leave a card or anything?"

"Nope. They rolled full California-covert in unmarked Range Rovers."

"Any idea who they're working for?"

"Whoever suspects I'm following in Layne Lackey's footsteps, I'd wager." Talking about it shook something loose. "Shensei made me fight three times. The first guy was dressed like the ones that roughed me up. I think Shensei was trying to warn me what I was up against without breaking his nondisclosure agreement with the Calabrias. He wants me to get to the bottom of this while also keeping his hands clean."

Ray soaked it in, trying to look serious but barely able to contain his excitement. He'd spent his life building toys for people to play pretend with and now it was happening for real. My quest to prove my innocence was the ultimate tinkerer's test.

"So where you off to next?"

I holstered my Quarreler and buttoned up. "It's time I paid Jove Brand a visit."

8

LUCKY FOR ME, BRYCE CRISP WAS IN THE STATE, summering at his hobby vineyard in wine country. It was too hot, dry, and dusty for my car's meager AC.

After a half hour my shirt was soaked and the bulletproof blazer was laid out on the backseat. It didn't breathe much. I tested out the Bluetooth earpiece catching Missy up.

"So was Runshaw was giving you clues? Then why try to beat you up?"

"To make sure I'm ready for what poking around is going to bring down on me. Whatever is going on, Runshaw wants it stopped. He tried using Layne Lackey first, and it got Layne killed."

"It seems strange they talked to him at all."

It only seemed strange to Missy because she didn't know the whole story behind *Near Death.* "Working with Lackey was a good way to find out what he was after. I might need to meet with Runshaw again, once I know more, which is why I held back a question. To force an audience."

"Will that work?" I could hear Missy chopping vegetables. She was always chopping vegetables. It was her lot in life, being a gluten-free vegan.

"If he's to preserve face, yes."

"Is that like honor?"

"More like image. Think of it as maintaining a persona."

The sound Missy made told me she understood exactly what I was talking about. "So we need to figure out who these private, uh, contractors are."

I nodded, then remembered I was on the phone. The Bluetooth was darn convenient.

"That would be good, but more important is who they work for. They came looking for me the day I got started. That's a pretty big coincidence."

"I'll ask around and see who people are using to discourage stalkers these days."

"You're getting the hang of this faster than me."

"You'll catch up," Missy said.

"I'd better. I'm almost there. Bye for now."

Bryce Crisp's estate was a Frank Lloyd Wright dream built into a craggy, artificial hill complete with falls flowing into multilevel pools. Bryce could enjoy the fruits of seven successful Brand films from a master suite overlooking acres of vines and orchards. I went through the open gate and up a winding path to park in the multilevel garage built into the hill.

Vehicles were another of Bryce's passions. My old beater lowered the tone.

As I was heading toward the elevator, I caught him out of the corner of my eye, standing proud among the six-figure classics. His majesty stopped me dead in my tracks.

The White Stag, Jove Brand's signature ride.

There had been more than a dozen Stags, evolving to fit the era that fostered them. The first was a stock Triumph with minor cosmetic additions and only two gadgets: a shotgun mount and oil slick. Over the years the bikes, like the films, became more elaborate and fantastical to outdo their predecessors. There have been White Stags that rode under the water and White Stags that danced in the air. Their antler racks have held grappling hooks and missiles and lasers. Their hooves have trailed fire and kicked up smoke.

This particular Stag was my favorite: the classic from *Most Dangerous*, with swept organic lines and graceful flanks. It was like stumbling across a unicorn. Despite his age, he looked fresh from his maiden voyage. Eventually, I tore myself away and stepped into the elevator.

Only the third of four floor buttons was lit up, so I pushed it. When the doors closed, the Jove Brand theme started playing, the one from *Flings and Arrows* with the Spanish guitar. The doors opened into a huge room with a glass wall so clean it gave the illusion of open air. The oppressive heat only added to the effect.

Bryce was waiting for me in a vintage black leather lounge chair. Despite the temperature, he was wearing a smoking jacket and slippers. Freshly dyed, coiffed and shaved, he was more suave than a man in his late seventies had any right to be.

I sat in the matching chair opposite him, angled to be intimate but also oblique, to discourage improper eye contact. A pitcher of tea sweated through the lace mat and onto the glass-topped table between us, the edges of the ice cubes still sharp. It was accompanied by a plate of cucumber sandwiches neither of us intended to eat.

"I love what you've done with the place," I said, filling both our glasses. It had been less than a minute and I already wanted to rub the pitcher all over my face.

Bryce gave a perfunctory smile. "You jest, but this was once fallow field. Where now stand trees lay not even a sapling. Of course, by the time the boughs were suitable, my climbing days were done. As one of the gentry, I always longed for a castle, so I raised one."

"You were smarter than a lot of guys back then." I took a long drink. Bryce liked his heat dry. "They thought the good times would last forever."

"Connor Shaw included, may his soul rest in peace," Bryce replied. "We were all typecast. My blacklist was not as dark as yours, but after Brand, I was never considered for a role that didn't involve bullets or bedsheets. Gone were the dreams of King Richard, laid to rest with the aspirations of Macbeth."

"You did more with Brand than anyone." I drained my glass. I was dying to get the blazer off, but if Bryce saw what I had strapped on under it, he was going to think I'd lost my mind.

"Oh yes. I tamed the brute. Civilized him. My Brand treated his paramours to his fingertips rather than the back of his hand. "

"You and Shaw created the ends of the Brand scale. Sir Collin's portrayal of Brand landed right in the middle."

"Perhaps Niles will add a new measure."

That Bryce had heard about Niles Endworth's casting wasn't a big surprise, nor was it that he was aware of Niles's existence. Endsworth was a shoe-in to one day be voted sexiest man alive.

Back then people didn't know how good an actor Bryce was, convincing the world he loved the ladies as much as they loved him.

I refilled my glass from the pitcher. Bryce still hadn't touched his. "Did Missy explain why I wanted to meet?"

"She suggested Layne Lackey's fate was tied to Sir Collin Prestor's."

"They were killed the same way, by a person who knew what they were doing." I could hear whoever Bryce had shaving him and brewing his iced tea these days puttering around in the kitchen. "Layne Lackey was working on what he felt was a big story, related to Brand."

"As were all his tales, true or not," Bryce replied.

"Whatever the story, Sir Collin could have filled in some blanks."

"And perhaps myself."

"A strong *perhaps*," I said between gulps of iced tea. "What did Layne ask about?"

"He was more indulgent than insistent. He let an old man drift, as old men are wont to do."

"Was there a topic he steered you toward more than once?"

I emptied the pitcher while Bryce thought. The ice cubes had become slivers. I sucked them to death as surreptitiously as possible. Around the time I began worrying he'd fallen asleep, Bryce spoke again.

"Interestingly enough, he wanted to talk about you. Well, your film, at least. The genesis of it. Was I present for discussions after *A Beautiful Disaster?* Did Kit Calabria court me as an investor or consult me on contract matters? I was once a barrister, back when I still believed gaining my father's approval was a possibility."

Now we were getting somewhere. Besides the Calabrias and the Fletcher estate, no one had ever read the infamous Brand rights contract in its entirety, only gleaned pieces of it from behind-the-scenes footage and interviews. "Did Kit show you the contract?"

"Portions only. He was rather circumspect in his inquiries."

"Was Kit concerned he had broken it?"

Bryce stopped to ponder, tilting his chin to search his memory with careful consideration. He still had the moves. It was a good performance. He already knew the answer, from when Layne Lackey had asked him.

"In recollection, it seemed to me more he was preparing to. His inquiries surrounded the boundaries of transferal of rights."

"Which were?"

"My conclusion was that the film rights to Jove Brand could only be transferred to a member of the Calabria family. Though, as I recall, there was no stipulation about that member being born into bloodline."

It was a line written by an actor. Too many words, but perfectly delivered. It had the desired effect, hitting me full force. "So if you married into the family, that would work?"

Bryce gave a measured nod. "At the time, if Kit broke the contract, the rights would revert back to Bowman Fletcher, who was still alive."

"Don't remind me," I said. Fletcher died shortly after *Near Death* was screened in Hong Kong. Extremely shortly after. Layne Lackey once suggested seeing the movie was the cause. "If the contract was broken now, where would it go? To his estate?"

Bryce inclined his head. "None of Fletcher's many supposed heirs have passed the required DNA test. Yet."

"Fletcher did get around." I drained the last drops from my glass. Bryce wasn't even sweating. What was it with English thespians?

Bryce dropped his next bomb casually. "He also inquired about exactly what elements were necessary to constitute a last will and testament."

My mouth somehow managed to get drier. "Did you help Kit write a will?"

Bryce shook his head. "I did not want to impose, and he never broached the subject again."

Another five minutes in here and I was going to empty Bryce's glass for him. To hell with decorum. Sweat was starting to run into my eyes. "I'd like to freshen up if I could."

Bryce made a vague gesture toward a square mile of house. "There's a water closet past the kitchen."

I got up, conscious of the wet spot I left on the leather, and charted a course toward the kitchen. It was a little better in there, with the sun on the other side of the hill.

Every surface was spotless. His and his places were set on the farmhouse table.

Bryce, you sly old fox.

I was turning the corner toward the half bath when it occurred to me to refill the pitcher while I was up. I ducked back into the viewing room to find the Black Knight sneaking up behind Bryce.

My battle cry was as ineloquent as it was involuntary.

"Nope!"

The Black Knight spun to face me. The helmet concealed his expression, but everything in his carriage signaled hatred. The Quarreler was already in my hand—I didn't remember drawing it. It was a long shot. If I hit Bryce instead of the Black Knight, I was going to kill my predecessor, another Brand first. I closed the gap with my weapon at port.

The Black Knight paused to consider, then broke and ran.

He was flat-out faster than me, ignoring the elevator to vault over the railing. The drop was twenty feet, ending on water-kissed stone, and he landed it like a gymnast. By the time I was aiming the Quarreler over the rail, the Black Knight was out of sight. I didn't know where the stairs were, or if there even were stairs, so I ran back to the elevator.

"Comeoncomeoncomeon," I shouted at the doors. When they opened I smashed the garage button and leaned on the door-close button, except I got the triangles wrong and kept the doors open instead. I caught my mistake and got the elevator moving, kneeling to take up a firing stance. The Jove Brand theme kicked on again, this time the synth mix from *Cupid's Bow*. It was my least favorite Brand film, after *Near Death*. Jove Brand did not belong on the moon.

How had the Black Knight found me? He must have tailed me from Ray's compound. He'd probably jumped for joy when he found Bryce's gate open.

When the elevator doors parted, I saw plenty of cars but no Black Knight. I pointed the Quarreler around like I knew what I was doing. A Triumph's engine roared. I ran after it to watch the Black Knight corner left, skidding around the back of the hill to take the rocky stair down to the vineyard.

Even if my beater somehow survived the stairs, it wouldn't be able squeeze through the rows of grapes. I hoped Bryce would forgive me for what I was about to do.

I jumped onto the White Stag's back and depressed the ignition switch on the antler-bars. Nothing happened. The gas gauge read full. I was thinking the battery was dead when I remembered Viviane Lake's exposition from *Most Dangerous*. The handlebar ignition was actually a fake that triggered the self-destruct. Good thing Ray wasn't 100 percent accurate with all his props. I slapped the hidden flank switch and the bike roared to life.

It had been eighteen years since I had been on the back of a bike. At the time, Hong Kong cinema was kicking out these insanely dangerous motorcycle stunts. Guys firing machine guns while standing on the seat, guys diving off the saddle to tackle each other in the air, guys barreling full tilt into unexplained pyramids of cardboard boxes, that kind of thing.

I was as much a product of the times as Jove Brand. The Chinese stars were doing all their own stunts. To stand aside and let a stuntman take the risks would have been an irrecoverable loss of face. Not only as the lead, but also as the fight coordinator. Being completely inexperienced had already set me back plenty. To command any respect, I had to be the best of them.

So I did all my own stunts in *Near Death.*

Including the bike scenes.

I cranked the throttle and spun the White Stag about-face. His torque almost bucked me off. Handsome as he was, the Stag sure had it where it counted. I narrowly avoided dumping him on the suicide turn around the hill. We got to know each other navigating the stairs down to the vines. I couldn't see the Black Knight, but he was leaving a clear dust trail.

The Stag handled the transition from the concrete walk into the dirt rows without a bump. Detecting wasn't my strong suit, but this I could do. The near-invisible windscreen attached to the antler rack sheltered me as I gunned it. I went from staring at a dust trail to passing through it. When we hit the orchard, there was no more dust to kick.

The Black Knight was a hundred feet away, weaving through the trees, avoiding ditches and roots as if he were psychic. I eased off and trailed after him. I had a full tank of gas and he had ridden his bike here. All I had to do was keep him in sight and run him dry.

The Black Knight took a sharp turn when he hit the property line, bouncing onto a double-row trail made by the tractors. The corner gate was open. Whoever he was, the bastard was using up a lifetime of luck. He pulled out onto the two-lane road that bordered the property and doubled back to pass me on the far side of the fence. I let go of the antler-bars long enough to shout into my watch.

"Call Ray."

"Yello."

"I'm on a White Stag chasing the Black Knight. I need to know what it can do."

Ray didn't skip a beat. "What movie?"

"*Most Dangerous.*" I wove into the opposing lane to pass a tractor. "It's the one Bryce Crisp owns."

"Ah. He bought that Stag at auction. I retrofitted it for him, jeez, gotta be more than twenty years ago."

"Well Bryce took care of it." The Black Knight rode the double-yellow line, squeezing between a Jeep and a pickup going opposite ways. I managed to thread through, but swinging out to get the angle cost me.

"Always good to hear," Ray said.

"Any forward-facing artillery on this thing?"

"Nah," Ray grumbled. "I took out the snout cannons and the grenade launcher. His mouth still opens to emit the tube though."

"Not a big help at the moment." Five miles passed in three minutes. When the freeway on-ramp came into view, I swore and swore into the wind.

"Whoa. Tender ears here, buddy," Ray said.

As the Black Knight took the on-ramp, a green Range Rover came skidding off the exit side. A second Rover joined it, both coming right for me like they had been given directions.

Unbelievable.

I buried the throttle, leaning low, measuring the gap. If I could pass them, I could lose them in traffic. But they didn't advance. Instead, they angled parallel to block both lanes. The passengers exited before the Rovers were done braking. Each of them held the fat, revolver-style shotgun police used in riot situations.

I broke the White Stag into a skid and reversed direction. A check in the side mirror showed the gunners jumping back into the Range Rovers.

"Ray?"

"Yeah."

"What about rear-facing ordinance?"

"He's hiding a few surprises, what are you up against?"

"Pair of Range Rovers. Probably security reinforced," I said.

"Too heavy for the oil slick. Try the toggle on the left handle. Might stick a little. It's not electric."

I cranked the raised depression downward but it refused to budge. My stomach dropped as the Stag wavered from the unbalanced pressure. I stood in the saddle for leverage and worked it down in pulses.

Batches of skeletal pyramids tumbled onto the road. The first Range Rover soaked the spikes and took a header into the drainage ditch. The second one used the shoulder to edge around the thicket.

"Got one," I said.

Ray's celebratory cheer rattled my eardrums.

"Any other surprises on this thing?"

"I'll have you know that bike was pretty tricked out for 1972."
Ray snorted. "Anyway, didn't I load you up for bear?"

The gate back into the vineyard was in sight, the path to escape
open. No way a Ranger Rover could pursue through the orchard.
There was no shame in running away when you were outgunned.
Ken Allen would have lived to fight another day.

But Jove Brand wouldn't have.

"I've had about enough of these guys." I skidded to a halt and
broke the Quarreler open. The remaining Range Rover slowed in
response to my sudden reversal. I switched quivers from yellow to
green. When the Range Rover came to a stop, I buried the throttle
to get close enough before they got their doors open.

I aimed and squeezed.

The first shot hit high on the windshield. The second hit dead
center. The windshield spiderwebbed as the fléchettes detonated.
I dropped the Quarreler into the mount on the antler-bars as I
passed the Range Rover. The mercs were out by the time I circled
around. A cross between a baseball and a beanbag smashed into
my windscreen. The Stag wobbled but stayed the course. I reached
behind my back to search for a certain texture.

I tossed a green ball at a Latin guy in a tan windbreaker. He hit
the ground to dodge it. The ball continued on, into the interior of
the Range Rover. It bounced off the dash and stuck to the ruined
windshield.

I watched in the sideview as the mercs fled the cloud of oily-
brown gas. They were too busy puking to bring their weapons up.
I swung back into the gate and took it easy on the way back to
Bryce's garage. It was a victory lap. A draw was as good as a win
for me. The Black Knight had escaped, but Bryce was alive. Which
meant Bryce could clear my name. A call alert rang in my ear.

"Gotta let you go, Ray. Stag still runs like a dream."

I switched over to be greeted by my favorite law-enforcement officer.

"What the hell are you doing, Allen?"

"Afternoon, Special Investigator Stern."

"Are you at Bryce Crisp's vineyard?" The anger in Stern's voice told me she already knew the answer to her question.

"I'm going to have to decline to answer on the advice of counsel."

I pulled around the suicide curve to find Stern staring bloody murder at me. At least her gun wasn't out. I sensed a snake in the grass. The Range Rovers' timely arrival was beyond suspicious. Stern happening to be in the neighborhood at the same time was preposterous.

Stern pointed me into the garage. "You put that back and do not dare leave."

"Am I under arrest, Investigator?"

Stern almost lost it but recovered nicely, gritting her teeth as she aimed a finger at me.

"You're lovely when you're angry," I said, pulling the Stag back into his den.

Stern took a breath to master herself. "I am going to go interview Crisp. It would be helpful to my investigation if you remained on scene."

"You know I can't say no to you."

I dismounted the Stag reluctantly. Going back to my old beater was going to be tough. After Stern disappeared into the elevator, I stashed my harness and blazer in the trunk. The garage was more lived-in than the rest of the place, with bottles of unfinished sparkling water strewn about. Whoever was drinking it stopped when the bubbles did. I found the mini-fridge they came from and helped myself.

Stern came back when I was on my third bottle. I offered her one so we could toast my innocence. "How'd it go?"

Stern came for me, dropping into a shove that sent me into a vintage Jag worth more than I was. She pinned me with a straight arm, her rear hand resting on her weapon. "Did you threaten that old man?"

I was too stunned to talk. When Stern processed my genuine bewilderment, she backed off. Having made it all the way through *Near Death*, she knew I wasn't that good of an actor.

"What did Bryce say?" I asked.

"Not a damn thing. In fact, he is leaving for England immediately. A car is on the way."

My stomach churned. "No way. He saw the guy. He can clear me."

Stern blocked my path as I stepped toward the elevator. "You aren't going anywhere, Allen. You want to explain why you stole that motorcycle?"

Somewhere, Mercie Goodday was scolding me. I kept my mouth shut for the half hour it took for the limo to arrive. The minute it did, Bryce Crisp strolled out of the elevator. He was positively disheveled, with a loose cravat and crooked buttons.

I stared a plea at Bryce. He looked away with a hint of apology. The driver opened and closed the door for him. The limo began to pull away, then stopped. I dared to dream as the rear window slid down.

Bryce handed me a State of California Certificate of Title. "The Stag is yours."

Stern wasn't sure what to make of it all. I didn't blame her. I barely believed it myself. Together we watched Bryce Crisp embark eastward. Stern asked me before I asked her.

"You want lunch?"

ONE OF THE best things about California culture was how gracefully waitstaff endured fad diets. No meat or all meat. No fats. No, wait, no carbs. No wait. Extra butter but no nuts. Fruit instead of fries, and no nightshades. If cavemen didn't eat tomatoes then neither would I. Hold the dairy and how many grams of sugar was in your Greek yogurt? Could I substitute sweet potatoes for rice?

I was finishing up a tasty sausage-and-cabbage stew, skipping the beans. Stern's ahi tuna, nothing on the side, was long gone. She wanted to smoke, but was worried if we got up I would leave. She jerked a thumb over her shoulder at the White Stag, parked next to her unmarked.

"Going method, Allen?"

"Against my will. None of this was my idea." I waved the server over. "Cheese plate, don't bother with the fruit or crackers, and coffee for us both."

"Excellent," said my server.

California servers were also top notch at faking approval. I could have ordered a turd sandwich, hold the bread, to my waiter's enthusiastic endorsement.

Stern broke the stalemate. "I think you cracked. Getting humiliated by Collin Prestor and Niles Endsworth in front of millions was the thread that unraveled your sweater. You get away with the first murder and here comes Layne Lackey, harassing you for the umpteenth time. Except now he has something on you. You walk on two murders, so what's next? Kill the last surviving Jove Brand."

The server set down the cheese plate and took his time pouring the coffee. He'd overheard enough to want the rest. Stern watched me for tells while I downed a wedge of Tillamook. After the coffee was poured, the server left the carafe and fussed around with the settings of nearby tables.

I wet my whistle before responding to Stern's charges. "So why didn't I kill Bryce? If I wasn't chasing anyone, why run? I had him right where I wanted him, according to your Ken Allen Goes Method theory."

"How the hell should I know?" The coffee made Stern go for her pack, but she beat her monkey. "Maybe you had a change of heart, or maybe you've got two people bouncing around in there: nice-guy Ken Allen and Killer Brand."

I almost spilled my coffee laughing. "The old 'you don't even know you're doing it' bit, huh? What's next, the 'we have the footage from the convention lounge' move? Or maybe the 'did you know Bryce Crisp had a state-of-the-art security system' rap? You're barking up the wrong tree, Stern. I wish those little lies were true, because then you could go after the real killer."

Stern picked up a wedge of something creamy, smelled it, then tossed it back down. "So this is you playing vigilante?"

I poured another cup. "If no one is going to fight for me, then I'm going to have to fight for myself."

Stern sat back and crossed her arms. "Not all by yourself. I checked your financials. You can't afford Mercie Goodday."

"Have you interviewed anyone who actually knows me?"

"Sure."

"And?"

Stern rolled her eyes. "You're a hell of a guy."

"Look, this is bigger than your psycho jealous wannabe theory. Someone is trying to tank the Brand franchise."

"And you're the only who one can save it."

I didn't take the bait. "Doing something sure feels better than doing nothing. And this isn't about me."

Stern's self-satisfaction bothered me. I had given her something.

"Whoever is holding Mercie Goodday's lead is holding yours too. You on a quest, Allen?"

"Not everyone is out for themselves," I replied.

Stern sensed she had hit a nerve. "And I think when someone asks you to jump, you ask how high. If someone needs you, you'll do anything, no matter what it costs. I saw *Near Death*. You were willing to die for that heap."

"Someone did die for that heap," I snapped. Stern was damn good. She almost had me spilling. "You got me. We all have our flaws. Look at you."

"Uh-huh," Stern said around biting her nails.

"You're on me for playing vigilante, but here you are, chasing me around all alone. I wasn't sure when we met, but now I know. Growing up, other girls dreamed of a white dress, but you wanted the white hat. How'd your parents take it?"

Stern looked bored. Looked. She started tapping an antique lighter on the table.

"You haven't smoked in what, three hours? Why not make it four?"

"Let's not talk about me," she said.

I tried to decide what to tell Stern. It was bad having her behind me, but having her ahead of me would be worse.

"Layne Lackey was onto something. He was trying to tell me about it, but was too paranoid about being hacked to leave a message. I thought he was angling for an exclusive over Sir Collin's death so I never picked up. Did the convention center end up having cameras?"

"Yeah."

"Well that's good news for me. You've seen the Black Knight."

Stern toyed around with her lighter, flicking it open and closed. "Guess your lawyer will tell you anyways. Lackey disconnected the cameras in the VIP lounge when he came in. He also had the room cleared prior to meeting you."

And also prior to meeting the Black Knight. I fumed over my coffee. "Layne came to that con to chase me down, but the killer got to him first."

"Why you?" Stern leaned in, all ears. She was back playing ally. I liked that she hadn't given up on long hair. It was hard to find anything I didn't like, and I was trying.

"I wish I knew. Maybe he wanted to know if Sir Collin said anything to me, or maybe he thought I had a piece of the puzzle. Maybe he wanted me to throw in with him, now that I was a victim of the plot."

"I'm not the conspiracy theory type."

"Neither was I, until I got cast as Oswald."

Every time Stern looked at me I was already looking at her. I didn't want to get up either, so I found a new topic of conversation.

"How up are you on the local private security operators?"

"You turning me into a source, Allen?"

"Look, do you want to be able to use all these words against me later or not?"

"I'm familiar," Stern admitted. "Having your own little private army is the new fad. There's no shortage of ex-military floating around, or guys pretending to be."

"Any of them drive green Range Rovers?"

"They white guys?"

"Half of them."

"Not the Daredevils then. Sounds like Chevalier." When Stern pronounced the word, she left off all the right letters.

"How do they rank?"

"Top five. They know what they're doing. Former French Foreign Legion. Use a lot of nonlethals. So far they've managed to avoid any felonies."

Then it was Chevalier. The demographics, vehicles, and use of nonlethal weapons matched, if hundred mile-an-hour sandbags counted as nonlethal. "They must do okay. Range Rovers aren't cheap."

I got up and dropped some cash on the table. All play and no work would make Ken Allen a convict. Stern walked me to the Stag. I climbed on and patted the seat behind me. "Care for a spin?"

For a second there I thought she was going to say yes. Instead she pulled out a cigarette case. "Get a helmet, Allen. It's illegal to ride without one."

I was thinking of a parting line when my brain clicked on. "You were at Bryce's property lickety-split."

Stern shrugged while she lit up.

"Maybe you should be wondering who's tipping you off and how they know where I am." Instead of patting myself on the back for my delivery, I should have been asking myself the same thing.

9

THE OPENER BUILT INTO THE STAG GOT ME INTO
Bryce Crisp's garage. In beating a hasty retreat, Bryce forgot to set
his security system. It took me a long time to search his place. It was
loaded with Jove Brand memorabilia, a lot of which looked like actual
production props. In spite of his resentment over being typecast, Bryce
had embraced his time as Brand. Then again, unlike me, playing
the role had been a positive experience. The fandom loved him.

Fortunately, Bryce's beau had cleared out and saved me from
making awkward excuses. From the state of the guest bedroom, it
appeared they didn't share a bed. Not nights, anyway. The guy was
a stud, if the weights in the exercise room were to be believed. I
didn't find any secret rooms or hidden safes or discarded notepads

to run a pencil over for clues. What I did discover was that poking around in Bryce Crisp's private life made me feel gross.

I transferred the balance of Ray's cases—the reloads, batteries, and sundry—into the White Stag's saddleboxes, then emptied my bags in my trunk and sorted through the remains of my life. There wasn't much from before all this I cared to keep, but a guy needed underwear.

My beater stayed in Bryce's garage. It wasn't like it was cramped in there. That old car had taken me a lot of places, but none I wanted to be. I wasn't going to miss it. I found the helmet from *Most Dangerous* under one of the workbenches. The hood piece was a little scuffed up and Connor Shaw's cigar smoke lingered on the mouthpiece, but it fit like it was made for me. Much to my surprise, Bryce didn't have the matching gloves. Maybe Ray could make me a pair.

THE FIRST MOTEL I passed called out to me. I placed pencil cameras in strategic locations, sure to keep the Stag in frame in an attempt to alert me to any ambushes.

I came out of the shower to my phone vibrating with a call from Missy. She skipped the greetings.

"I got the flash drive."

"Don't plug it in. It has a security thing."

"I don't know any computer people."

I could hear her putting groceries away. "Do you ever stop shopping?"

"Oh, I like shopping for produce. The colors, feeling them, smelling them, seeing the change of seasons reflected in them. There's a wonderful farmers' market up here."

Even if Stern had managed to make me suspicious, two minutes on the phone with Missy would have dispelled it. "How's the Ashland place?"

"Exactly the way I left it. After the break-in last year, I upgraded security. It was a scary one."

There were a lot of things to envy about Missy. Being able to rate all your break-ins wasn't one of them. "What made it so scary?"

"Nothing was taken."

I made a sound like I'd drank spoiled milk.

"Now, who do we get to hack this thing?" Missy asked. "Is that what you do with these, or do you crack them? What's the difference?"

"I have no idea. Ray Ford might know a guy. The gadgets he gave me are state-of-the-art."

"I bet he was excited."

"Yeah, he finally has what he's always wanted: a living, breathing crash-test dummy." Missy's sigh forced me to once again lie to her for her own good. "Don't worry, I'm being careful."

"Okay." Missy hung up without saying good-bye. They never did, those stars of the big screen.

And Ray didn't bother with hello. My phone didn't even finish the first ring. "Tell me everything and don't skip nothin'."

I swear he took notes while I gave him the play-by-play.

"I'm putting cameras on your next coat and belt," he said after I wrapped up. "And all over the bike I'm going to build you. I got this idea to use adhesive foam—"

"Do you know any hackers? I need someone trustworthy to tinker with that flash drive I told you about."

"Have Missy overnight it to me. I'll see what I can do."

I texted Ray's address to Missy, then fell into bed with the AC blasting. I wasn't too worried about leaving the Stag parked outside. With his bugs on it, Ray could track it anywhere.

———

TURNED OUT CAR chases took a lot out of you. I slept like a baby for thirteen hours. The room was too cramped so I went through a stretching sequence in the parking lot. One of my custom, do-it-anywhere routines—think the martial-arts version of yoga.

My ribs were sore where the third demon kicked me, but the soreness felt good, like a workout that broke a plateau. I was munching pecans and turkey jerky when a notification came in. The Super-Friends had posted the footage of our fight from the con in Fresno.

They didn't come off too good in it, but hey, channel hits were channel hits, and Street Justice could always rebrand themselves as a comedy troupe. The video was good news for me. They acted first and I responded with minimal reasonable force, even when confronted with a deadly weapon. I hadn't hit anyone in the face or the girl anywhere. Equality aside, people react differently to a man punching a woman than the other way around. Myself included.

The girl had honored my request to tag me, and now my channel of poorly sound-mixed instructional videos had a hundred thousand new hits. Only about 75 percent of the commenters called me a murderer so that was an improvement.

Hearts and minds, baby.

A rare good idea passed through my head. I started the video at the beginning, where they were detailing their surveillance with our table behind them. I cringed through me chopping away at my "fans" until I found what I was looking for.

There he was, the Black Knight. The cheeky bastard had paid forty bucks for me to chop him. I texted the time-stamped link to Stern and went to get cleaned up.

Missy had a knack for calling when I was showering. Her voice mail informed me Dina Calabria had an opening today around brunch. I wondered if Missy had talked to Dina, or if the scheduling was done through intermediaries. Neither of them had taken Kit's death well, with Missy so close and Dina on the outs.

The next voice mail was Ray telling me what the White Stag drank to keep running, along with the station closest to me. It was no surprise he was tracking me, probably through my new watch.

I fed the Stag rocket fuel and headed south towards Big Sur. My heart rate rose as the distance closed. I hadn't seen Dina since Kit's funeral. As far as Kit and Missy knew, I'd only met Dina briefly, when she paid an unwelcome surprise visit to the *Near Death* set.

Neither of them knew that she hung around after the blowup, or about how much time we ended up spending together. And how we spent it.

Then Kit died before he and Dina could heal their rift. It didn't make sense to blame me, but emotions and associations didn't have to make sense. Dina lived less than an hour from Missy and they hadn't spoken in eighteen years.

The wall was the first sign I'd passed onto the estate. Ten feet of tapering stone frosted with jagged quartz. You couldn't see Calabria Cove from the road, and even modern satellite views wouldn't reveal much.

By the time the fifth film was released, the Jove Brand franchise was a worldwide phenomenon. Life imitated its art, from fashion to design to architecture. Everything on screen was real—the gadgets, the vehicles, the sets. When the audience sat down in the theater, they were staring into the future.

Endless Watch was Big Don Calabria's magnum opus. He tapped into his network of ex-privateers to carve a castle into a cliffside. Crews drilled for weeks while a constant stream of ships delivered materials. The lighthouse at the top was only the tip of the iceberg, with dozens of glass-walled rooms facing the sea and a private marina nestled into his very own beach.

Endless Watch was the highest-grossing Brand film yet. The investors were over the moon. No one minded much when the Calabrias moved in after filming wrapped. Big Don had built his dream home on the movie's dime and used its massive cost to absorb any recorded profits. When the tax men showed up, he drowned them in shipping invoice after shipping invoice. To this day, *Endless Watch* was still in the red, on paper.

An unseen gate guard raised the portcullis. The path looked like gravel but rode like silk. Neither helipad was in use. Airborne toys waited behind the open hangar doors. A branch broke off the main drive, curving down to the beach. I stayed the course toward the lighthouse.

It looked like something out of a fairytale, three stories of rounded white stone, its top crenellated like a battlement. The sea breeze hit me hard, filling my ears. The waves were high. Good surfing, if you liked that kind of thing.

The girl coming out of the lighthouse was the picture of Mediterranean beauty. She still had the tautness of youth, not old enough to have either developed or mistreated her body, firmly in those golden years where she was sure she would look the way she did forever. Everything about her face was generous, with an unapologetic nose and dark eyes that didn't shy away from the sun, even on a day like this. She walked like she was trying out her curves but knew exactly how far away to stand to be heard over the ocean. Brushing wet curls braided with seaweed behind her ear, she asked "Returning our bike?"

"This one isn't yours."

"They're all ours, really." She tilted her head at my outfit. "Are you an impersonator or something?"

"Or something."

"Dean's birthday is going to be next level." The girl motioned for me to follow with a tilt of the chin as she turned toward the door. That move she nailed. Eighteen years ago, I would have scaled walls for her. Now all I saw was a kid pretending to be all grown up.

The bottom floor of the lighthouse was dominated by a single round room. A fire pit encircled by a leather couch anchored the space. My greeter stepped down to join three of her sisters.

Bowman Fletcher wasn't the only man of his era who embraced arcane contractual requirements. In his will, Big Don stipulated only a male heir could inherit the Calabria fortune. Though Dina was firstborn, the Brand legacy had gone to her brother. After that, the best she could do is produce a son and hope Kit didn't do the same.

It took Dina seven tries to get a boy. She must have really loved her first husband, because she gave him two attempts before she dumped him. The next four husbands only got the one. Sometimes Dina dumped them before she even gave birth, as if she could sense another daughter was on the way. Then, the summer after Kit died, her last husband gave her Dean. She stayed married to that one.

Just in case.

Those months after Kit's death were the closest the rights to Jove Brand ever came to defaulting back to the Fletcher estate.

In court, Dina argued that she was bearing a male heir and thus the Calabrias still maintained the rights. Fortunately, the case was argued in Italy, the capital of all Catholicism. The ruling came back that if she bore a son, the rights would fall under her conservatorship until Dean turned eighteen. A birthday which, according to his mermaid sister, was just around the corner.

"Mom's all the way up," my greeter informed me before resuming banter with her sisters. While they were loved, each of them was a failed attempt. I knew how they felt.

The second floor was a combination of dining room and kitchen. No outsider did the cooking in a Sicilian family. The top floor was where the work got done. How many Brand pictures had been planned out on those bowed couches? How much film history was made, overlooking the waves, a glass in one hand and a cigar in the other?

When I told Missy to leave Dina for last, I left out half the reason. I didn't ever want to see her again, and, to hazard a guess, she felt the same way. But here we were. Dina was waiting on the terrace, taking a call with her back to the sea. The dowager queen never rested.

She put her phone down but kept her drink, appraising me with the frankness of a woman who had masterfully cast six Brand films, including handpicking the last two Jove Brands. I appraised her right back.

Dina was what her daughters would one day be if they did everything right. She indulged in the vices so many lived for without giving them free rein. A proper balance of exercise and diet kept her skin and hair healthy. You'd never know she was a mother seven times over. The little work she had done kept everything how it was, rather than transforming her into a different creature.

Her looks were only half of it. The other half was the knowledge of who Dina Calabria was, what she had accomplished. Her brother may have saved Jove Brand, but Dina restored him, secured his place alongside Robin Hood and King Arthur. Except better. Robin Hood needed Sherwood Forest and King Arthur Camelot. Jove Brand changed with the times, a man always one step ahead of the present.

But the only way to make a myth was to kill history. Seeing her again erased eighteen years of forgetting. The proper response was probably anger, but weakness beat it to the finish line. Right then and there, I wouldn't have been able to lift a gallon of milk.

"You held up pretty good," Dina decided.

"Clean living."

I stepped through the glass doors to join Dina on the terrace. Like her daughters, she was solar-powered. I was jealous. The sun didn't kiss me as much as it spat in my face.

"No, I mean it." Dina took me by the chin to turn me into profile. "You're a dead ringer for Brand now."

I didn't mind the hand. Dina always did like taking control.

"Maybe on a book cover," I said.

Dina betrayed the trace of a smile. I couldn't recall ever seeing her laugh, even before Kit died. Even in play she was all business.

"You know, people thought I was crazy, casting Collin Prestor," she said. "Market research indicated men found him nonthreatening and women comforting. Not very Jove Brand."

Dina had steered us toward Sir Collin all on her own. I said something to stay the course. "Sure, but what had he been in before *A Gentleman's Play?* The butler in a few period pieces and those romantic comedies where the American girl moves to the English countryside?"

"They hadn't seen him onstage." Dina peered into her glass like it was a scrying pool. "When I saw his Marc Antony, I knew. The stunt stuff we could sell. Pop sold it seven times with Bryce Crisp. That crap doesn't matter, the punching and shooting." She remembered who she was talking to and threatened to smile again. "No offense."

"Oh, I'm with you. Jove Brand isn't about choreography or spectacle, not anymore. It's about properly executing the myth, reenacting the—"

"The ritual," Dina finished. She looked at me like she was seeing a whole new person. "You weren't this sharp back when we were sneaking around in Hong Kong."

She hadn't changed a bit. Anyone else would have tried to pretend it never happened, avoided the topic completely. Not Dina. Dina walked right up to the elephant in the room with a bag of peanuts.

"I've had plenty of time to reflect. Along with a multitude of helpful people pointing out my shortcomings."

Dina dismissed my modesty. "You looked good on the poster. Kit kept the dogs off with that one-sheet and the distribution trailer."

"Good thing there was plenty of footage where I'm not talking."

"*Near Death* looked like Kit fixed everything *A Beautiful Disaster* caught heat for. You were young. You looked good with your shirt off. You could throw a punch and ride a motorcycle. That shot where you flip out of the helicopter and kick Moon-Tzu was something else."

I forced my jaw to unclench so I could reply. "Yuen almost died."

Dina drained her glass with a shrug. "That's show business. Want one?"

I swallowed my first reply and reminded myself that I needed to find out what Dina knew about the murders if I was going to clear my name. "Too much sugar."

"Then I must have a sweet tooth." Dina went back in to reload, pouring from the same crystal decanter her father drained for fifty years. The drinking was the only sign my presence had any effect on her. Dina had never been much of a boozer.

I leaned over the rail to gape at the many decks and terraces built into the cliffside. The rest of Dina's daughters and their toddlers were playing on the beach. She came back out with a club soda in her off hand.

"To Jove Brand," Dina said, clinking my glass for me before handing it over.

"May he live forever, no matter how many times he dies," I added before taking a drink. It wasn't flat, which was a minor miracle considering it had probably been sitting in the bar fridge longer than her son had been alive. "Did Missy tell you why I wanted to meet?"

Dina studied the depths. "I didn't talk to Missy. Missy's people talked to my people."

"Missy wasn't trying to get between you and Kit, you know."

"She didn't have to try." Dina took a drink. "They were effortless together. The moment they met, I became an outsider."

"Kit loved you, Dina."

"Yeah, well, we always hurt the ones we love, right?"

In the silence, we looked to the ocean as a ship disappeared into the horizon, its sails waving white. I caught her eye before I spoke again. "I didn't kill Sir Collin, and I didn't kill Layne Lackey."

Dina looked at me like I was an idiot. So much for the newfound respect my insights had won. "I know that, dummy. Do you think

I'd meet with a murderer? Open my door to a guy whose hands are deadly weapons? Let him near my children?"

"Oh, yeah."

"Oh, yeah." She slapped my forehead. "What did I ever see in you?"

Someone you could wrap around your little finger. "I could do those handstand push-ups."

"Oh yeah," Dina said. She took a drink to hide her muted smile. I was glad I never battled the bottle, with the way people leaned on it. "It was the bastards who killed them, Ken. The same bastards who have been trying to steal Jove Brand since my father made him into something worth stealing."

"Who?" I kept my part short. Dina was ramping up and I didn't want to slow her down.

"The same types that tried it back with *Near Death*. The studios, the mob, the commies, the Asians. These media empires are buying up every property in sight, proven or not. They've made a movie out of any show that got as much as a second season thirty years ago. They make movies out of video games that were rip-offs of movies. You don't think they want Jove Brand?"

I put on my considering face. "Is Brand worth killing over?"

"*Final Bow* grossed a billion, before home video and merchandising," Dina said. "Jove Brand plays worldwide. Higher grosses in Europe than in the States. The Shensei brothers gave us a big leg up, distributing us in Asia. Jove Brand grew alongside their market. *Final Bow* was huge over there. China loves anything with wheels in it. Niles began training the day he was signed. Over there, the biggest stars do their own stunts."

"You don't say."

"Quiet, dummy," Dina said. "Niles is you, if you could act."

"Yeah, I saw *Raid the Roof.* He's a legitimate martial artist, on top of being fearless. I broke out in a sweat watching that scene where he scales the skyscraper."

"And he came cheap. We paid Prestor forty million for *Final Bow.*"

I whistled. Sir Collin's paycheck was quadruple *Near Death's* budget.

Dina consulted her glass for portents. "Niles is something else, you'll see. We'll get seven films out of him easy. And he has a family tie to Brand. His grandfather was Bowman Fletcher's editor. As a kid, he was Brand every Halloween. The pictures are a marketing jackpot."

"Makes for a good story—Brand superfan grows up to land his dream role."

Dina tacked into the wind to save her curls. "Superfan is right. Niles was dying to meet all the old Brands. It was his idea, using you on *Beautiful Downtown Burbank.*"

"Remind me to thank him."

Dina smirked. "Don't embarrass the kid. I think he did it so he could meet you on the sly. Ham Price dying was a blessing in disguise, God forgive me for saying it."

She wasn't talking about pork products. "Hamilton Price, the singer?" I asked.

We realized at the same moment Dina's liquid lunch had loosened her lips. She tossed the contents of her glass over the rail. The wind pushed most of it back at her. "You have privilege?"

"Born with it, according to the internet."

"No, attorney-client privilege, moron. Are you licensed?"

"No," I admitted.

"We're going to have to do something about that. It will come out eventually anyway. Before we cast Niles, Ham Price was set to be the next Brand. Then he hung himself jerking off. Stupid bastard, he could have had it all."

"Price spent his childhood in a boy band before making it solo. He knew what having it all meant. You sure it was an accident?"

Dina's brow could still wrinkle, if it had enough cause. "You think the pressure of being the next Brand got to Ham?"

"That's not what I'm suggesting at all."

"Jesus," Dina said, rolling air around in her empty glass.

Even with the wind I was starting to sweat. The sun was putting a nice sear on my face. The armored blazer might as well have been airtight. Dina didn't notice, so I shielded my forehead as if I were making a visor for my eyes.

"Let's have a pretend conversation, because saying this out loud seems bonkers," I said.

"I like hypotheticals," Dina replied.

"Let's pretend someone has been trying to tank the Jove Brand franchise. For whatever reason they decided now was their big chance."

Dina was an old hand at brainstorming to break story. "Maybe because Collin Prestor announced his retirement from the role."

"I like it. But Sir Collin's murder wasn't the first action taken. The ball was always rolling. Maybe it rolled over Hamilton Price."

"Still, Collin was marked." Dina toasted her glass at me. "He had to go. The killer is waiting for the perfect moment."

"Then they see me onstage, and they decide to improvise."

"Sure," Dina agreed. "The skit is all about you chopping people to death. That's not too big a jump."

"Now they have a patsy. As long as I'm close to whoever they want dead, I'm the default choice. A man acting alone. No conspiracy, just a jilted washup who's finally snapped."

"Ken Allen Oswald," Dina said.

"I already used that one." There was no way to ask the next question subtly, but it had to be asked. "Did Sir Collin's death void the contract?"

Dina shook her head. "Nope. We filmed his exit while shooting *Final Bow,* the same way Pop did with Bryce Crisp."

"How many people know that?"

"Not many. Me, the director, the screenwriter. Most of it we shot in the middle of production, in bits and pieces disguised as deleted or extended scenes. The money shot we kept quiet."

One hand wasn't hacking it as a sun visor, so I added the other. "Sir Collin dies?"

Dina watched the tide come in. "Brand has to die. You can't have two Brands at once."

So that was part of the contract. It was long rumored among the fandom that there could only be one Jove Brand at a time. That Jove Brand could never step down, never abandon his post. He had to die in service of the Crown.

"You must be busy lately," I said.

"You don't even know. I'm used to putting out fires, but this one, it's like the gates of hell have opened. Niles is freaking out. I'm on the phone with him three times a day, talking him off the ledge, assuring him the franchise is safe. But . . ."

"But maybe it isn't." I rotated in an attempt to cook evenly. "Layne Lackey was investigating Sir Collin's murder. From what I can tell, he was getting close to figuring it out."

Dina was paying attention now. "What makes you think that?"

"Well, I think that at least the killer thought Layne was getting close. He was interviewing all the right people. Which reminds me, did you meet with Layne Lackey recently?"

"Yeah." Dina sighed. "As much as he drove me nuts, Lackey made himself a necessary evil."

"He was good at that."

"Layne Lackey." Dina turned his name into a curse. "Leaks are strategic, with strict timelines to fuel interest and control the cycle. All that little shit cared about was growing his web traffic. Much as we tried, none of our fan sites could compete."

"The fans can always sense a shill," I said. "What did Layne Lackey want to talk about?"

Dina finally noticed me cowering from the sun. "You're burning up, aren't you? All right, I'll take mercy on you."

She led me back inside and pointed me toward a wide couch. The corner of a blanket poked out from under it. Dina probably spent more nights up here than in her own bed. She refilled my club soda and poured one of her own before joining me, taking up the opposite end. We had never shared a piece of furniture so far apart. She stretched her legs toward me but they didn't quite reach. I waited for her to lead.

"Mostly Lackey asked about *Old Game, New Rules*."

"Niles Endworth's debut has a title already?"

Dina threw her head back, groaning in self-aggrandizement. "Remind me to make you sign an NDA before you leave. We haven't leaked the title yet."

"I'll take it to the grave. What did Lackey want to know?"

"The normal stuff. Who was cast, locations, set pieces . . ."

"Contract questions?"

Dina sat up a little. "Yeah, I guess so."

Being this close to her brought sense memories I had fought hard to kill back to life. At least this time, I was the one prying for information. The methods Dina employed back then were definitely more effective than the ones I was using now. The tension I felt told me they probably still would be.

Dina finally made up her mind what she was willing to share. "Layne asked plenty about Dean."

"Because he's coming of age."

"And about to inherit the whole shebang," Dina confirmed.

"Eighteen is a little young."

Dina threw her head back. "Could you go back in time and tell my pop that? And while you're there, remind him I was right about *A Beautiful Disaster*. But no Calabria man, father, brother, or son, has ever listened to a Calabria woman."

Dina was reclined too far for me to get a look at her face. I was tempted to move, but standing up might have signaled our meeting was a wrap. "You going to retire, Dina?"

Dina snorted. "Hardly. Dean's a good kid, but he's still a kid."

"Kit was only twenty-four when he made *Near Death*."

"And look how that turned out. If he would have given me a seat at the table, listened to me, we might have made something special."

I wanted to reply *or taken both of you down, instead of just him*, but that might have triggered an argument I had no hope of winning.

"What if Dean sells?"

"Dean's not going to sell," Dina assured us both.

"What would he get if he does? Three billion? Four?"

Dina's gaze could have killed. "Dean's not going to sell."

I leaned forward and rested my elbows on my knees. Getting the jacket off the back of the couch felt good, but I still couldn't read her expression. "Did Layne bring it up? Ask what will happen to you when the clock strikes midnight?"

"It's a big scoop." Dina swung off the couch and headed over to her laptop. Not long after, a printer built into the desk started spitting out papers.

"When's the big day?"

"Next Friday," Dina said, not looking up. "We're having a big to-do here."

"You're opening up the Cove?" There was no hiding my surprise.

"For the first time since filming *Endless Watch*. We got all kinds of stuff planned. A media presentation. Oh, and get this: I'm going to have a bunch of Jove Brand types, decked out to the nines, serving the guests."

"Coronations demand such extravagances. Is Dean upset his big day is a public relations event?"

"He'd better get used to it," Dina turned a ream of paper towards me. "Standard NDA."

"I haven't talked yet."

Dina shoved a pen into my hand. "And you never will."

When I'd signed and initialed to her heart's content, Dina fed the stack into a scanner also built into her desk. It bought me a little more time.

"Missy mentioned you had a Russian-based production problem last time out."

Dina took a moment to decide how much trouble she wanted to get me in. "A problem named Grigori Fedorov."

"Sounds evil already."

"He's been laundering his dirty billions buying up international properties. Got into the German film business off some tax dodge they had over there. Imported the concept to Russia, where he founded Veles Productions."

"The Veles that makes the Brand knock-offs?" I asked.

"The very same. Fedorov is the guy behind the Cherno Perun movies." Dina blew raspberries. "Buncha schlock."

I didn't say so, but I liked the Cherno Perun movies. Schlock had its place. "I'm listening."

"Five years ago, during pre-production on *Named Brand*, Fedorov made overtures. Wanted to cofund. I humored him, but we do all our financing in-house these days."

"Which is quite the accomplishment," I pointed out.

Dina gave a bow. "Thank you very much. Anyway, Fedorov was also feeling out if we would sell."

"How much?"

"Two point five," Dina said.

"Billion?"

"Dollars, not rubles." Dina waved a dismissal, which was her version of air-quotes. "It was all hypothetical of course. He never came out and made an offer."

"Lot of that going around."

"When we turned him down, which we did by pretending we never got wind of it, a certain amount of muscling occurred."

"How serious did it get?"

"We won't be filming anywhere near Russia anytime soon," Dina replied. "Fedorov's got his own little army. Hires Russian ex-military, gangsters. All guys with confirmed kills. I had to hire my own ex-military guys to fend them off."

The type of people who would know how to crush a throat. "Sounds like a peach. Where can I find him?"

"He bought a defunct offshore oil rig. At the time people thought it was nuts. The well had long run dry."

"He mounting missiles on it or something?"

"Offshore gambling," Dina replied. "The rig falls under international waters, so he opened a casino for wannabe one-percenters."

"Can you get me in?"

Dina gnawed on her lip. "I don't know. Fedorov has been after Brand a long time. Maybe even back when you were filming *Near Death*."

Her accusation made sense. Like Niles Endsworth, I had replaced the first choice for Jove Brand, who had overdosed in Fedorov's corner of the world. I watched Dina waver. She still cared. The time for me to act tough had come.

"Hey." I used a finger to lift Dina's chin and caught her eye. "I can handle it."

Dina shook her head to chase away the birth of a smile. "Your acting hasn't improved any, but okay. It's your funeral."

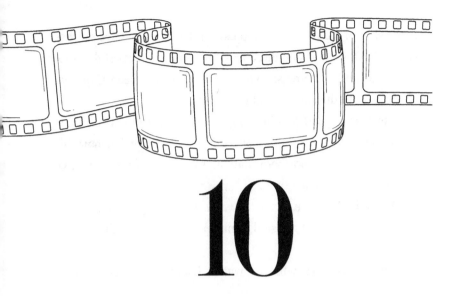

10

ON MY WAY DOWN THE STAIRS, I GOT A LOOK AT THE family room from above. The layout formed a bull's-eye. In the center of the room, a round fire pit burned. It was encircled by an inner ring of couch, behind which was a band of marble flooring. It had to be on purpose.

Every Brand film opened on a white screen. The silhouette of Jove Brand's hand holding his Quarreler raised into frame in first-person, as if the audience were Brand. In an explosion of fire and smoke, the audience took an arrow's-eye view, gliding through stylized depictions of the coming scenes, which provided clues about the plot. As the title theme rose to a climax, the audience zoomed toward a distant bull's-eye, piercing its center to land in the first shot of the film. As I stepped off the stairs, the fire pit rose up from the flag-stones on three legs, stopping six feet off the floor to reveal a hidden staircase. This was how I met Dean Calabria, heir apparent to the Jove Brand franchise.

Dean was a good-looking kid, but he didn't much resemble his mom or sisters. Tall and lean with tight curls of fair hair, his features were more northern Italian. Michelangelo might have carved him, once upon a time.

"Damn it, Dean, use the elevator like everyone else," the sister who had greeted me said, fanning the air. "Now there's ash everywhere."

"Goldpecker does what he wants, Diana," a different sister said.

Dean and Diana. Like many monarchs before her, Dina had named all her children after herself.

A fine-boned girl slipped out from behind Dean to join his sisters on the couch. She was maybe four years older than Dean, but there was no such thing as too early when it came to working your way into a dynasty.

Last out was Niles Endsworth, the next Jove Brand. He was wearing a vintage short sleeve button-down, left undone to display his chiseled physique. His white swim trunks were likewise drawn from a bygone era where the shorter the leg was, the better.

"Can't let Jove Brand leave without shaking his hand," Dean said, hopping out of the secret stair with practiced grace.

When Dean extended a hand, I knew what was coming.

I hated shaking hands. It wasn't just the useless ritual or that so many guys spent the day cradling their crotches for comfort. I couldn't stand the arm wrestling. The unspoken fight for domination, as if a handshake meant anything.

Having nothing to prove, fighters employed a light touch. A career fighter didn't have ego problems. Any delusions of grandeur got beat out of you coming up. All that cockiness was an act to sell tickets. Being liked was fine, but if you could get people to hate you enough, they'd pay anything to watch you lose.

Fighters had their own handshake. They made their living with their hands, so they took care of them. Hands were fragile things, with all those little bones. All of mankind's know-how and we've never managed to build a machine as adjustable or articulate as the human hand. Not even Ray Ford, and you better believe he'd tried.

Dean's fingers brushed past mine as he delivered the fighter's faint, secret squeeze. I returned it with a grudging smile.

I could feel Niles's gaze locked on me as he studied my every move. If he was looking for a Jove Brand role model, I hoped I was last on his list. Not wanting to leave him out, I offered my hand. His shake mirrored mine perfectly.

When we broke grip, I nodded at his ensemble. "*Hunter's Moon*, right?"

Niles froze at my words. It was a stark reminder that most of the world believed I was the killer. I kept talking to prevent further awkwardness.

"Your outfit. It's what Bryce Crisp is wearing in the cyborg shark-attack scene. I'm buddies with the guy that built that shark."

Niles snapped back to the moment with a caught-schoolboy grin. "You've found me out, old boy."

"Nothing wrong with dressing for the part you want."

Niles crossed his arms. "You never know when you're in for a swim."

I tilted my head at his non sequitur. It sounded familiar. Not only the words themselves, but also their delivery.

Dean stepped between us to break our moment. "Thanks for stopping by, Niles. I'll text you about that thing."

Niles took the offered escape route with a nod. "No rest for the righteous."

Again, his reply tickled at my memory. Still, the way Dina's daughters watched Niles leave told me he was going to be box-office gold.

"Come on down to the man cave," Dean said. He tugged on my blazer as he turned, pulling me along like a little kid aching to show off.

I had to admit it was hard to say no to him. "I guess I got a minute."

"No guests below, Dean-o," Diana said. "You know the rules."

Dean rolled his eyes. "Oh, please. There's going to be two hundred people down there next week. What's one now?" He looked at me like I had a say in the situation. "Anyway, Jove Brand never talks, right?"

"Right."

Dean smiled like I had given him something and disappeared into the staircase. I copied his eager skip down.

"Goldpecker strikes again," Diana said to our backs.

The spiral staircase lurched as the fire pit lowered back into place. I snatched the handrail for balance. Dean was watching me over his shoulder.

"Sorry, man. I should have warned you. They're right, you know. I could have taken the elevator, but come on."

Once stabilized, I got busy gawking. The cavernous space was more than two stories tall. The walls were natural rock but the floor had been tiled in stormy blue. The pattern would seem random to anyone who hadn't seen *Endless Watch*, where Roman Brackish, during his infamous monologue, revealed it to be a map of the bottom of the sea.

"Mom cleared everything out for the party." Dean's voice echoed through the empty chamber as I stopped to stare.

Calabria Cove hadn't changed since its appearance on film more than forty years ago. The hallways, softly lit from hidden recesses, whorled like the inside of a conch shell. Navigating their uneven curls was disorienting. We passed a half dozen circular iris doors on the journey to the one that capped the passage.

Dean typed a code into a clamshell pad and the door twisted open, groaning and screeching. That caught me off guard. In *Endless Watch*, the iris portals had hummed softly. They must have muted out the racket during post-production.

"They don't make them like they used to, huh?" I shouted over the metallic whine.

"I don't think they ever made them like this," Dean shouted back.

We stepped into a room with more square footage than my condo. It also had a hell of a better view—the far wall was completely windowed to look out over the sea. Familiar as the room looked I couldn't place it, probably because Dean had converted it into a gym.

Weight racks stood against one wall, each bar stacked with poundage appropriate for Dean's age and build. There was a lane set up for sprint and shuttle runs, along with a stationary bike and a rowing machine. A big trampoline sat next to a pipe-framed structure designed for a variety of body weight exercises.

A full-sized ring and cage occupied the far side of the room, past an obstacle course of hanging bags. Gloves and headgear waited on shelves. Flat screen televisions and speakers were mounted at regular intervals along the walls, their remotes holstered on the equipment throughout the room. Even with brisk ventilation and sparkling gear, the dried sweat lingered through the bleach. Dean spent a lot of time in here.

It was a fighter's paradise, but I felt for the kid. Growing up in Calabria Cove must had been like living in a submarine, but Dean was too valuable to let roam.

"What do you think?" Dean asked. "What am I missing?"

Dean could swim in the ocean and he could run on the beach. But he wasn't asking me about getting a cryo tank. What I saw behind his smile made my heart hurt.

"What do you train?" I asked.

Dean snagged a remote velcroed to the jungle gym and tapped a button. Iris doors groaned open to admit a well-built guy ten years my junior. Shaved and tattooed, he was already in a rash guard and shorts, on standby whenever Dean whistled.

"Stavros, what do I train?" Dean asked, walking over to where the gloves were shelved.

"Everything," Stavros said. I had a suspicion his accent wasn't real.

Dean pulled off his shirt to show the base coat of what would one day be an impressive physique when his body matured. He was balanced throughout, not ignoring his legs the way kids his age did, chasing big biceps. He geared up right, first strapping on his shin pads then gel wraps. He slipped on one glove and was going for the other when he remembered something.

"Check this out," Dean said around the glove hanging from his mouth. It made him look like a puppy. He keyed the remote. The screens lit up and I had no choice but to gaze upon my sins.

Dean had been watching *Near Death*.

"I don't care what people say, this is the best one," he said.

It was queued up to the office-building fight, which routinely won online polls as the most notorious scene in Jove Brand history. Along with budgetary issues and tight time constraints, *Near Death* was light on story. With his cast and funding stripped away, Kit had been forced to rewrite the script on the fly. This led to comically long set-piece fight scenes in order to pad the movie so it would reach the contractually required ninety minutes.

There were two such scenes in *Near Death*. The first was staged in a warehouse, where the trial to prove myself worthy of being Jove Brand took a deadly turn. That one went for eighteen minutes and was immediately followed by a motorcycle chase scene that went on for another twelve, before the zipline sequence and helicopter stuff.

Those scenes together weren't objectively terrible. They stood up alongside other late-nineties low-budget genre films. Of course, those were the ones we shot early, rapidly burning through time and money.

The scene currently on Dean's screen was pure filler. We had sixty-seven minutes of movie and needed ninety, before title sequence and credits. Had those counted, *Near Death* would have had the slowest credit roll of all time.

I'll never forget the morning when Kit came to me for help, palm glued to his forehead, hair standing wild—the look of a man who had freshly compromised his vision. He stared right through me, straight into creative hell.

"Ken, I need you to stretch this out. Whatever works, man."

The result was twenty-three straight minutes of me beating up stuntmen, as Jove Brand worked his way, floor-by-floor, to the top of an office building. I punched and kicked my way through the lobby, stairwells, and cubicles. We rotated the ten stunt guys we had through wardrobe like an assembly line, recycling the cannon fodder. Different jackets and jumpsuits. A mix of hats, sunglasses, and facial hair.

It didn't help much.

Layne Lackey ran the numbers once. In those twenty-three minutes, I single-handedly took out one hundred and ninety-nine foes. It worked out to eight and a half guys a minute, or a bad guy every seven seconds.

I did my best to mix it up, putting all the styles I knew or could fake into play. The office-building fight had it all. Jumping and spinning kicks of every flavor. Kung Fu, boxing, and judo. If it was found in an office, it got smashed over someone's head: chairs, monitors, keyboards. I slammed those same ten guys through doors, desks, and copiers.

I broke fourteen necks, twenty-three arms, and thirty legs. I dislocated shoulders and snapped wrists. I also violated every rule of the ring: breaking fingers and gouging eyes and fish hooking. I bit and I head butted.

But above all, I chopped throats.

I honestly couldn't tell you what it was with me back then, but *Near Death* made me the Michael Jordan of throat chopping. I attacked the neck from every angle. Whatever I needed to do to get at your windpipe I did: pulled your tie, uppercut your chin out of the way, ripped your hair back from behind. Nothing was keeping me from landing on that airway.

If you forced me to answer, I guess I had it in my head that a secret agent like Jove Brand would be a quick, efficient killing machine. In movies, guys took a dozen punches to the face without them leaving a mark. They got booted like a field goal and popped right back up ready for more. Going for the throat felt vicious and final. Being too close to the material, I failed to realize how much I was leaning on it at the time.

God bless those stuntmen. *Near Death* was my first and only movie. I had no idea what worked on camera, what looked good. Those Shensei guys sold the hell out of my moves, hitting everything full tilt, reacting to my blows as if Hercules was behind them. If not for their expertise, the flick wouldn't have been anywhere near watchable.

Even so, the sequence was a tonal mess. A monotonous grind with no sense of beginning, middle, or end. There was no indication of when it was finally going to stop, the painted floor number on each staircase going up and up.

The viewer got the point around floor three, but the scene wasn't even getting started. There was a frat game where you took a shot every time you saw a new staircase. A proud convention patron once told me every fall it put at least one of their rushes in the hospital.

"I can't tell you how many times I've seen this, man," Dean said, his eyes glued to the screen.

"I'm sorry to hear that." Staring at the floor was my only reprieve. If only Ray had made me earplugs.

"Are you kidding? This is what got me training. Those older Brand movies, I mean, I get the appeal, but those guys couldn't fight their way out of a wet paper bag."

Oh, the folly of youth.

"The first Brand was actually a pretty tough guy," I said. "He was SAS before he got discovered from those cologne ads. There are stories about him clearing out bars when the punters would give him lip."

"Nah, I mean, I hear you, but you got to give yourself some credit," Dean replied. "Your switch knee counters are so clean. And you were like, what, only three years older than me then."

Stavros snorted. It didn't bother me. I'd suffered Stavroses my whole life. Dean faced up on a banana bag and laid in a decent combination: jab, cross, low-kick, high-kick. A good sequence, on paper. Slick but sterile.

Dean looked at me with stars in his eyes. "Want to get in a round?"

Oh boy. I was in it now. Here was the decision tree of death I had been forced to navigate my entire professional career as the so-called Sensei to the Stars. There was no winning. Say no and I lost Dean's respect, maybe made an enemy. Say yes and rough him up and surely make an enemy—if not Dean, then Dina. Say yes and let myself get roughed up, then I lost Dean's respect and it got around Ken Allen was a fake.

I should have looked for a way out of this, but there was something about Dean that made him hard to refuse. It was clear how much he wanted it, the way he was bouncing up and down. For whatever weird reason, gloving up with me was on his wish list.

"All right, kid," I said, heading over to the shelves. "But for Christ's sake don't tell your mother."

"Deal."

I faced away as I bent out of the gel-jacket, but there was no hiding the harness and holster.

"Holy shit, dude," Dean said. "You walk around like that?"

"Don't tell your mother," I replied, laying the blazer over the stockpile.

"Badass."

"What weight gloves?" I asked.

"Let's do fours. I just want to play around."

Dean would pick the lightest gloves. Nobody was hitting the golden goose or complaining when he hit them. I slipped on shin pads and gloved up before sliding into the ring.

"Where's your headgear?" I asked.

"Aw, come on."

Dean paced around while I loosened up, running through static then dynamic stretches. I didn't rush it. The longer Dean waited, the more anxious he was going to become. Impatience was a killer in the ring.

"I'm a long way from eighteen," I apologized. There was no harm in highlighting our age difference. Young guys thought it was their big advantage. But the trade-off was experience. I'd been training almost twice as long as Dean had been alive.

Goldpecker, his sister called him. The prince of Calabria Cove. Here I was, in a position to teach him a lesson. One I could have used at his age.

"One round," I said.

"Three minutes." Dean nodded.

Stavros hit a button on a remote and the screens switched to display a three-minute timer. A beat later a bell sounded through the speakers.

Dean skipped right into range and aimed a low kick at my lead leg. It was a common move at his level, a noncommittal way to measure range that also had psychological value. It gave you the sense you'd scored. That you got a shot in.

I didn't bother to check it. Instead, I lifted my leg to let Dean's kick pass under before extending my foot to catch him high on the chest. I made the kick a shove rather than setting anything into it.

Off balance and on one leg, Dean stumbled back.

"Nice," he said, smiling.

I gave Dean nothing, neither returning his smile nor mean-mugging him. He was trying to set the mood, to get in his comfort zone. By remaining totally neutral, I kept the engagement uncertain. Never provide your opponent information, not even so much as what kind of fight they were in.

Dean got his feet under him and crept back into range, feinting with a low round kick before switching high. He did everything right: turned his hip over, got his head out of line, kept his hands up.

I ignored the feint and closed the distance, checking his kick with an elbow as I stepped behind his base foot. A little application of my hip and down Dean went.

I kept my guard up while I withdrew. I learned the hard way, sometimes when you're doing a partner a favor and letting them off the hook, they would still tag you on the way out.

Dean rolled backward, bridging into a handstand to regain his feet. He kept his distance, formulating an approach. I liked what it told me about him. He wasn't at the mercy of his emotions. And he wasn't a brat, because he wanted to keep going.

I stepped into my phone booth. Imagine you are trapped in a phone booth barely wider than your shoulders. You could only be hurt if an attack came into your booth. Attacks outside the booth couldn't reach you, so you didn't chase after them. You guarded your booth.

Dean tried a jab. I checked it with a lead hand chop to the underside of his wrist. His jab-cross got another chop, rolling into a scything elbow that sent his rear hand sailing off course. Dean grimaced and tried a body kick. Instead of a parry, I dropped my elbow, the point colliding with the top of his foot. Without foot pads, it was a break. With them it was merely excruciating.

Dean shook it out and started circling, but without the same pep in his step. His power leg was starting to cramp and his foot was swelling. He was going to wait for me now, as uncomfortable as it made him. Offense was easy. Lots of guys won fights on pure aggression. It was defending that was hard.

I didn't hit Dean. I played him like he was a set of bongos. Left to the body, then right to the body as my left trapped his arm, left to the jaw, right to the temple. The whole sequence took maybe two seconds. I kept tight on his leg the whole time, sticking with him as he failed to retreat. Eventually, he turned his back and put his hands up, the universal sign for *enough, enough already!*

I slapped him on the shoulder. "Not bad, kid."

"Yeah, I really had you there." Dean sulked.

I took a seat on the mat. "Let's talk about it."

Dean sat down with me, rubbing the knot out of his leg. The bell went off to signal the end of the round.

"Control the engagement, so you can pick your moment," I said. "Don't let your opponent choose when and where."

Dean quit looking at me, but not because he wasn't listening.

"Once you control the time and space, let your tools flow. The goal is to remove any decision making. To make technique an instinct."

"When's that happen?" Dean smirked and we laughed together. "Hey, can I show you something?"

I got up and helped Dean to his feet. "Sure."

Dean led me into the room where he stored Stavros: a den with leather furniture, a dry bar and a galley sink.

"You follow fighters?" Dean asked.

"I do."

It was the answer Dean was hoping for. He pointed to the corner left of the door, the blind spot Mom wouldn't see if she ducked her head in. "Check that out."

There was a grappling dummy set up in a ready stance, dressed in gloves and fight shorts. The broad gold belt strapped around the dummy's waist declared it to be heavyweight champion of the world.

"You like Alexi Mirovich?" Dean asked.

"Who doesn't?"

Alexi Mirovich had appeared out of the primeval forests of Russia to conquer the fighting world. He was the greatest of all time. Anyone who disagreed was a contrarian by nature. I moved in to get a better look at what was scribbled on the shorts. The only word not in Cyrillic was a name.

"This is signed to you."

"Yep."

"Isn't Alexi Mirovich in prison right now? In Russia?"

Dean scratched his head sheepishly. Stavros snorted to announce his presence. I was treading into his territory.

"Want water?" Dean asked.

"Sure," I said.

Dean went over to the fridge himself to get it. He had turned out about as good as someone could, growing up under house arrest.

Stavros leaned against the wall with his arms crossed, which made his already big forearms massive. We played a round of Don't Blink.

"Calm down. I'm not looking to evict you," I said.

"You can't," Stavros replied. He raised his chin as his pectorals jumped in sequence.

I nodded toward the glass wall. "You push gear on this kid and I'll throw you out that window without opening it first."

Dean must have noticed us jawing on the way back because he had a glimmer in his eye when he handed me the water bottle. "Why don't you guys go one round?"

"I should get going," I said, stepping back into the gym.

"Yes, you should," Stavros said. "Take your fake fighting and run away."

I came to a stop with a wince, weighing the situation. What kind of lesson did I want to teach Dean? Should I be the bigger man here? Those questions were swept away pretty quick. I had one major weakness. One vice. For some people it was booze and for others it was blow. There were people who chased tail until it ruined them, and others who dove after adrenaline out of airplanes and off bridges.

Me, I couldn't say no to a fight.

I set course for the ring. "I don't have three minutes. But this will only take one."

Dean hobbled double-time to grab the remote before I changed my mind. Stavros slid into the ring on his stomach and bounced to his feet. How a guy was built was a tip-off. It told you what kind of workouts they did. There were guys who worked out for form. They had a pronounced V shape: big arms, full chests, but slim waists. Other guys trained for function. Those guys looked more like a block, their torso a straight line from armpit to hips.

Stavros was a function guy. He was concerned with moving a lot of weight as fast as possible. He bent deep, folding into himself, tucking his chin into his shoulder with his hands high—the stance of a guy looking to get inside and make use of all that power.

I knew what Stavros was thinking.

He had suffered through Dean emulating *Near Death* and other movies full of fancy, useless crap. Stavros had been praying for the opportunity to show Dean all about real fighting. Now he finally had his chance. The gods had smiled upon him and delivered Dean's false idol to the sacrificial altar.

"Ready?" Dean asked.

Neither of us acknowledged him. I gave Stavros exactly what he wanted to see: a traditional stance, dominant foot forward, fairly upright, facing in profile. We stared each other down. I knew better than to call for the bell. When I opened my mouth, Stavros would pounce and later justify his gun jumping to Dean as a lesson about the real world.

Stavros broke and rushed in. His left hook was meant to anchor me in place more than knock me out. He had gone and made the mistake of thinking he was fighting the Ken Allen of eighteen years ago, before the mixed-martial-arts boom. As if a guy who had spent his entire childhood traveling from *dojo* to *kwoon* wouldn't later step into the cage.

I slipped the hook and was already turning the corner when Stavros shot for the takedown. I took his back before he was done scooping for my leg. His left hand came up to block his throat but I was already there.

I became a human backpack, my heels locked on Stavros's hips, as I squeezed hard and inflated my chest to further shrink the space between us. Give a guy time to start thinking maybe he could escape and he would fight until he blacked out.

Stavros slapped my thigh three times in under a second. I turned him loose, bridging him while we untangled, in case he got any ideas. For the same reason, I kept in his blind spot when I stood up.

Dean's mouth was hanging open. He had forgotten to ring the bell.

Stavros spun up to face me, his hand snapping out to offer a shake. If he had aspirations of being in the next Jove Brand film, it was time to give them up. The second I put my hand out, he shot for the takedown again.

I replaced my hand with a knee, driving it forward with a skip, my elbow chambered to counter the torque. Dean was right—the switch knee was my best counter.

My target was the solar-plexus, but Stavros was too fast for his own good and I caught him square on the chin. He was instantly teleported to the shadow realm all fighters dreaded, an abyss that forever devoured any illusion you were invincible.

I rolled Stavros onto his back and straightened his legs out. Bodies did weird stuff when the mind was on vacation. You could tear things, twitching around. "You have medical staff on the premises, kid?"

"Uh. Yeah," Dean replied. His eyes were popping out of his head.

"Get them here."

By the time I had buckled on my harness and holster, Stavros was winking back into existence. I swung my blazer on. "Time to go."

"I'll have to unlock the elevator," Dean replied.

On the walk to the doors, I could sense Dean wanted to say something. He finally got it out when I stepped into the elevator.

"I tried to get you, when I found out you were a trainer, but Mom said no."

It was at that moment I started to suspect why.

"Mother knows best," I managed as the doors closed.

I was back on the White Stag when I realized what scene Dean's gym had been in *Endless Watch*. It was the dining room where Jove Brand and pirate king Roman Brackish broke bread, measuring each other's depth while the tide rolled in and the sharks circled.

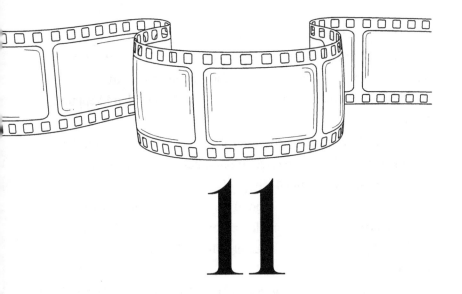

11

I WAS HUNTING FOR A HOTEL WHEN MISSY CALLED. I tried to fill her in on my meeting with Dina but all she wanted to hear about was Dean.

"Does he look like Kit?" she asked.

"Not really."

Kit had been a notch better looking than his dad, who had the charisma and clout to fish above his league. Dean was a notch above Kit. The rich were the new royalty. They got progressively better-looking as the generations passed. If you want to know who founded the fortune, look for the ugliest portrait in the mansion.

"There's a little of Dina in there, but I'm guessing he takes after his dad."

"The Venetian art dealer?" Missy asked.

"The Genoese banker. Good thing she got Dean out of him. The ones who gave Dina girls paid for it in divorce court."

Dean also looked a lot like someone else I knew, but I kept that to myself.

"Kit and I were going to start right away. I was hoping our first would be a girl." Missy paused to pulse her food processor. "Dina was so striking. Kit wanted a boy, of course."

This would have been a good time to ask if she and Kit had gotten married on the sly in Hong Kong or if maybe she had any leads on the location of Kit's secret will, but I couldn't summon the gumption.

"Dean's got a good head on his shoulders, for being the boy in the bubble. Jove Brand will outlive us all." A Range Rover cruising into my sideview caused me to tense, but it was blue with a phone-wielding mom at the wheel. "Hope Ray made progress with the flash drive. I'm done with Layne's dossiers."

"This Russian producer, Fedorov, was he on the list?"

"No," I admitted, "but Layne interviewed Dina before Sir Collin was killed. Maybe she was trying to keep Layne out of trouble."

Missy knew better than to directly ask me to throw in the towel. "Meeting with a person like Fedorov is dangerous, Ken."

"Yeah, and no one has had their throat crushed in like five days. Maybe I'll retire. Emigrate to Bali, or wherever presumed serial killers settle down."

"I'm starting to think you're enjoying yourself," Missy said.

She was right. Every meal, even the ones that came out of vending machines, was a joy. Colors were brighter. The air had more oxygen in it. I didn't miss my condo or my clients or the conventions. I was even happy when my phone rang. The less I acted like Ken Allen and the more I acted like Jove Brand, the better life felt.

But there was more to it. Among fighters, sucker punching was a cardinal sin. It required a response. Framing me for two murders was one hell of a sucker punch, and I had hit my lifetime quota for cheek turning.

"I have to see this through. If I go down, whoever is behind this gets away."

Missy went quiet. She knew plenty about unavenged deaths.

"I need to find a safe place around here while Dina works her magic."

"Use my beach house," Missy said. "I'll text you the codes."

"You sure? Nothing has blown up today. I'm due."

"That's what insurance is for." Missy ended the debate by hanging up.

A minute later an address and two key codes flashed on my watch screen, one for the gate and the other for the door. I set course in the GPS and called Ray, who picked up on the first ring.

"Any luck?" I asked.

"You first. Daddy needs his details."

I filled Ray in, including all the fighting parts I had kept from Missy.

"I got to improve your jacket," Ray said after I finished. "Having to take it off all the time leaves you vulnerable."

"If it could also be air-conditioned, that would be great. Now, about the flash drive."

"You shipped me a brick," Ray said.

Cliff diving would have been gentler on my stomach. "No. No way. That thing had a whole deal on it. An interface and dossiers and who knows what. Did you read Missy's note?"

I could feel Ray restraining himself. "Yeah. I didn't go and plug the damn thing in all willy-nilly. How about you?"

"Ah, jeez. In my defense, I pulled it out with like two seconds left on the countdown."

"Two whole seconds?" Ray asked. "You know what, forget that for now. Did you eject the thing or just yank it out? It might have been set up to delete if you ripped it out during a security check."

"Ah, jeez."

Ray went quiet for a moment, and I got the distinct impression he was listening to someone else.

"A flash drive has to be plugged into something," he said. "What did Lackey use to take notes?"

"He had an app on his phone." I didn't remember seeing a phone anywhere near Layne Lackey in the VIP lounge. I told Ray I'd call him back, then hung up and dialed Stern.

"Allen." She sighed. "Let me guess: There's a black helicopter chasing you."

"Not yet. Did you find a phone on Layne Lackey?"

"No," she said. "Why, have you seen it?"

"I think the killer took it."

"Why?"

From the background noise, Stern was on the road too. I checked my mirror, fully prepared to spot her unmarked, but I was all alone.

"Lackey used it to record interviews, take field notes, that sort of thing. Can you trace it?"

"You watch too many movies, Allen."

That's when it hit me what Niles Endsworth had been doing. During our conversation, he'd spoken exclusively in quotes from the Jove Brand movies. Either he was the biggest Brand fan this side of Layne Lackey, was going next-level method, or was having fun screwing with everyone. Whatever the reason, it made me like him.

"You still there, Allen?"

"Yeah. What were we talking about?"

"If I could trace Layne's cell phone," Stern replied. "No go. Location is disabled and no one picks up."

We both went quiet, following our thoughts.

"Did you call it when we had lunch?" I asked.

"And when I had you in the backseat," she replied.

"Did you look at that video I sent you with the Black Knight in it?"

Stern stopped to exhale. "I gave it a glance."

"Believe me yet?"

"Anything else, Allen?"

"Thanks for both your protection and service," I started, but she hung up on me after *protection.*

It was a long ride back to This Town, but I didn't mind it the way I did all of four days ago. Ray had put a Jove Brand playlist on my watch to stream through the Bluetooth. The muffled sounds of the White Stag eating up the highway only added to the ambiance.

I stopped at a sushi place for a bowl of sashimi and a side of avocado that cost the same as an entire roll. I was getting back on the Stag when Ray called me with a suggestion.

"If you're looking for leads why not search Layne Lackey's place?" he asked.

Big detective I was. "The cops must have combed through it. Packed up all his devices, collected his papers."

"Well with them looking out for you, why bother?"

"You're right," I admitted. "Don't know where he lives though."

"I'll see what I can do about that."

"You need to make yourself a robot suit so we can trade places," I said.

"Who says I haven't?" Ray replied and hung up.

It was full dark by the time I got to Missy's Malibu beach house. It was a little place—all her places were—close enough to the studios to take meetings. The guards didn't look at me after I typed in the gate code.

Inside the gate was a self-contained enclave with a full staff, including a community chef and doctor. The little houses weren't much more than two-room cabins, with one of those rooms being the lavatory. Each cabin was walled off from the others with a stockade fence.

Once upon a time it had been studio housing, where the old moguls locked up their problem children. This was where they sent actors to dry out and chained up writers to force them to finish scripts. These days it served as a stash for misters and mistresses, a don't-ask-don't-tell motel.

I set up the pencil cameras in case someone came calling, scooped up the complimentary swag bag standard on all A-list celebrity doorsteps, and punched in the key code. All my clothing minus the bulletproof blazer went into the hamper for laundry service. After texting in a room-service order I jumped in the shower.

My meal was waiting when I got out, a hearty seafood stew with a side of nothing to sop it up. I stared at my phone while I ate, trying to decide if what I was thinking was a good idea. The problem was, I was running low on ideas, good, bad, or in-between. I picked up my phone and sent a text to Layne Lackey.

Watch your back, Black Knight.

I checked all the locks before sliding into a bed with two layers of blanket and about twenty pillows. Everything but the flannel top sheet went on the floor. I was drifting off when my phone vibrated with a text alert from an unknown caller.

I'm not the Black Knight.

Then who are you, sir? I texted back.

Not sir. Gamesman. Gamesman Brand.

I placed my phone down gently, as if its contents were under pressure. The enclave was gated, but the guard wasn't the questioning type, not in a getaway reserved for clandestine visits. No way the Black Knight was able to track my phone, right?

I made a body out of pillows on the bed and threw the comforter over it. Then I used the rest of the pillows to make a nest on the floor, on the side of the bed opposite the door. It was a good thing Missy liked big clouds for pillows. I barely felt the Quarreler underneath mine.

I SPENT MY forced day off doing interval sprints on the beach, avoiding what I knew needed to be done. I hoped Dina would finagle me access to Fedorov's lair or Ray could hunt up Layne Lackey's address and give me an excuse to procrastinate. The smart watch's heart rate monitor let me know I was already losing my edge. Between short bursts of terror, the bulk of this gig was driving from place to place and eating crap.

I got plenty of looks from my neighbors and gave plenty back. Looking was fine. Touching wasn't. The women I recognized were trouble and the ones I didn't were more. There was a reason harems used to be guarded by eunuchs. The sultans did not tolerate interlopers.

After my too-long shower, I was completely out of excuses. Jaw clenched, I searched every inch of Missy's beach house. There was no reason to believe any evidence of a secret wedding or forgotten will would be present. This was only one of her many residences, and if her wearing my watch from *Near Death* that Kit had gifted her was any indication, Missy kept her precious things close.

The combination of the small setting and Missy's minimalist tendencies made my invasion of privacy relatively painless. The only item of interest was a DVD left in the player labeled *Kit*. I sat on the edge of the bed, close to the screen, and hit play on the remote.

The first video was brief, with Missy acting through audition pages and Kit behind the camera. The ones that followed were a mix of candid moments and one-scene plays. Most of them were Missy alone, though Kit was in some with the camera on a tripod. He wasn't much of an actor, but after about thirty seconds of watching him I had to pause the tape. The lens of time had mercifully blurred my memory. Seeing him in sharp resolution cut deep.

There were hours of footage. Kit grew up in the independent film explosion and it showed. It was clear he had ambitions beyond Jove Brand. I kept my eyes peeled for clues, but didn't spot a secret will or marriage license laid out on a table in the background.

Near the end of the footage, I made a cameo appearance. In the video, Kit and Missy are spitballing character names for whatever project they were dreaming up after *Near Death*. From off frame, I tap on the door and lie to Kit, telling him I'm going to grab a bite and crash and that I will see him in the morning.

It was a lie of omission. I leave out that his sister will be accompanying me. As far as Kit knew, Dina had left Hong Kong after her surprise set visit and the resulting blowup between them, awkwardly witnessed by the entire crew. Kit had a lot on his mind and my betrayal went undiscovered. Though you never see me on screen, I sound exactly as naive as I was. Young men never realize when they are being seduced. They always think they're the seducers.

I remembered the last night we were together in Hong Kong. Dina practically dragged me from the hotel, kept me up all night. My ego was at an all-time high. I really believed her intensity had everything to do with me.

I knew I should watch the DVD again, see if I missed anything, but I didn't have the energy. I burrowed into the nest I made on the floor and tried measuring my breaths to clear my head. It didn't work. Hours later, as I was drifting off, in the limbo between waking and dreaming, it came to me that Kit and Missy were not spitballing names for future movie characters.

They were picking baby names.

———

I WOKE UP to missed calls from Dina and Ray. I called Dina back first.

"I swung an invite to Fedorov's offshore operation through a friend of a friend," she said. "You're on the list as Connor Shaw."

"Pretty cheeky alias."

"Had to think of a name on the spot. I'm going to give you some GPS coordinates. If you have to write them down you better eat them when you're done."

"I'll carve them on these almonds," I said.

Dina told me where to go and what to do when I got there, then asked, "How are you going to get Fedorov talking? Or even get close to him?"

"Same way I did with you. I can still do those handstand push-ups, if I'm near a wall."

"Hope you can swim," Dina said and hung up.

Ray was next.

"I've got Layne Lackey's address," he said.

"How is it you know computers better than me?"

"That I got a guy for. Layne's place is less than an hour away," Ray said. He fed the address directly into my GPS. "You got a good workout in yesterday."

Ray was monitoring more than my location. "You see my heart rate in real time?"

"Big Brother loves you," Ray replied.

"Why do I even bother to call you?"

"To maintain an air of propriety."

"Good-bye Ray."

Ray sent me a location to gas up on the way to Layne Lackey's place. My clothes were clean and pressed with a paper band wrapped around them like a ribbon. I got dressed and loaded a yellow quiver into the Quarreler. The gate guard didn't make eye contact when I left. I almost asked if being a eunuch solved any of his problems.

I wove the White Stag through traffic, laughing in the face of the gridlock while reclaiming hours of my life. With the helmet on you couldn't tell it was me, which was good because plenty of people were taking pictures of the famous bike. My appearance would probably get written off as a public relations stunt for the next Brand movie.

Judging from his place, Layne Lackey had been doing a hell of a lot better than me. His condo was converted from a local landmark. They kept the veneer but knocked down walls and put in staircases, turning ten rooms into five units. Layne's was a corner unit. The second-floor turret gave a panoramic view of the boulevard that once defined This Town, though these days the location wasn't a selling point. Quite the contrary.

I pulled into the spot directly in front of the door on the presumption it was Layne's. His car was gathering rust in police impound. That was too bad. If I remembered right, it was a nice ride, the same model as Viviane Lake's in *Right of Way*, back before every film turned into a product-placement extravaganza. It was a shame, but Dina had to do everything she could to mitigate the series' progressively inflating budgets.

I set up a few pencil cameras on the Stag, one facing the condo and one facing the road, then made for Layne's door cool and casual. Just a friend stopping by to feed the fish. There were a lot of cars around, considering the time of day. In This Town, people kept weird hours, if they kept them at all.

I slid the vibrating pick into the deadbolt. Ray's little gadget set the tumblers in about two seconds, but turning it was awkward. It took two full twists. I hoped no one was watching. Stern was looking for a reason to slap me in cuffs and this was an actual crime.

The bolt popped. Loudly. I let myself in and closed the door behind me. The power was still running, which was good because Layne liked curtains. Opening them for light would have created more witness opportunities. The alarm box staring me in the face read *Disarmed*. Either Layne forgot to set it or the cops did. Either way I got lucky, because I had no idea what I would have done if it was on.

All the normal house sounds seemed suspicious. I drew the Quarreler. Either this place was empty and no one would catch me being overdramatic, or the Black Knight was hiding around a corner and I was right to be.

I cleared the closet to my left first, learning Layne liked coats and believed in umbrellas. His place had a weird layout, a result of the renovations. The entry led into a combination kitchen-dining room with a half-bath tucked around the corner. A spiral stair in the other corner went up. I decided to finish checking the first floor.

There was a living room past the kitchen, separated from it by a half wall. One long wall was dominated by a huge television and the other shelved movies. A sliding door was set into the short back wall. It looked out into a half-decent atrium. I got the impression the living room didn't see a lot of use, which was kind of sad. It was the place Layne had designated for company.

I headed upstairs, Quarreler first, and almost shot Sir Collin Prestor. A cardboard stand-up of him, at least. It was from *The Gamesman's Grounds*, where Jove Brand—after spending two acts being hounded around the globe—led his pursuers back to his ancestral home, not realizing that was what his foe wanted the entire time . . .

Sir Collin sold the costuming, looking natural in a big-game hunter outfit in which 99 percent of the population would come off as pretentious. He angled his Quarreler low so we could see his desperate but determined expression. He didn't look like someone who would be caught off guard on a rooftop.

Layne obviously spent his time on the second floor, which was both master suite and Jove Brand fan museum. The walls were lined with vintage posters and signed photos, including one of Kit and I posing on the set of *Near Death*. How he had gotten his hands on it was beyond me. Blurry and with a slight reflection, it was a poor print. The only other photo with me in it was from my first convention appearance. Layne and I were standing outside a meeting room, having just co-hosted a screening of *Near Death*.

This was six years ago, right after *Near Death* leaked online. For the dozen before that, there were whispers about a mythical Jove Brand movie released overseas for a single weekend. A lost Brand film never screened in America or Europe, with no home video run.

Kit might have gotten away with it, protected the brand—pun intended—without hurting its market. Kept the franchise as worldwide blockbusters instead of straight-to-video fodder. But there was no predicting the internet.

Fortunately, by the time *Near Death* spread through cyberspace, there were already four hugely successful Sir Collin Prestor installments out. Those films created a buffer that transformed *Near Death* from franchise killer to cult classic. The movie was everywhere inside of a year. Not only the entire film, but edited highlights and countless GIFs.

If there was ever a flick made to be viewed in five-second bursts it was *Near Death*. Whether it was me executing a twenty-four-punch combination—referred to in the movie as the "full quiver"—or me pulling off the helicopter jump-kick that almost killed Yuen, or me emptying dual Quarrelers point-blank into a squib-vested Tzu Warrior. If you saw one clip, you wondered what the heck you were looking at. If you saw five, you told yourself you had to find the whole thing. Invite your friends over. Make a night of it.

It didn't hurt that Missy Cazale was in it. Missy, who had played queens and indentured servants and Nobel-winning scientists. Missy, who won an Oscar portraying a mother forced to steal her own embryos for the stem cells to heal her dying child. Now you could see her cowering in a wet tank top.

Poor Missy. The sad truth was the haters were waiting in the shadows, eager to take you down. And the internet was nothing but shadows. If you Googled Missy Cazale, in the first ten results you would find a clip of Missy ripping off her bloody blouse in defiance. In the next ten, you'd see her mouthing "By Jove!," as all Jove Brand's lovers must, per contractual requirement.

Half of the problem was Missy acted the hell out of *Near Death*. You believed her terror or vapidness. The other half was, due to a combination of casting and contractual issues, Missy had to play twins. One of which embodied "an upstanding English girl of breeding" and the other "a trollop who, after a tryst with Brand, must pay the price for her loose morals."

The first *Near Death* rips were Thai-dubbed bootlegs sold at comic cons. Then an English print was dumped online, booty for the pirates. Finally, in an *If You Can't Beat Them, Join Them* move, Dina included *Near Death* in the Jove Brand fifty-year anniversary boxed set, digitally remastered and sound-corrected in a futile attempt to polish a turd.

To everyone's surprise and dread, that boxed set sold like hotcakes. To this day, it is the only way to legally own *Near Death*. Not long after, Layne Lackey contacted me via email. Had I heard of the convention circuit? Would I be willing to make a paid appearance? Did I retain my wardrobe?

I remembered the moment we took this picture. I was shell-shocked. The audience loved *Near Death*. They roared with laughter and clapped. Every time they couldn't believe what they thought was about to happen, it happened.

Standing there, in Layne's little Jove Brand museum, I got a little choked up. In the end, Layne Lackey had done a lot for me, both good and bad. I was going to miss him. Eventually.

Besides the cardboard stand-ups and posters, Layne had a decent collection of Jove Brand memorabilia. Not of the same quality or quantity as Bryce Crisp's, but respectable. I made my way past his waterbed—someone should have told Layne he was asking for trouble putting it in an upstairs bedroom, or, you know, anywhere—toward where his home office was set up. He had a beautiful reproduction of Tender's three-fold desk, complete with the Herne the Hunter and stag inlays. I sat in the chair—also a reproduction—and started searching.

The cops had seized the computer and any papers. The drawers were raided, minus the office supplies and an occasional Bowman Fletcher paperback. It was silly of me to think I could find anything law-enforcement professionals had missed. Of course, how many of them were hardcore Jove Brand fans? Did they remember the scene in *For Love or Money* where Tender fought off an assassination attempt?

I ran my fingers over the carved relief of the long bow, then drew the string back. A latch released and the hidden drawer knocked into my leg.

"I do my best work from here," I said, quoting Tender as I reached inside. I knew what it was by feel. There was nothing else in the secret cubby. As far as replica Quarrelers went, this was a good one.

But mine was better.

I set the replica down on the desk. Here I thought I was onto something. This shamus stuff sure had its ups and downs. Turning in the chair, I took in the rest of the room. Twin posters for *Ungentlemanly Warfare* flanked the sliding door out to the terrace.

The poster's images were sliced up by a Brand bull's-eye, depicting all the classic tropes in silhouette: Brand aiming his

Quarreler, the two types of girl, the White Stag. But Brand was bleeding from multiple wounds, the wrong girl lay dead, and the White Stag was in flames. The poster looked good. Professional.

Except *Ungentlemanly Warfare* wasn't ever a Jove Brand movie. It was Layne Lackey's fan-fiction screenplay. He was always trying to get me to read it.

How good of a replica was Layne's mock Quarreler? I broke it open to find a dummy quiver loaded. When I shook it, there was a dull rattle. I pried the cap off the quiver and dumped a flash drive into my palm.

Layne had made a backup. I looked back over to the photo of us, then to the one of me and Kit. Missy had taken the shot. How had Layne gotten it? The only person who had it was Missy, and there was no way Missy had shared it willingly.

Someone knocked on the door. Three friendly taps. Not loud or urgent. I pressed the button on my video watch to active the pencil cameras.

I couldn't see the guy knocking from the front camera view, but the guy behind him, facing the street, had his arms crossed over a pistol. The rear camera showed twin Range Rovers angled behind the Stag to pen it in.

Once again, Chevalier had found me a little too fast for coincidence. I whispered into my watch.

"Ray, call 911. I got company."

I was trying to remember if I had locked Layne's front door when it slammed into the wall. So far, there were always two goons per car, which meant the other pair were coming up behind me. I put my back against an *Ungentlemanly Warfare* poster and shifted the curtain over the sliding door. A Chevalier goon was pulling himself up onto the second-floor terrace.

I buttoned my blazer as the downstairs got the full no-knock treatment from the mercs clearing rooms. The Quarreler was in my right hand. I unlocked the sliding door with my left.

Three seconds later, the door slid open from the outside until it was wide enough to admit one broad-shouldered soldier of fortune. The Chevalier goon stepped into the room, and turned toward me to clear the corner.

I posted his arm with my free hand to block his aim and put two darts in his leg. I only meant to pull once, but I was nervous. The Chevalier goon seized up, canting over onto his side. Unsure how long the fléchette batteries would last, I slammed an elbow into his temple. He went limp but didn't stop twitching.

The spiral staircase vibrated a warning. I took cover behind Tender's desk and aimed the Quarreler. It was a long shot, but a grenade would have ruined Layne's memorabilia. When the merc came off the stairs, he did the same double-take as I had when confronted with the cardboard stand-up of Sir Collin. It saved me, because my first shot missed. The second got him in the hip and down he went, tapping out an involuntary SOS with his heels.

I swapped back and forth between watching the sliding door and stairway, awaiting the next wave. After maybe thirty seconds, my ambusher from the BART parking lot yelled up.

"Allen?"

I didn't answer.

"You're boxed, Allen. I got a guy out back and I'm watching the stairs. It's only a matter of time."

It sure was. Soon, the cops would be here. To arrest all of us. Whoops.

The Cavalier commander kept trying. "Throw your gun down and we keep this nonlethal. My guy up there, check him out. That's a Taser in his loadout."

I risked a glance at the goon twitching by the sliding door. Lying on the floor next to him was a space gun with a yellow hatch instead of a barrel.

The commander called up again. "But this act you're pulling is pissing me off. I've got a throwaway with your name on it. They'll find it next to your corpse and me with my lawyer's card in my hand. Toss your kit off the back deck and we'll play nice."

What was either a brilliant or stupid idea came into my head. I set down the Quarreler and started stripping off my harness.

"All right," I yelled. "Give me a minute."

"Take your time. My guys okay?"

"One will have a headache."

I crawled onto the terrace. The fourth Chevalier goon was standing outside the ground floor sliding doors. I tossed my harness in a high arc, then sent a Quarreler on the same trajectory. When the goon turned his head to track it, I sent two darts at his way. One of them hit his neck and he went down.

Score one for the replica market.

I soaked the drop from the terrace with a roll. I didn't used to need the roll, but gravity got heavier every year. Scooping up my harness, I averted my gaze from the guy with a fléchette sticking out of his neck. Hope Chevalier provided medical coverage.

I turned onto the narrow walk beside the condo with my Quarreler leveled. I was amped up and raring to go and still lost. The Chevalier squad leader fired as he cornered, the twin darts from his Taser hitting my jacket dead center.

He threw an arm over his face as my last dart thudded into his windbreaker to no result. Neither of us had stopped moving toward the other as we traded fire. We emptied our hands as we closed on each other.

The space between the wall and the privacy fence was maybe a foot wider than my shoulders. Fighting here was like two trains dueling. I had all of a heartbeat to get a read on the squad leader. He had an inch and fifteen pounds on me, none of them extra. There had to be a vest underneath his windbreaker. A trauma plate limited my options. No doubt those were steel-toed boots on his feet. He didn't say a word. He wasn't looking to talk me out of this, because he wanted this.

Well so did I.

He went straight for the groin. It was the right kind of kick— arcing up and in, like a whip. I checked it the only way you could, by moving in and sliding my front knee over. He sent speared fingers before his foot was back on the ground. It was the classic one-two of Jeet Kune Do: nuts then eyes, delivered together in less than a second.

I slipped the gouge and put a straight right into his ribs— skinning my knuckles but good on his vest—then rose up with a backfist, the heel of my hand snapping into his orbital bone.

It was all downhill from there. I rolled an elbow into his other eye socket and shouldered him into the fence. Ray's miracle blazer soaked the knee he put into my ribs as I shoveled a left into his liver, then snapped his head up with a right uppercut. As his chin came down, I launched it back up with a skip knee. He didn't need the knee, but I didn't need to be suckered with a Taser in that BART lot either.

I went to collect everything I'd dropped, not bothering to check if the commander was out. If he got back up from that knee, I was dealing with an android. I made a mental note to send him smoothie recipes. Straws were replacing silverware in his foreseeable future.

Either the sirens hit earshot right then or I was just noticing them. I hung my harness over the antler-bars and squeezed the Stag out along the front walk. I kept to side streets and obeyed all traffic laws as I fled the scene. A mile from Layne Lackey's condo, I pulled over to slip my harness back on and make sure the second flash drive was still in my pocket.

It was a bummer I didn't get to see what happened when the cops rolled up on Chevalier security, laid out all over someone else's property. They thought I was out of their league. Turned out they had it backward.

12

I OVERNIGHTED THE SECOND FLASH DRIVE TO RAY before heading back to Missy's cabana. I was halfway through a riceless stir-fry when Stern called.

"I've missed you. Did you miss me?"

"Can it, Allen. We picked up four Chevalier guys at Layne Lackey's place off an anonymous tip."

"You get a lot of those."

"They were beat up and shot full of darts," Stern said.

"Did they name their attacker?"

"They did not."

I savored the flavor of beef. "That's a real shame. So, how was your day?"

"You're losing your mind, Allen."

"Yeah? Did any of these guys have their throats crushed?"

Stern blew out before saying, "No."

"Imagine that. Don't be a stranger," I said as she hung up.

I forced myself to nap the day away so I would be fresh for prime time. My ensemble now included a white button-down shirt, but everything else was the same, which made my boxing shoes even more gauche, but what could you do? Show me a dress shoe that wouldn't escape orbit when I kicked and I'd buy it.

The sun faded on the ride toward Long Beach. I kept to PCH, weaving the Stag through the congestion to lose any tails. I was on my way to catch a boat headed outside of United States territory in order to snoop on a guy responsible for who knew how many deaths. Also, I had no plan.

I was expecting a bare-bones dock walled by chain-link. Instead I got miles of ornamental wrought-iron fencing. The lone gate was open, with opposing bears on their haunches on each side. When the gates came together, the bears would embrace. That should have been my first warning.

I queued up behind the biggest collection of sports cars I'd ever seen outside of an auto show. My old beater would have been a red flag in such a procession, but the White Stag held its own. The guard waved me through without confirming I was really Connor Shaw. There was no point. No one attending a secret offshore casino was using their real name.

I maintained several car lengths between myself and the Ferrari ahead as we wound down to the shore. The single residence inside the gate was a mansion that owed more to Crimea than California. It might have been the situation, but the place reminded me of the type of joint you had to shove a witch in an oven to escape. The doors were probably made of chocolate bars and the windows rock candy.

The carports lining the shore matched the mansion above, four long roofs each sheltering fifty or so spots, few of them empty. I took the open space closest to the docks, in the event I had to make a run for it. Every little bit helped.

The boardwalk to the dock was also covered, with the perfect amount light to keep everyone in shadow. Ambience was everything. I was watching the waves lap against the harbor when my watch flashed another text from an unknown caller.

I've left a royal surprise in your lair.

My heart became a frog looking for a way to escape my throat. The Black Knight had planted something in my apartment. Nothing dangerous, like a bomb or a barrel of tarantulas. He needed me alive to frame me. So something incriminating. The ferry out to the defunct oil rig-*cum*-casino drifted into view. Leave now and I might not get a second chance.

I started back toward the Stag, then stopped. It was too late to do anything about the Black Knight. Rushing to my condo and into whatever trap he laid was exactly what the Black Knight wanted. The only way out was to delve deeper.

The crew clipped the velvet rope back into place behind me. I headed for the stern as the ferry pulled away. Back toward land, a latecomer was waving from the dock. He looked used to boats turning around for him. This one didn't. There was a lighted helicopter pad on the far side of the mansion, along with a private dock suitable for small watercraft. No chance I was going to run into Fedorov on the courtesy shuttle.

I stepped into a lounge finished in brass and wood, set aglow by light filtered through frosted glass. There was a full bar and an ornamental cage for buying chips. No one bought in for less than my net worth. I headed over to the bar and ordered a club soda. A Russian girl who could have walked the runway asked if I wanted lime.

"Only if you slice it fresh. When does the last ferry leave for shore tonight?"

The girl shook her head with a hint of a smile. It wasn't clear if she had answered me or blown me off. It also wasn't clear if she was inviting more conversation or wanted me to go away. I set a bill I hoped wasn't too insulting on the bar. She didn't touch it.

"Only chips," she said with a tight head shake.

"Sorry." I scooped the money back up. I didn't like what the staff being restricted from accepting cash told me. It also meant I was going to have to trade with the coin of the realm.

I went over to the cage and emptied out my pockets, using my body to block anyone who might be watching. The results weren't promising. The White Stag rode like a dream but he drank deep. I got seventy-three bucks back because a hundred was the smallest denomination accepted, leaving me with a total of seven chips worth forty-seven hundred dollars here and here alone. At least my pockets wouldn't have any unsightly bulges.

"Good luck," the caged girl said, but she didn't really mean it, because she really didn't care.

"Same to you," I replied, meaning it.

I used the drink as cover to examine my peers. It was an interesting mix. Sure, there were the gray-haired men paired with excited girls who weren't their daughters, but there was also the nouveau riche. The tech guys whose start-ups had made it and the high-stakes gamblers stretching way past their bankroll, hoping a sea voyage would net them a whale. But it was the fighters who surprised me.

They weren't here as guests. Everyone one else was sporting evening wear and they were in their warm-ups. Fighters couldn't afford these stakes anyway, regardless of wardrobe. There were three of them. Each sat alone, their hood up, trying to keep their mindset.

I headed toward the bow. The front lounge was a replay of the rear, except the clientele was a little rowdier with anticipation. Sitting in front meant you were impatient for the destination. The booze was flowing more freely here. I spotted two more fighters. One was napping with his earbuds in. The other had his shirt off and was chatting up the bartender about what all his ink meant.

The distant lights of the oil rig came into view. It was a complex of four platforms connected by generous walkways. The superstructure glittered with hundreds of golden lights. The helicopter pad was currently occupied. At least fifty watercraft of various sizes were moored around the base, from yachts to speedboats. More were approaching from every direction. Despite the late hour, the party was still warming up.

The ferry docked with nary a bump. Once the rope was opened, the passengers filtered off briskly. Lollygagging meant an hour round trip to shore and back.

There were two elevators up, along with a lighted staircase no one was using. I chose the stairs, preferring a view of the complex's underbelly to the nighttime sea. The only other person on them was one of the fighters. I gave him berth as he jogged past. I could empathize.

You walked a knife's edge before a fight, wanting to be warm and loose without tiring yourself out. Struggling to keep your adrenaline from firing prematurely and leaving you blown out before the bell ever rang.

I took it slow to get a look at what was happening at sea level. There were four guys on dock duty, roping off boats and keeping watch. None of them were visibly armed. A man in a tuxedo greeted those arriving in their own craft and rode the elevator with them, probably to work the buttons. I didn't see any boats get turned away and I didn't see anyone get thrown over the side, which wasn't saying it didn't happen.

There was a lot of activity in the water around the platforms. I heard splashing but all the lights killed my night vision. Yuen once told me cruise ships created their own little ecosystems, from the sea life orbiting them for scraps. Then the sea life who ate the other sea life showed up. The same went for this place. You dumped whatever didn't get eaten over the side and let nature take its course.

My head kept going back to what was waiting for me onshore. I was sure that by now the Black Knight had tipped Stern about incriminating evidence in my condo. My guess was Layne Lackey's phone. I probably gave him the idea when I texted it.

Ground and center, Ken. Focus on what you can control, I told myself. The climb helped clear my head. The elevator crowd had beat me to the top by a wide stretch, leaving me all alone.

Each platform had a single multiple-story building standing on it. The one closest to the elevator looked to be a nightclub at sea. Muffled electronic music vibrated through the walls. I decided to skip it. I wasn't sure how I could poke around in there and not look like I was poking around. Even if I ran into Fedorov, the volume being what it was, I wouldn't be able to spy on him without sitting in his lap.

The second platform accommodated an upscale gaming house, the granite veneer clashing with the steel superstructure.

A guy in a tuxedo opened the door as I approached, greeting me with a deferential smile. Reflexively thanking him was probably a mistake. Darn me and my plebian manners.

Blood-red carpet ran from paneled wall to paneled wall. The ceiling was sprinkled with skylights. A haze missing from modern casinos completed the atmosphere. Maritime law must have lacked a provision against indoor smoking. I went aisle by aisle. It was all house games: roulette, craps, blackjack, and keno. There was also a game with two croupiers and cards I didn't recognize, along with a bank of vintage mechanical slots and another of pachinko machines.

This was the attraction designed for thrill seekers. The place where the rich could impress their misters and mistresses with how much they could lose without a care. Lingerie-clad girls who weren't old enough to indulge themselves served drinks, taking their gratuities in chips. Nothing or no one caught my interest. I glanced away from anyone who tried to attract it. The less attention I drew, the happier I was.

I drank in the sea air on the walkway to the next building. Smoke was great for mood but that was about it. The third structure was much like the second, this one devoted to card games. Poker of all flavors and baccarat were popular, but there were other, more complex games I didn't understand. Games using nontraditional cards with wizards and dragons and castles on them. The tech guys were eating it up. If I was reading the stacks right, there was close to a million bucks on the table.

I didn't have the head for card games. I'd done okay during the poker boom by reading people, but I lacked the love of the game to put in the hours it took to become better than adequate. Anyway, it was mostly clients who invited me to play and I wasn't about to win myself into the poorhouse. I couldn't testify as to the quality of players, but every hand opened with more than what I had in my pocket. I didn't even have enough to ante.

The players in this building were a different breed. They had come for the games. The serving girls were largely ignored here. There was less alcohol and more food. Gambling was a rush, and the problem with a rush was your tolerance only went up. You had to play for enough so the next card made you sweat. The gamers celebrated and commiserated, talked trash and thought deep. Rivalries were born and friendships forged, based on grudging respect and shared experience. Built on mutual, consensual attempted destruction.

The best kind.

I didn't see anyone who looked like they owned the place, so after feigning interest in several hands, I headed out the door to the last building. Even if I hadn't already reasoned out its purpose, stepping through the door would have told me. From the muffled gasps and horrified cheers. From the smell of sweat and triumph and fear. The years I had spent around all of it had penetrated every fiber of my being.

The last building was an arena.

The doorman waved me in as the humid air welcomed me. There was no view from the doors, which was smart. If there were, the casuals would pile up in the threshold, not willing to fully participate but not able to look away. Instead I was facing a digital screen mounted in a curving hallway. The screen displayed the faces of the fighters, their specifics, and the odds.

The hall was finished in old-school padded leather, making it look like the back of a swanky couch. It led into a lobby lined with betting cages. Screens were everywhere, showing sporting events from around the world. The days of chalkboards were over. Monitors displayed the odds, updated in real time.

The odds boards for the bouts were different from the norm. The upcoming fighters were stacked against each other as usual, one at a minus and the other at a plus, but each fighter also had a second number, set across from *to 1*. The first fighter was *6 to 1*, the second *8 to 1*. That's how I knew what kind of event I had walked into.

A brass handrail split the lobby stair down the middle. I walked up. In place of stadium-style seating, there was a series of boxed booths, each one sheltered from the others by a curved half wall. The booths were only 50 percent occupied. The main event was yet to begin.

The cage I was expecting wasn't there. Instead, I was looking down into a fighting pit. The wall was eight feet high and made up of rectangular panels, which made the arena a twelve-sided bolt hole. The mat and walls were canvassed off-white, to display any spilled blood without the lights glaring off them too harshly.

The fight world perennially generated rumors of underground matches. Secret tournaments fought to the death. Private duels held between two patrons for huge purses, each with their chosen champion. Gladiator events with teams or weapons. It always turned out to be grifters blowing smoke or wannabes spinning yarns to impress the ill-informed. Soldiers had stolen valor, fighters fabricated honor.

Had someone described to me what I saw, I would have written it off as a tall tale. But here I was, standing in a modern coliseum. Standing for too long. I slipped into the first empty booth and thought about what to do next. I was on the right track. Here were the fighters Runshaw Shensei had warned me about. This was where I wanted to be. The clubs and casinos, those were for the VIPs. This place was different. This place was a labor of love.

I was studying the screens mounted over the pit when a Russian stepped in front of my booth. He had classic Slavic features: a high forehead with a strong brow that cast his eyes into shadow, a long blade of a nose and a slash for a mouth. The only way to tell what century he was from was by his clothes. His gray blazer displayed rather than obscured the solidity of functional strength. Russians could give a shit about muscle tone. They just wanted to be able to move bodies.

"I cannot believe it! It is you. Brand. Ken Allen Brand!"

The only thing scarier than a stoic Russian was an excited one. The man spread his hands in my direction as if he were revealing me to myself.

Denying it was pointless. The few times I had been spotted on the street it had never worked, and on those occasions I wasn't running around dressed as Jove Brand.

"Please, don't rise," the Russian said as he slid in next to me, pointing to a giant man who had followed in his wake. "Anatoly, he says it can't be. But me I am sure. Anatoly, I say, have you seen *Near Death* thirteen times? No. Do you wish to wager then? No."

Anatoly loomed to the right of the booth, saying nothing despite his reputation as a chatterbox. I guess it was hard enough to train a bear to wear a suit, much less teach them to speak on command.

"But Ken Allen is not on the list, he says. Ah, you are right Anatoly, but Connor Shaw is. And who was Connor Shaw? Second-best Brand. Think, Anatoly. A big star like Ken Allen does not use his real name."

"I don't like a fuss," I managed to get in.

"Grounded," replied the Russian. "He is no prima donna. This is not a charlatan who needs fast cuts to look tough. Put the camera on Ken Allen, wide shot, and let him do the rest."

I rooted around for a pen. "Who should I make this out to?"

"Good, very good. He's funny, Anatoly. To your new friend, Grigori Fedorov."

I was hoping he wouldn't say that.

"I keep a pen here," Fedorov said, reaching into my jacket near the breast pocket. "So it does not poke." He pulled the Quarreler out of its holster and studied it. From his casual competence, it was clear this was not his first time around a firearm. "Now, this is method. Become the character. Wear his skin."

Fedorov leaned back, stretching his arms along the top of the booth, which aimed the Quarreler right at my head. I figured Fedorov might recognize me. He was ready to spend billions on the rights to the Jove Brand franchise. He'd know it like the back of his hand. What I wasn't sure about was how I was going to get an audience. But Fedorov seemed as eager to talk to me as I was to talk to him.

A girl in a fur-lined teddy, whose great-grandmother likely fled the Bolsheviks, brought over two club sodas with lime. She didn't make eye contact with either of us. I took a drink to be polite. It didn't escape me that Fedorov knew what I had ordered on the boat.

"This is a dream come true—the chance to watch fights with Ken Allen. I love this country. You are hungry, Ken?"

"Ever since I can remember."

Fedorov reached across himself to pat me on the shoulder. Using his close hand would have meant putting the Quarreler down. "Yes. Serve dinner to your enemy. You have a little Russian in you, Ken."

Thankfully Fedorov didn't ask if I would like some more. He kept his hand where it was, clamping down on my shoulder. "Very good. Thick. Solid. You've kept tight all these years. I hear you never stopped training."

"It gets to be a habit," I said.

"A warrior does not know any other way." Fedorov pulled out a brick of a phone and used it like a walkie-talkie. I didn't speak Russian but all the warmth he'd shown me was absent in his tone. "Are you a fight fan, Ken Allen?"

"I like to keep up."

"Keep up, yes." Fedorov nodded as if I had given some sage insight. "So much has changed. At first the Brazilians had dominance. But only because no one knew their style. Except us, of course."

I saw my chance to get in two words edgewise. "With Sambo."

"Yes, with Sambo! You do not disappoint me, Ken Allen." Fedorov sampled his club soda. His expression didn't change but when he put it down, he said, "A warrior."

"Striking is opening back up," I said to keep it going. Whether by design or not, Fedorov had chosen one of my passions as the topic of conversation.

"Yes, because now all fighters know how to wrestle," he said.

"The fear of the takedown is gone."

"Exactly, exactly. You know who brought kicks back into practice, Ken Allen?"

"Eastern Europeans."

"Right again. Because they do not fear."

I would have argued it was because Thai boxing was so big in Holland or cited the thriving full-contact kickboxing scene in Japan, but I didn't want to smear the polish I had going. The arena was filling up with surprising speed. Attendance was around three hundred.

"But not all change is progress," Fedorov lamented. "Now with the gloves and the rules. America is the worst offender. No knees on the ground. No football kicks. No stomps."

"Because of boxing," I said.

"Because of boxing," Fedorov confirmed. "Now it is less a fight and more a sport. I will never understand boxing. For a decade my people have dominated the ring, exposed what a farce it has become. Soon we will have killed it."

I took a drink to hide my reaction. Did Fedorov just tell me he conspired to destroy boxing because he didn't like it? Whether he was full of it or not, it was hard to wrap my head around a guy with an ego that big.

The announcer came out, entering the pit through a door secreted behind one of the panels. He was exactly who you're thinking.

"Wow," I said.

"Real fights, Ken Allen," Fedorov replied.

Wall panels opposite each other opened up to admit the fighters. Handlers in the tunnels beyond pulled the panels back into place. The fighters were announced. The one I recognized was a contender before he caught a year's suspension for PEDs. From the shape he was in, he looked to be back on the cycle.

The announcer retreated through a panel, which closed behind him. As the bell sounded, I realized someone was missing.

"No official," I said.

"No official," Fedorov confirmed. "No corner men shouting instructions. No rounds. The fight stops when it is over. And no judges. The winner is the man who can walk out."

"Real fights," I said, my jaw tight.

In the pit, the two fighters cautiously stalked each other, each man acting as if he were caged with a cobra. Neither was wearing gloves. I began to feel the sympathetic tension I always felt watching, my hands drifting, my shoulders making miniature slips and rolls. Knowing the rules, or lack thereof, put an extra edge on the bout. I slipped into fight breath, regulating through the nostrils with my lips sealed.

The once-contender rushed in, seeking the clinch. Once he got it, he didn't let go. I lost count of how many knees he connected with after ten. He dumped his unconscious opponent on the mat and decided against a soccer kick, which spared the loser a coma.

"If you can break, the pit will break you," Fedorov commented, clearly not impressed with the loser. The should-have-been-a-princess brought us refills. I got a new club soda and Fedorov got something also clear but higher proof.

The doors opened as what I hoped were licensed medical professionals entered the pit to wheel the loser out on a collapsible stretcher. Above the pit, the four screens boxing in the lights came to life. I watched as the odds were adjusted, one fighter wiped off as the other's chances rose.

"The winner might make it to the next round," I said. "He didn't take much damage."

Fedorov leaned back as he appraised me. His eyes were black beads devoid of concern for social convention. "You have spoiled my reveal."

"You like tournaments."

"We all have our weaknesses, Ken Allen."

The next two fighters came out. I didn't recognize either, but I also didn't follow freestyle wrestling or submission grappling closely.

Their fight dragged on for three-quarters of an hour, all of it on the mat. Both men were looking to avoid damage, but in doing so they burned each other out. The loser ended up involuntarily asleep. It took the winner three tries to get on his feet, rolling up then lying back like a turtle in trouble.

"He's not moving on," I said. "You have alternates?"

"The need occurred to me," Fedorov said.

The next fight got underway. The fighters were both strikers. They went high movement, low volume, jousting as each hunted for a walk-off knockout.

"Were you ever tempted, Ken Allen?" Fedorov asked, nodding toward the pit.

I shook my head. "I got back from China in '99. I'd heard of submission grappling, but went west of California instead of south. By the time I caught up on mat work, I was over thirty."

"Fighters have started later," Fedorov said.

"But also sooner. The guys you're talking about were wrestling at seven, eight years old. I considered coaching, but by then I had my first A-list clients."

"Still you must wonder, being untested."

"Not much," I shrugged. "I know right where I rank. I'm a highly experienced amateur, which does not equal a professional."

The fight between the two jousters ended with predictable suddenness and finality, with one man landing a massive overhand right that instantly dropped his opponent. I heard the winner's hand break on the other guy's skull. We all did.

Faced with a tournament-ending injury, the winner gave his unconscious foe a kick out of frustration.

"He will continue," Fedorov said. From his certainty, he knew something I didn't.

"What's the purse?"

"Five hundred thousand American," Fedorov said.

"And for second?"

"Often fighters bet on themselves." Fedorov didn't get a chance to set down his empty glass. The princess was waiting to exchange it for a fresh one.

The last two fighters came out. I blinked hard, sure I was mistaken, but then the announcer called out his name and removed my doubts.

Alexi Mirovich, the Bull of St. Petersburg. Once heavyweight champion of the world, before his title was stripped.

"Isn't he in prison?" I asked.

"Work release," Fedorov said. His self-amused exhale fogged up his glass.

Alexi Mirovich was the what-might-have-been in the combat sports world, smashing his way up the rankings with apathetic precision. Raised by his father—a former Olympian—from the moment of his birth to be the perfect fighting machine. People speculated Alexi was secretly a cyborg, citing that he never bled and could function anaerobically.

Five years back, Yama O'Hara fed Alexi a right hand that would have dropped an ox. It only made Alexi mad. O'Hara was staring up at the lights less than a minute after. A year later, Randal Cobb suplexed Alexi so hard it left a dent in the mat. Alexi transitioned immediately into a lock that about tore Randal's arm off. Randal was never the same after. It wasn't just his rotator cuff. It was permanently disheartening, giving a guy the best shot you've ever dished out and them eating it with a yawn.

I missed who Alexi was fighting. I was too busy studying the greatest of all time. He looked bored. He was so immune to stress it made me wonder if he was on the spectrum. He didn't acknowledge the crowd or his opponent. He made no attempt to study or intimidate, which was demoralizing all on its own.

Alexi's opponent was scared and it showed. The fear pushed him into going for a takedown from too far out. Alexi sidestepped, sprawled, and threw a right hook all at once, ending up in the blind spot behind his opponent's hip, where he choked the guy unconscious without bothering to set his hooks in. Convenient, because Alexi didn't have to untangle himself when the poor slob went limp. Alexi stood up like a robot, knee before foot, the fight instantly forgotten. He turned a slow three-sixty looking for an exit. When one of the wall panels opened, he vanished through it.

I whistled under my breath. Alexi had it all. Perfect timing and speed. Incredible efficiency. There was no plan, only instant reaction. He had attained what all fighters strove for: technique transmuted into pure instinct.

"Now we must set matchups for the semifinals," Fedorov said.

My mouth had gone dry from hanging open. I took a drink while I thought. "The good news is you have two fairly fresh fighters, likely your finalists, though anything can happen. The bad is you have one guy with a broken hand and another who can't continue. Looks like you'll need two alternates."

Fedorov rocked slightly as he nodded agreement with my assessment. "Broken Hand will have to continue, as I have only one."

It was the first oversight Fedorov had shown. As a fight fan, he must have known tournaments were affairs of attrition.

"To be truthful, I had none." Fedorov looked at the Quarreler he was pointing at my head like he had forgotten it was there. "But here you arrive, delivered by fate."

The idea was so absurd I almost laughed, but I didn't find Fedorov's expression the slightest bit amusing. He raised his eyebrows with the barest suggestion of a smile, which was the Russian equivalent of a Cheshire grin. The maniac thought he was doing me a favor.

"I'm not prepared," I said.

"A warrior is always ready," Fedorov replied.

It was an effort to swallow my club soda. The ice cubes rattled around in the glass like dice in a cup. My adrenaline was already spiking at the thought of having to fight, which was bad. A professional bout wasn't only about being physically prepared, which I was not, for a match at this level. It was also about being mentally prepared.

"I don't stand a chance on this notice," I said.

Fedorov snuggled in to put his arm around me, resting the Quarreler on my shoulder. "This is not what I hear. I hear you have honed your skills, all these years. That you have done well against professionals. Very recently."

He knew about me and Chevalier. "They weren't prepared either."

"Nor are these fighters," Fedorov replied. "I want real fights. The participants do not know who they will be facing. They receive only three days' notice. There is no training camp, no chance to cycle or to peak. No time to cut weight. Of course, without weight classes there is no need."

There was a reason why weight classes existed. If you took two guys of equal skill, the bigger guy won. Sure, there was always luck. But luck ran both ways. Two of the remaining fighters had twenty pounds on me. Alexi was small for a heavyweight, but he had at least thirty. That was on top of him being plain better than me. I was leading in the one category you didn't want to be.

I was older.

"At least it will be quick," I said.

"Good. Confidence is good," Fedorov replied. "You will give a good fight. It is all about motivation."

"Going to make me paddle home?"

Fedorov beckoned with two fingers and Anatoly produced a full-sized tablet from under his jacket. Probably had a shotgun and a pot roast under there too.

"Threatening a warrior is useless. They do not fear pain. They defy death. You must employ other methods," Fedorov said.

He swiped the tablet to show a sharp, clear image of a private room. Everything was green because of the lowlight lens, but the booth said nightclub. It sat six people comfortably. None of the four men were Russian and all of them were the right type of harmless handsome. The two women were co-eds.

One was Dina Calabria's youngest daughter, Diana. The other was her fine-boned friend, the one who was cozied up to Dean.

"You should have visited the discotheque," Fedorov said. "I had what I am told is called a 'meet-cute' planned. Very natural."

"She's not old enough to drink."

"Here she is old enough for everything," Fedorov replied.

I started to threaten him but caught myself before I made that mistake. I'd have better luck intimidating a blizzard. All of the losers and half of the winners had left the pit with injuries it would take weeks, if not months to heal. If the same happened to me, my days of tilting at windmills were over. "The fighters bet on themselves?"

"Themselves only," Fedorov answered.

I emptied my pockets, splashing the chips across the table.

"I'm all in," I said.

13

FEDOROV'S PEOPLE WERE KIND ENOUGH TO ESCORT me around back to the service entrance. Couldn't have me getting lost. The room they stuck me in would have violated the Geneva Conventions if it was a prison cell. A pipe fitting which opened right into the sea served as a bathroom. I didn't bring my cup or mouthpiece and there weren't any extras lying around. They did provide shorts, however. The fact mine were salmon was not lost on me.

Neither my watch nor my phone had reception. Those and my harness went into a sheet-metal locker. I hung my jacket, shirt, and pants all on the one hanger and pulled the shorts on. With Jove Brand removed, Ken Allen alone was reflected in the streaked, full-length mirror. He looked terrified.

There was no way of knowing who I was matched up with. Fedorov probably figured having it narrowed down from "anyone in the world" to "three" was already polluting the purity of the event. I couldn't prepare for my opponent, but I could prepare myself.

I warmed up doing jumping-jacks, then moved into a stretch routine, taking an honest toll of my condition. The surprising thing about this whole insane adventure was how little damage I'd taken. Besides skinned knuckles and some stiffness from being kicked at the Shishi Opera House, I was the solid 90 percent where guys who trained all the time hovered. You never hit the fabled hundred, because in pushing yourself toward it, you wore something or other down.

I shadowboxed next, feeling the movement, letting my hands and feet flow. I didn't think about the future. I didn't think about any opponent except the one imagined before me, reacting to the threats my subconscious created. You learned to listen to your inner voice. It spoke of your strengths and weaknesses. Right now it was exposing my fear. I was moving away a lot, countering the younger, stronger guy about to manhandle me.

Don't create the situation you fear, I told myself. *Instead, stop it from starting.*

When I was loose but beginning to breathe hard, I slowed down and moved through techniques with measured precision, timing my strikes to land perfectly with my body mechanics. I slipped away from time and place, quieting myself. It worked, until my handler wrenched the door open and made my vitals spike all over again.

I took deep, measured breaths. Anxiety made for hollow breathing, which was the opposite of what your body needed to perform.

Fedorov's backstage guys were different from the workers who interacted with the guests. They moved with the lazy predator pace, saving their energy until it was time to kill. I was led down a tunnel of supply lines and conduit, past caged bulbs, feeling the steel grid under my bare feet. The rooms weren't finished out down here. They probably cleaned with a firehose. As I got close, a guy unscrewed the door leading into the pit by its wheel. He kept his weapon covered as I squeezed past him.

The first step out under the lights blinded me. The canvas was pulled tight and had good traction, without any sponsor logos slippery from sweat. I bounced a few times to get a sense of the springiness. There wasn't any. If you went down, you were going to feel it. If you were slammed down, the fight was over.

My sight returned enough for me to get a look at who I was facing. Either I got lucky or Fedorov had a finger on the scale, because it was Broken Hand. He was eyeballing me while unconsciously shaking his damaged paw.

As the announcer began doing his thing, I shuffled to the center before sliding laterally, measuring the space. When I hit a wall it didn't give anything back. My guess was canvas-covered sheetrock on top of a repurposed metal framework. There was a reason for ropes or a fence, beyond visibility. Ropes and fencing could be used defensively, to lean away or soak momentum. Not these walls. These walls were weapons.

I backed toward where my door was, wiping my feet to dry them off. I took slow, deep breaths from the diaphragm. It was hot from the lights and would only get hotter. All I'd had to drink in the last six hours was maybe twenty ounces of club soda. I should have asked for water, but if I was going to start should've-ing I was going to pass *should've let Stern do her job* on the way back to *should've said no to an appearance on* Beautiful Downtown Burbank, stopping at *should've told Kit Calabria thanks but no thanks.*

I tuned back in to the announcer singing our praises. Broken Hand was first. I wished I had watched his fight more closely. He was right-hand dominant and while his best weapon was damaged, it wasn't going to stop him from using it if he had to.

Not everybody fights for their body type, but at the professional level you tended to make the most of your natural gifts. Broken Hand had long reach for his height. He stood tall, which told me he liked to kick. He was thin for his frame. Twenty pounds would have helped his chances with the ladies, which meant he wanted to be thin. He was standing with his left foot forward, bowing to instinct and keeping his wounds as far from me as possible.

In return, I did my best to give him nothing. My biggest advantage was being an unknown, though the announcer was working on that.

"Hailing from This Town, California, standing at an even six feet, the Sensei to the Stars, Jove Brand himself . . . Ken Allen!"

I didn't acknowledge the crowd in any way while the announcer stretched out my name. Not only were the lights up there, but the sooner I forgot about being on display the better. I had enough problems as it was without concerning myself with public humiliation.

The announcer disappeared into the wall. I took a southpaw stance, opposite my opponent, resting the edge of my rear foot against the wall for reference. My lead arm was low, deliberately leaving an opening to tempt him into using his wounded hand.

I wasn't listening for the bell. I didn't care about the bell. Timers only mattered when there was a time limit. My attention was entirely on Broken Hand. Not his eyes or his shoulders or his hips, but everything. It was the opposite of focusing: taking the wide-view instead of zooming in.

He looked European, lacking all the mutt features us Americans don't realize we've acquired. I needed to know if he fought in the ring or in the cage. Overseas they preferred the ring. The cage was an American innovation—I blamed professional wrestling. From what I recalled of his first bout, Broken Hand kept well off the walls and counterfought, making his jousting passes when his opponent closed on him. Wall phobia said ring guy.

It took a while, but eventually Broken Hand came forward, closing a stride at a time until he was a lunge outside of reach. He wasn't sure what to do because I hadn't given him any information. You either liked to lead or counter. Broken Hand liked to counter, so I would force him to lead. I wanted him out of his comfort zone.

Broken Hand feinted a jab, pawing as he inched in, trying to draw an attack out of me so he could counter. I didn't budge. Next was a snap kick, long and quick but another noncommittal tester. I soaked it, keeping my arm loose rather than bracing.

Broken Hand used the kick as a bridge to enter the pocket and bring more options into play. His right hand wanted in but he squashed the instinct before it got away from him. I stayed in my phone booth and waited. I was going to have to make a guess soon and guessing meant you could get it wrong.

He tried a rear round kick, keeping it low. There were two ways to go with a low kick. One was to be like Dean and use the kick as a feeler to set up your offense. The other was to go for it the way I did with Street Justice and blast off full tilt, maybe catch your foe sleeping and land a crushing blow out of the gate. Seeing as Broken Hand had already tested the water twice, I suspected he was going to go for it. I drove my knee forward to meet him halfway, my shin down and toes pointed.

I guessed right. He put everything into it, turning his hip over for maximum power to chop my base away.

My shin caught him on the knee like a slicing blade. All the force he had generated fueled the collision. I felt his kneecap clank out of place. Broken Hand staggered away, eyes on me in case I chased after him. But I didn't move. I stayed right where I was, gaze unfocused, in no hurry at all.

It was all by design. I was worming into his head through a crack created by a legitimate fear. He already had a busted paw and now he was worried his knee was torn up. It was the same tactic I used on Dean, except I took it easy on the kid. This guy, I needed to crush.

Broken Hand hopped around, testing his leg. He thought about switching leads, trying out both stances to discover he didn't like either. It was a no-win situation. Use the damaged knee as your back leg and you had to drive off it. Use it as your front and it was out there, exposed. The less he had to move the better, so he took a page out of my book and stood in place, waiting for me to take the lead. I didn't oblige him. I had all night. I wasn't the one with the rapidly swelling appendages.

The crowd started booing and hissing. Screw them. Like I cared what they thought. People had been doing a lot worse to me both online and in person for years. Broken Hand cared though. He was a professional. He had been conditioned to please the crowd. Such was the cost of maintaining a reputation as an exciting fighter.

Fighters were paid based on how many asses they put in seats. How many pay-per-view buys they drew. There were thousands of guys out there slurring their speech from waging wars in the name of entertainment. If you went digging, you'd find skeletons under the coliseum scored up with trident marks caused by falling prey to the same temptation.

Broken Hand gave up and shuffled back in. I lowered my lead, creating an inviting opening for his left. He was running out of options he considered safe and I wanted to help his decision along.

He came with the left jab. I rolled my elbow up and over, putting my hip into it. I wasn't aiming for anything in particular, just sending my elbow out on an intercepting path. Even if I caught nothing, the rotation of my upper body had still moved my head out of line. In boxing it was called the shoulder roll. Kung Fu guys named it wing arm, because of the way it looked with your elbow rotated up higher than your shoulder. It was the same thing. A rose by any other name and all that.

My rising elbow caught Broken Hand right on the bare knuckles. I felt one of his fingers—probably the pinkie—pop. I heard him react more than saw it, his whimper scaling into a frustrated growl. He was a tough bastard. He'd proved it, coming back for the semifinals.

He went for the follow-up body hook, circling his punch under my raised arm. He was aiming for my liver, one of those magic spots that ended a fight if you tapped it right. Getting hit in the liver was worse than a kick in the nuts. There were a lot of nerves surrounding it and all your blood passed through it. You couldn't work out your liver to toughen it up. There was a reason why boxers hiked their shorts up to their rib cages.

I snapped my arm down, simultaneously dropping with my shoulder and hip. The point of my elbow caught him on the top of his wrist, two cars hitting head on. Maybe it was enough to snap a bone, maybe not. That was for the X-ray technician to work out.

As I executed, I let my rear hand drop, leaving my jaw exposed. You'd have to erase years of training to ignore the opening, busted paw or not. And that was without being frustrated and desperate.

The temptation was too much. Broken Hand swung for the fences, putting everything he had into the punch, betting it all on a knockout. His rear cross was a picture-perfect blur, fast and on track. I would have been put to sleep, if I hadn't drawn the attack out purposely.

I slipped underneath it, stepping out nice and low, sweeping my foot up as I went, like I was kicking a field goal. With his damaged knee, Broken Hand was already light on his injured leg, on top of having shifted his weight to his front in launching the big right bomb.

My kick sent Broken Hand's base leg into the air, which made the rest of him lurch forward. His cracked hand crashed into the weaponized wall at full speed. He screamed in involuntary horror as he sank to his knees.

It only worked because he was a ring guy. He wasn't used to worrying about checking his punches. It was all air on the far side of the ropes. He sank to his knees, exposing his back as he cradled his hand. When my shadow fell over him, Broken Hand extended his good arm toward me, a begging gesture more than a defensive one.

I knelt next to him and rested a hand on his shoulder.

Broken Hand nodded surrender. We waited for medical together. The life-or-death moment over, I tuned back in to the spectators.

There wasn't much to hear. The sequence of events had stunned them into silence. There was a sprinkling of excited shouts mixed with sour grumbles, the former from those who had bet the dark horse and the latter from the ones who had played it safe. As if there was such a thing as a safe bet in the fight game. Applause akin to golf clapping issued from a group of Japanese in a show of appreciation for my calculated execution.

Then a girl yelled out "Gooooo Jooooove!"

I squinted up into the lights, accidentally looking tough. Dina Calabria's youngest daughter, the mermaid who'd greeted me at Calabria Cove, had her hands cupped over her mouth to form a bullhorn. She was in a booth with Dean's girlfriend and two of the harmless-looking guys.

Coyotes looked harmless too. One would call out to your dog, scamper around, invite him to play. When the pooch followed, that lone coyote led them into the brush where the rest of his pack were waiting to tear old Rover apart.

As much as I wanted to tell Diana all that, I just waved. Even if she could have heard me, the parable would have been lost on her. She was sure the wall her grandfather built kept the wolves at bay.

———

I ASKED EVERYONE I passed on the way back to the "locker room" for water, the whole time trying to remember the Russian word for water. The fact I only knew the word for good-bye struck ominous.

I sat on the grill-top bench and worked to ease myself down, regulating my breath and wrestling my heart rate back to normal. I escaped my first bout unscathed, but let's face it: the odds were stacked in my favor and I had survived through sheer trickery. The room was suddenly freezing. I started to shiver as the sweat dried on my skin. What good was winning a fight if you ended up dying of hypothermia after? The door unscrewed to reveal either another Russian or someone doing a bang-up job in their character acting class.

"Bring your things," he said.

I bundled everything up inside my blazer. My guide led me into a communal shower with a fixed temperature perfect for poaching eggs. It would get me clean, but I wasn't about to drink it. A rough, used bar of soap was provided for my grooming needs. Good thing my hair was short.

I listened to the next bout unfold through the skeletal ceiling as two sets of feet drummed out an intimate tune. The crowd's cheers rolled in like waves before climaxing in an eruption.

I dried off with a rag you'd normally use to wipe the grass off your lawnmower and got dressed. The multi-tool and grenades were missing but at least they left my watch. I didn't bother putting the Bluetooth in. Fedorov himself was forced to use a walkie-talkie out here. The guard reappeared as I was working my way back into my blazer.

"Come," he said.

He led me out to the boardwalk toward the ferry dock, then up to the helipad. I wondered where we were going with one fight yet to be fought. There was no one to replace me in the finals. My opponent was done, both physically and mentally, and the crowd knew it. There was no selling I had withdrawn—I didn't take any damage—and from what I heard from the showers, the fight after me had a definitive ending.

I didn't have long to ponder what Fedorov was up to. He came bounding up the stairs, arms swinging like the world kept handing him everything he wanted.

"Ken Allen you do not disappoint me."

Anatoly wasn't as fast on the stairs but they relented to his assault. He rumbled past and opened the helicopter door for us.

"It is better to get in before the rotors start," Fedorov said.

He put a hand on the back of my arm, gesturing for me to precede him into the passenger area.

I got in as if I went on helicopter rides all the time. There were four places to sit, making every seat a window seat. I picked the one I figured would be the hardest to shove me out of the doors from. Might as well make Anatoly work for all those pic-a-nic baskets.

Fedorov sat next to me. Anatoly got a side all to himself, to keep us from rolling. As soon as he closed the door, the rotors started up. Fedorov pointed to the hanging headsets and we all put them on.

Anatoly didn't bother to adjust his mouthpiece.

"You must tell me about your strategy," Fedorov said. He focused on me, leaning forward, elbows on his legs, hands steepled.

"If a guy has an injury, target it."

Fedorov didn't acknowledge my cheek. "Very good."

I looked around but didn't spot an ejector-seat button or hang glider or anything else that might save me from Anatoly. With the room I had to maneuver, I might as well have fought him in a coffin.

"There has been a change of plan," Fedorov said. "After your bout, interest is rising. I am giving it time to boil over. Tonight, you will be my guest. Tomorrow, you fight in the finals."

"Is Alexi staying over too?"

Fedorov leaned back to get all of me in his eyeline. "There is no view from the showers."

"A crowd of Russians isn't going to cheer their hero's defeat."

Fedorov looked at me, looked at Anatoly, looked at the ocean. I would have had better luck guessing what a mailbox was thinking.

"I was right about you," Fedorov announced. "A true warrior."

"Alexi is going to wipe the floor with me."

"Only winter is certain," Fedorov said.

When we landed, Fedorov got out first, then Anatoly, then me. It was a short walk from the helipad to the witch's house, which was good because it was as cold as her tit. Everything inside was dark wood, like it was finished and furnished from the forest that once stood around it. There was also a lot of wrought iron. It kept the elves away from the shoes.

Fedorov led us into a starkly furnished den. The leaded windows radiated night. There was a barren fireplace and a lot of books too fancy to have titles on their spines. He poured the drinks himself, leaving both bottles. No one liked being the only guy with a bottle. Our chairs faced each other. Fedorov made an art out of awkward eye contact. I waited until he drank to drink. I waited until he refilled to refill.

I waited until he talked to talk.

"Any more predictions, Ken Allen?"

"You're setting up a limited broadcast, giving all the time zones a chance to buy in and place bets. I don't remember signing away my likeness."

"There is always the prize money," Fedorov replied. "And you may continue to bet on yourself."

"How did I make out?"

"You turned your forty-seven hundred into forty-two thousand three hundred."

Eight-to-one against a guy with a broken hand. My odds against Alexi were going to smash the record.

Fedorov looked at me the way I looked at aquariums. "Do you wish to leverage your winnings?"

"Let me sleep on it."

"Yes, I should allow you rest." Fedorov paused to give me time to stand with him. "Forgive me. You are good company, Ken Allen. We will talk at breakfast."

Fedorov muttered a syllable into his walkie-talkie and the doors opened.

I scooped up my bottle. "Thanks for putting me up."

Yet another Russian girl in fancy underwear acted as my guide. She was in no hurry to lead me up the stairs. The temperature being what it was, you'd think she would have wanted to get her blood pumping. She gestured to my door like the prize I'd won was behind it.

"I'm out of chips, sorry," I said.

She smiled because she had to. I didn't so I didn't. She didn't offer to join me, seeing as there was already a girl in my bed.

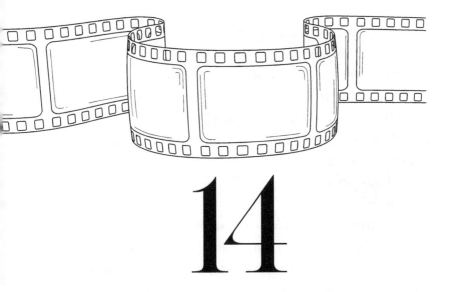

14

"TURN THAT THING ON," DINA'S DAUGHTER SAID,
nodding toward the fireplace. She was rolled up in the blankets like
a little Italian burrito.

I went over to the hearth and checked the flue. The logs had
been sitting there long enough to host a feudalism of spiders. I
pulled one of the books off the shelves. It was in Russian. From the
way it was laid out it, it looked like a play.

"Hope it's not a first edition," I said and tore a handful of pages
out. There was a box of matches in a drawer with an ashtray. I
shuffled the logs around to make an opening and crumpled a few
pages in it, then set a match to the pages. The whole first act was up
in smoke by the time the logs caught flame.

"Your name is Diana, right?"

She nodded from her blanket cocoon.

"What are you doing here, Diana?" I asked.

"Nat got us in. Don't tell my mom, she'd freak."

"Was coming out here Nat's idea?"

Diana worked herself into a sitting position. "No, that was Pino, a guy I know."

"A guy you met through Nat?"

Diana nodded.

I faced the flames. "Nat works for Fedorov."

"Oh come on. I've known Nat for years. Since like—"

"Let me guess. Since like the last Jove Brand film was in pre-production. You met her while your mom was out scouting locations. You were bored and hanging out at the hotel. My second guess is it was on a summer trip to Europe."

"Shut up. Nat's my friend." Diana abandoned arguing with me in favor of arguing with herself. "And she's Dean's girlfriend. She's like family."

"Since when?" There was no food in any of the drawers and no phone to call room service. There wasn't even a little bell to ring.

"Since she moved to California."

"After Sir Collin's last movie wrapped?"

Diana started running the timeline on their friendship. "Yeah."

"And—oh my gosh how cool was this—she was going to school not too far from you." I angled my palms towards the heat. "It's a classic spy trope. You should watch more movies, kid."

Diana shivered. The Calabrias weren't built for the cold. "That fire isn't doing much."

"Get closer to it. And bring the blankets with you."

Diana rolled out of bed and hopped over to toast herself.

It was no wonder she was shivering. Her curls were jeweled with drops of water, same as when she escorted me into Calabria Cove.

"How'd your hair get wet?" I asked.

Diana peered into the flames. "Nat said you wanted to see me. You know, after you waved at me. So they took me back here in Pino's boat. He drives like an ass. We didn't bring extra clothes. All they had is what the girls who work here wear."

I poked at the fire. It didn't need it, but I liked poking at fires.

"Yeah, what a crazy set of coincidences. And seeing as Fedorov is running short on rooms in this enormous mansion we'll have to share."

"It's a dacha, not a mansion," Diana said before going quiet.

It was going to take Diana a while to sort through three years of false friendship. Not wanting to unwrap herself, she tried to blow her drying hair out of her face. When it didn't work, she was forced to slip an arm out of her swaddle. Under the layers, she was probably wearing more than when I met her, but context was everything.

I attempted to put her at ease. "Me and your mom used to know each other."

"Yeah, Dean told me. You were in Uncle Kit's movie. Can I do that?"

"Poke away," I said, handing over the iron.

There were logs in the wood box, which saved a shelf's worth of books. I'd never been much of a reader, but throwing books in a fire didn't feel right.

"I'm sorry I thought you were like, pretending," Diana said.

I wasn't sure if she was talking about when we met or my fight. Probably both. "I am pretending, Diana. Sometimes pretending is the best way to get through a tough time. Plenty of people do it their whole lives."

"Yeah." Diana's one-word reply was enough. Growing up where she did, it would be hard not to relate. She welled up but didn't spill over. "You know, Nat told me she thinks Dean is going to propose. She used me to get to him. I feel like an idiot."

"That's the sensation of growing up." I fed a log into the hearth. "This is a bad place disguised as a good one. The girls who normally wear what you're wearing are prisoners. They're marooned on that casino. And they get paid in chips, which keeps them from saving up."

There was fear and then there was horror. Diana was experiencing the latter. "What about Nat?"

"Nat's different. She's allowed to leave. Either she's a trusted part of the team, or they have some other leverage. Maybe a family member."

"Oh God," Diana said. "Poor Nat."

"Yeah, poor Nat, but don't let sympathy lure you back in. Nat will use that. She won't be able to help herself. From where she's sitting, looking at your life, she's gotta be pretty jealous, maybe even mad."

When Diana didn't say anything for a while, I asked, "You still in there?"

"Yeah. Okay." Diana steeled herself, nodding at whatever she was thinking. She sat up a little straighter. She'd be fine. Life hadn't asked much of her, was all. But she was Dina's kid. She'd catch up fast.

"They're watching us, aren't they?" she asked after a while.

I nodded. If Fedorov had cameras in his club, it fell to reason he would have them everywhere else. Operation Casino Kompromat.

"And listening, in hopes of me doing something stupid. Then they would have something over me and over your mom too."

"Oh God."

"There's a reason why your mom didn't do business with Fedorov when she had the chance. It's a bad idea to make a deal with the devil when the devil is an atheist."

"You talk weird, Ken."

"You don't watch enough movies. I watch too many."

Diana sack-raced to her bag. When she came back she waved a tablet at me.

"Pick something for us to watch, then."

I took the tablet from her at the farthest possible point. "Does this get reception out here?"

"No I tried, but a ton of stuff is downloaded already." Diana gave a mischievous smile. "Nat swiped it off Dean. Just for the weekend."

If the window opened, I would have hurled the tablet into the sea. Diana had enough on her mind, so I didn't tell her Dean's tablet was likely going home host to a herd of Trojan horses.

The tablet had cellular service, which meant along with emails, there were texts. It also had a messenger app. I grappled with my conscience. What kind of detective respected people's privacy? In the end, I decided my invasion was for Dean's own good.

All the histories were deleted. No call record, no email archives. Why did Dean feel the need to wipe out his tracks? I went through his email search bar one letter at a time, letting the past addresses auto-complete. None of the five email addresses that appeared gave a hint as to the identity of their owners. Dean had the same number of contacts in his messenger app. CoachCrushem must have been Stavros and Nat_4_U was Nat. Niles_to_Go must have been Niles

Endsworth. With Dean about to inherit, it was no surprise he was buddying up with the next Jove Brand. The last two contacts had handles that would have made great passwords. I tried to message them to see what happened, only to be reminded there was no service.

Having broken the creep seal, I went through the files next. There were no documents or pictures, but the tablet was crammed with videos.

"This has a ton of fights on it."

Diana let out a long sigh. "Dean's obsessed with guys in tight shorts groping each other. Can you imagine what would happen to the movie rights if Goldpecker ended up being gay? Mom's head would explode."

There were thousands of thumbnails to browse. Then I had the bright idea to search for *Alexi Mirovich*. Dozens of videos resulted, which was no surprise. Dean liked the guy enough to have a shrine dedicated to him. Which made me wonder where he had gotten Alexi's personal possessions in the first place.

"Did Nat ever give Dean a really nice present? Something one of a kind?"

Diana made the same face I made when asked about a sequel to *Near Death*. There were some things you didn't want to consider. "Are you asking if they've done it? Gross."

Rubbing my eyes helped erase the image. "No, like fighting stuff. A pair of shorts, some gloves, a big gold belt."

Diana thought about it. "Maybe. Nat brings a bag when she stays over and they're always sneaking off to make out."

Though I had access to every bout Alexi ever fought on camera—even his Sambo matches from before he went pro—there wasn't much. Alexi had logged less than three hours in the ring over twenty-one bouts. Such were the fortunes of being the unstoppable force.

"Is there literally anything else we can watch?" Diana asked.

"Sorry kid. We'll have a movie night another time, but this is research. These fights might save my life."

DIANA DRIFTED OFF next to the fire, her head resting on a cushion stolen off one of the chairs. I used the bottom sheet and mattress liner to bundle up and sat with my back to the hearth, studying Alexi's bouts until I had to dig the charger cord out of Diana's bag. I brought her clothes back with me and hung them over the mantle.

The fight footage only made me feel worse. Alexi had no weaknesses. His timing was razor sharp. His efficiency unrivaled. There was no wasted effort in his technique. His footwork was tight. In twenty-one fights he never kicked and never shot for a takedown. It was all punches and Greco-Roman style wrestling— body locks and throws. When he attacked, he went all in. There was no halfway, no hesitation.

There was a bathroom in what looked like a closet. I let the sink run for ten minutes before refilling my empty bottle. The water was as cold as water got without being ice. I dunked my head for a pick-me-up and watched the fights again.

Alexi rarely initiated. If his opponent refused to lead, he shuffled into range until the guy either threw something or they were in the clinch. He ate shots that would have shifted me into an alternate dimension. On only two occasions had he been rocked. The first was a head kick that came at the end of a crazy sequence. His opponent threw a Superman punch, fast and deep. Alexi slipped it, and the guy flew right past him. As they spun to face each other, the guy landed a kick right on Alexi's temple.

The other time was also a fluke. Alexi hit a picture-perfect throw, but his opponent's feet bounced off the ropes and gave him space to slip out the back door. As Alexi stood, he turned into a right hand that would have stopped a truck. He was going down when the follow-up left hook set off his alarm.

In both instances, once Alexi regained his composure, it was over quickly and viciously, his deliberation replaced by desperation. Alexi didn't seek to recover, to gather himself and restart. He pushed to end it as soon as possible.

I watched both moments again. Each time Alexi got tagged, he was getting up and turning. It would have happened to anyone. It was a vulnerable position. But Alexi weathered every other vulnerable position flawlessly.

A theory was forming. I watched all his post-fight interviews. He said little, while staring at the mat, unmoving. He never answered questions and made only brief, general statements. It was all very Russian.

Alexi's father stood close, always watching him, but they never touched. For a coach with an undefeated fighter, his father never looked happy. Never slapped Alexi on the back or shook his shoulders in celebration. Again, being Russian could explain that away.

I paused on a close-up of Alexi's ears. They were like horns, swollen and curling. Cauliflower ear. Wrestlers got it from having the cartilage crushed over and over, day after day, year after year. From lockups, from the exploratory slaps, from having your head ground into the mat. You saw a guy with those ears, you didn't get within grabbing distance. If you did, he was going to twist you into a pretzel.

Except Alexi never scrambled on the ground. There was a vast palette of grappling techniques Alexi must have been skilled at, or at least aware of, and his whole game revolved around avoiding them at all costs.

One of the fights was preceded by a video bio, detailing Alexi's humble upbringing in a wolf-infested forest. There was a yellowing still of him at ten years old, wearing a singlet, facing off against his father. Alexi's ears were already starting to curl. A polaroid showed Alexi at thirteen, looking much like he did now, those ears already in full bloom.

There wasn't much video of Alexi training. He worked out in the wilderness with the same three guys, none of whom were fighters and all of whom looked like they escaped from the zoo. He liked kettle bells. His rowing machine and bike looked homemade. There wasn't any sparring footage.

Alexi was a man of the people. He took the train instead of buying into the capitalist automobile fad. My Japanese was rusty but the narrative voice-over was more appropriate to a Godzilla film than a documentary.

I went through all the fights again, watching how Alexi defended every attack ever thrown at him on film. Every time he got hit, I studied how it happened frame-by-frame. Alexi loved the hooks. Hooks stopped guys from circling. Alexi never kicked. Kicks left you on one foot.

It had been a long day. Visions of Russian bears were dancing in my head. But my theory held up.

Alexi Mirovich was keeping a big secret.

15

DIANA SHOOK ME AWAKE. SHE WAS BACK IN HER clothes, which might have kept her legs warm but couldn't have done much for her midriff. It was sinking in that she wasn't free to leave.

"I'm hungry but I'm scared," she said.

"Me too."

I got up and did what could be done in the bathroom, then helped Diana into my blazer, which had never failed to keep me warm. Also, its swaddling effect could be comforting. One of Fedorov's guys greeted us at the stairs. He smiled like he learned how in a video tutorial and led us into a dining room set in the back corner of the dacha.

The three walls unconnected to the rest of the house were entirely leaded glass. The glass must have been custom stuff, because it looked overcast outside without a cloud in the sky. The offshore platform was out there. The waves were hungry. It was a good day to throw yourself off a cliff.

The room was colder in early afternoon than it should have been with all the windows. Stacked logs waited in a barren hearth.

"I should have brought a book," I said.

Diana stayed glued to me as we headed toward the table, with both her arms around one of mine and half her front on my back. She probably would have let me carry her if I offered. It made me braver, her being scared.

The table could have doubled as a bowling lane. I sat us at the end by the hearth, in case the logs spontaneously combusted. The second we settled in, the double doors burst open to admit models pushing carts. They set down a buffet of covered silver platters, lighting propane burners under most of them. Diana couldn't stop staring. I couldn't start. We shared the same expression.

"I know what I'm going to do with my life," she said.

I believed her. She had the same fire and determination that drew me to her mother, all those years ago. There were things so impossibly evil it was hard to believe they really existed. Slavery being one of them. "That's good, and I'll be your first donor. But right now isn't the time."

Diana unclenched her teeth. "I'm supposed to play dumb?"

"It's worked for me so far."

All but two of the girls filtered out, and those two waited in our blind spots in case we had a problem hefting the grapes. I took one of the burners from under a chafing dish and set it against the logs in the hearth. Then I started pulling the lids off everything.

I scooped a heap of scrambled eggs done with chives onto a plate and added half a dozen thick strips of bacon. There wasn't any avocado, which was the biggest sign we weren't in California anymore, Dorothy.

"That's a lot of fat," Diana said. She was eating cottage cheese straight out of a crystal serving bowl.

"Sure is." I poured myself some coffee. The butter dish was taunting me. I almost asked for an immersion blender but was worried what would happen if the girls couldn't find one. I ate faster than I meant to. It had been a while.

"I can pour my own water," Diana said, grabbing the pitcher from her girl.

I cleared my plate and drank three cups of coffee, downing a glass of water in between each of them. When the nuts in the centerpiece turned out to be real I filled my pockets. I was rearranging the twigs and berries to conceal my crime when Fedorov walked in.

"Was your night productive?" he asked.

"As can be," I said.

Fedorov took a seat at the end of the table. A girl immediately came into the room and set a covered dish in front of him. She lifted the lid to reveal an egg standing in one of those candle holders for eggs. One egg. Feed your enemy dinner, indeed.

Fedorov did a good job ignoring the logs as they erupted into flame. Diana was dying to say something but choked it down. I was tempted to start cracking nuts. They took up less space out of their shells.

"Your fight will begin at midnight," Fedorov announced.

"Peachy," I replied.

"If it is not too much of a distraction, I would like to discuss other matters."

I sat up straight. This was what I came for. "Sure. I got nothing going on."

"You are aware I produce films," Fedorov said. His blind-spot girl poured his tea. He took a drink right away. For her sake, I hoped it was the proper temperature.

"I've seen all the Cherno Perun movies," I said.

That pleased Fedorov. Good thing it was the truth. "Oh? What did you think?"

"Damn good, considering. Your guys accomplish a lot, keeping in mind what they have to work with."

"Yes, yes," Fedorov said. He set his teacup down on a saucer that narrowly beat it to the table. "We have so few skilled in film-making, and I abhor computer graphics. The spectacle is not the point."

"You're putting on morality plays."

Fedorov appraised me again. "You are like an onion, Ken Allen."

"That's just my breath. I forgot my toothbrush."

"I have studied the Jove Brand films endlessly," Fedorov continued. "They fascinate me. The forging of a modern myth, founded on factual basis."

"Have you seen the Burgess documentary?" I asked.

"Oh yes. And read all the biographies," Fedorov said, warming up. His blind-spot girl snuck tea into his cup. "Do you agree with Burgess?"

"Sure." The coffee had me yapping. "England needed a hero in order to feel relevant, sandwiched between superpowers."

"Rebuilding its psyche along with its cities," Fedorov added.

"Brand was the right character at the right time."

"Well said, and apt, considering your portrayal in *Near Death*."

Fedorov's egg was gone, though I couldn't remember him taking a bite. Here he was, broaching my topic of choice before I had the chance.

"Portrayal is a kind way of putting it."

"*Nyet, nyet,*" Fedorov replied. "The purity of *Near Death* is what speaks to me. A man is called upon by his superiors for one mission, almost certainly a suicide mission. He is chosen because of his skills. He is not a generalist. He is a specialist, a warrior in the way the last Brand was not. There is no consideration if he will be suitable for the next mission because there is no next mission. In this way, it is your story."

The way Fedorov was selling it, the passion and surety, made me want to see whatever movie he was talking about. In countless reviews, comments, and reaction videos—none of which I should have looked at—not one person had accused *Near Death* of being a deep flick.

Rightfully so.

"The entire film takes place over seven hours," Fedorov went on. "Every scene is about the mission. At the climax of each sequence you think, *This is where this new Brand falls,* yet he always prevails."

"We pretty much made it up on the spot."

"Again, *nyet.* The film is . . . *meta,* I believe is the term. Watching it, you are watching a man exchange his life for a legacy."

Diana caught up. "Are you talking about my uncle?"

Fedorov looked through Diana. "It is all there on the screen, girl. Your uncle's emotional journey. The mortal betrayal, delivered by very person he sought to protect."

The flames at my back did nothing for the chill running through me. How much had Fedorov uncovered about *Near Death*?

Diana held her fork like an icepick.

"Uncle Kit died in a plane crash!"

Fedorov wasn't bothered by her response. I doubted his expression would have changed if she buried the utensil in his cheek.

"Of course," he said to her before again addressing me. "Have you given thought as to Bowman Fletcher's true identity?"

What did this have to do with anything? I had a troubling sensation Fedorov was going to keep me here until it was time to get on the helicopter. But if I kept Fedorov talking, he might actually tell me something.

"Do you mean do I think that he really was a secret agent?" I asked. "Maybe. That would explain why the British government protected his identity."

"Franklin Garand was Fletcher's first choice to play Brand. Garand was a member of the Ministry of *Ungentlemanly Warfare*."

"At least he claimed to be."

"He was," Fedorov said with the offhand finality of a man who had done some checking.

I glanced over at Diana. She had been sick of hearing about Jove Brand around the time the training wheels came off her bike.

"I believe Fletcher was Roland Landalf," Fedorov continued. "Fletcher's taste for other men's wives was well documented, and Landalf was the ministry's resident seduction specialist. Elsbeth Brown and the Duchess Armand were among his conquests. Fletcher was addicted to courting the forbidden, even taking his editor's daughter as a lover well into his senior years."

"Which explains all these supposed heirs who keep popping up and trying to claim Fletcher's estate," I replied. Whatever Fedorov was getting at, he was sure taking the long way around.

"Exactly. Do you believe life imitates art, Ken Allen?"

"In This Town, life is art."

"You jest, but Jove Brand once dictated trends. What to wear, what car to drive, even how women styled their hair. When Connor Shaw eschewed a hat in *The Gamesman Afoot*, it was the end of haberdasheries."

"Also John F. Kennedy," I said.

Fedorov gestured at me as if I were proving his point for him. "But Kennedy was a Brand fan. He named *Fatal Range* as one of his favorite novels."

It was time to guide the conversation toward the two murders I was being framed for. "Do you think Sir Collin was a better Brand than Connor Shaw?"

"This has been refreshing," Fedorov said as he stood, "but duty calls. After your fight, if you are able, we will continue the discussion."

"I look forward to it," I said, rising with him. When Fedorov turned his back, I added "I'd like to place a bet, using my winnings from last night. All of them. On me."

I was hoping to bring Fedorov back to the table. Instead, he gave the slightest of nods and left. At that point in his life, he'd probably forgotten how door handles worked.

I turned to my blind-spot girl and asked, "There a bathroom around here or should I open a window?"

Turns out there was one next door. I treated it like I didn't know when I was going to see the next one. The candle on the vanity matched the dining room centerpiece so I stole the nuts out of it too.

Plan ahead, that was me.

Diana was addressing the girls when I got back. They were indulging her, but she wasn't getting anywhere. Unless she knew how to fly a helicopter, there wasn't much she could do for them anyway.

"I'm going to learn how to fly a helicopter," she told me.

"It looks pretty easy," I replied, putting out my arm. "Let's test our boundaries."

We weren't exactly followed as much as someone was either already in or happened to wander into whatever room we explored. The house was locked down tight. I thought about searching for clues but was worried that if actually I found one, it would get us killed.

We walked the grounds next. I turned us away from the parking area as we left, then circled back around. Nothing jumped out at me. There wasn't a secret diamond mine or a death ray, or if there was, it was well hidden.

The parking area was half full, which I suppose made me an optimist. The White Stag was still there. Waving around the replica Quarreler stashed in the saddleboxes wouldn't get me anywhere besides the afterlife. Guess I was also a realist.

I looked back toward the gates, calculating. Could I get us there? Could I get the gates open? How far would we have to get down the highway until they gave up the chase? How vengeful would Fedorov be if I vanished before the finals? If I ran now before getting any answers, what was the point of coming here in the first place?

"Should we try it?" Diana asked.

"Maybe if there was a ramp on one side of the gate and a stack of hay bales on the other."

On our way back to the room, I relieved every fireplace we passed of its display wood, which was a lesser crime than burning the furniture. Once inside, I went into low-power mode, shutting down my senses. Processing stimuli was draining. It was dim and quiet, which helped.

I tried not to contemplate Fedorov's role in the murders. Before a fight you didn't want to be distracted by anything new.

You watched your favorite movies. You only read from beat-up books. You listened to songs you knew all the words to.

Diana got bored and dug out her earbuds to watch Dean's tablet. She kept me between her and the door.

"You'll be out of this soon," I said.

"What about you?"

"I want to be in it," I replied before turning over to nap.

———

THREE HOURS BEFORE the fight bell would ring, I shelled nuts and sipped water. I wanted to work on my strategy, but the cameras made me nervous. While Fedorov was a fanatical purist, money was on the line, and who knows who else was watching. I stretched and visualized instead—inserting myself into the pit, rehearsing movement, practicing reaction.

In a real camp, I would have had a minimum of two guys acting as mimics, aping Alexi's style. They would also have the same build as Alexi and similar reach. I would have spent hundreds of rounds implementing my strategy to transcribe theory into muscle memory. Visualizing was better than nothing, but not by much.

After everything was good and loose, I shoved the furniture out of the way and started moving around. I built slowly, warming everything up before adding speed, until the motions were a blur and the bones in my hands felt like they were separating from the cartilage.

Every athlete deals with the reality of diminishing from their peak. My speed had declined over the last decade, but I never felt the loss as palpably as I did right then. If the timing I'd gained through experience didn't equal the quickness I'd lost, I was going to have a bad night.

At T-minus two hours, Nat showed up at the door. She was more tan and less tense than the other girls populating Fedorov's holdings, done up in club wear with a giant purse hanging half onto her back. Nothing about her screamed captive.

"Oh my God, there you are!" Nat said. She rushed into the room like she'd been looking for Diana nonstop for the last sixteen hours. "Pino is down at the boat. Let's go, it's drinky time."

Diana didn't say anything to Nat, which was both good and bad.

"Do you need this?" Diana asked me, holding up the tablet.

"Not anymore, but it really helped, so thanks."

Diana said thank you like Dina did, which was to not say it at all. Instead she flashed a smile like I'd caught her off guard. She started toward me, stopped, then jumped in and hugged me.

"Dumb's the word," I whispered in her ear.

I felt Diana nod against me a few times. She exhaled against my chest, gathering herself. She broke off but didn't look away until she had to.

"He's kinda hot," Nat whispered loud enough for the cameras. "I need them deets."

"Uck," Diana said, slipping into character. They both laughed. She was getting it now. She wasn't about to show her cards. There was nothing to be gained from accusation and confrontation. She was going to cash out ahead.

Five minutes after they left, a handler came for me. I was all alone on the helicopter ride back to the platform. So far, it had been the same helicopter. After checking the pilot was busy, I rooted around but didn't find a parachute or anything that doubled as a floatation device. I pulled the pin on the fire extinguisher and turned it to face across from me, in case I needed a useless gesture later.

Our approach allowed a good view of the platform complex. There were twice as many boats as last night and more than one mega-yacht, along with a handful of seaplanes. The boardwalk was bustling. Fedorov's delay to promote had paid off.

Faking it until you made it had its positives. Walking around like you were already beaten could be a self-fulfilling prophecy. I hopped out of the helicopter and marched toward the arena like this was all my idea. The handlers averted their gaze and opened doors. I made for the locker room like I was a VIP who wasn't about to take a leak through a hole in the floor.

I changed into the provided salmon shorts and did my darnedest to keep warm. The grated floor was no place to practice footwork, but that wouldn't bother Alexi. Wherever they had him caged, he wasn't dancing around. Instead of fast I went slow, with isometric tension in my muscles, flowing from one movement to the next like molasses. The arena above was a lot rowdier than it had been last night. The anticipation steadily rose, generating an ambient heat that raised my internal pressure. I felt like a horse at the gate, trembling to run.

I regulated my breathing in an attempt to get my heart rate under control. If my adrenaline dumped now, I might as well throw in the towel.

The handler peeked in this time instead of whipping the door open. I ignored him and strode with purpose, my gaze forward toward the pit beyond. When the crew saw me coming, they furiously unscrewed the portal as if they were worried I was going to trample the door down. I stepped into the pit, minding the gap. Alexi wasn't there yet. The champion always entered last.

Well aware a slick patch on the mat could spell my doom, I wiped my feet dry on the wall. I measured the pit in strides, sliding wall to wall and center to wall, internalizing the space. I was going to need every inch. The announcer had to jump out of the way twice.

It was hotter tonight, a combination of additional bodies and lighting. Fedorov had upgraded the cameras for sure. I envisioned him in a philosophical debate about digital versus film with apathetic IT guys, but pushed the musing out of my head. Now was not the time to lose focus.

The announcer introduced me. He got my height, weight, and country of origin correct, before reminding everyone of my shocking victory in the semi-finals.

"Sensei to the Stars, Jove Brand himself, Ken Allen!"

I restrained myself from showboating while the announcer belted my name into an opera. My slim chance for survival relied on complete surprise. There was almost no fight footage of me. The video from the juice bar two years back didn't tell you much. That guy didn't expect to miss and never recovered after my first punch landed. Then there was the con footage, but going up against Street Justice was barely a step up from hitting a heavy bag. You could watch *Near Death*, but in the end all you were left with was the question asked of every action star: *Was Ken Allen legit or not?*

It was conceivable Alexi's people had gotten footage from my fight with Broken Hand. It would be good for me if they did, because my strategy last night had nothing to do with my plan tonight. In poker, you played the player, not your cards. Fighting worked the same way. It wasn't about your strengths. It was about your opponent's weaknesses. Your job was to cultivate the tools that exploited their flaws. If all you had was a hammer, every problem became a nail.

The wall across from me opened to admit Alexi. He was small for a heavyweight while also less toned than most of his peers.

There was an ongoing debate about why he didn't lose fifteen pounds and dominate another division. But Alexi already ruled the premier weight class, so why bother? Reason one was it would take a lot of cardio. More than a stationary bike and rowing machine could provide.

Alexi kept his eyes down as he ground his feet into the wall to dry them. His head was freshly shaved and his body had been wiped dry of sweat. Some guys slathered on a layer of oil so they were hard to get ahold of, but Alexi wanted the opposite. I would have swam in Johnsons and Johnsons before coming out if I was given the opportunity.

Like Fedorov, Alexi's brow eclipsed his eyes. His wide mouth stayed closed. The Bull of St. Petersburg, with those ears like horns, swollen and curling and hard. He didn't lap the ring or shadowbox. He didn't look at me, not yet. He wasn't interested in intimidation. He kept his eyes fixed on the ground. It all supported my theory: Alexi was keeping a secret. I was betting everything on it.

The announcer started in on Alexi. It took a while to introduce him. We were opposites, in terms of notable accomplishments. Alexi didn't acknowledge any of it, which wasn't out of modesty, if I was right. When the announcer disappeared through the door, Alexi finally took his eyes off the mat. He watched me like I was a teller at the bank about to mouth *next in line.*

Alexi didn't respond when the bell went off. His hands didn't come up until I moved off the wall. There was no change in his stance from his past fights: orthodox with a wide base. He kept his hands at the midpoint between his shoulders and hips, the perfect height to throw hooks and uppercuts.

I came forward standing tall, closing the distance with my hands high. It had to look bonkers, going right at Alexi, but it was vital to completely adhere to my strategy. If I doubted myself, if I deviated in any way, I might as well have walked up to Alexi, given him a hug, and let nature take its course.

I threw a jab from way too far out. Only a guy with an eye patch would have judged he was in range, but it read like fear, so it worked. In all his previous fights, Alexi had seized the opportunity. A more cautious fighter might not have jumped at the bait so early, but Alexi needed the contest over as soon as possible.

I didn't wait for Alexi's overhead right, the thunder punch of the gods, the chosen blow of power hitters around the world. I started moving on the assumption it was coming. If Alexi decided to go to the body instead, I was done.

I stepped through, changing levels as I went, like I was ducking under a half door. Alexi's forearm skimmed the top of my head. I knew the punch was coming—I had drawn it out purposely—and still he almost got me.

We ended up facing away from each other. I torqued hard, bringing my shoulder and hip around together. The first blow was as clean as I was going to get, so I put everything I had into it. It was only a matter of time before Alexi figured out I'd figured him out.

Ideally it would have been an elbow, but I had ended up farther away than I'd intended. If my legs possessed veto power, they'd have kept on running up the wall and into the stands. I used the heel of my hand instead, keeping my arm loose, letting my body motion provide all the power. I connected exactly where I was aiming, dead on Alexi's crusted right ear. It was a waste to hit someone on the ear. If you had the angle, you wanted the temple. On any other opponent it would have been squandering a giant opportunity. But no one had ever hurt Alexi Mirovich when he had his feet under him and I had no illusions I was any different.

I didn't wait around to observe the results of my attack. I was already circling toward Alexi's back in an attempt to force him to turn. He cut the angle instead, stepping through to keep an orthodox stance. I squared up and we were back where we started when this all began.

There wasn't enough space for a punch, but there was enough for a slap. I sent it in a tight arc, cupping my hand on impact, my hip and shoulder snapping, making the blow a concussion, not a push.

I whacked him square on the other ear. The spectators had to be baffled. Ken Allen had just slapped the baddest man on the planet upside the head. Twice.

He had balls, they would one day recall. *They probably ended up wherever the rest of him landed.*

I circled with a wide dip as the blur of a left hook sped through the spot my head previously occupied. I glanced down at Alexi's feet and caught him shuffling to stabilize. My heart soared. That miniscule movement proved my theory.

Alexi hesitated. The fast way to get to me meant changing stances. The long way around meant rotating his head 180. Neither option was good for a guy with his condition.

He probably got sick as a kid. Out in the Russian wilderness, where the mantra of medical care was *If he dies, he dies.* Most likely an infection from rolling. It was impossible to wrestle your entire life and not catch one bug or another.

Usually, it wasn't a big deal, but Alexi never got the chance to recover. He was put through the wringer every single day of his childhood. Alexi's father had slapped his ears enough to warp them before the kid's voice changed. And it only got worse as he got older.

I was leading left and Alexi right, our stances opposite. His expression hadn't changed but he had to be wondering if I knew or if it was all a big coincidence. I shifted outside Alexi's lead shoulder, throwing a left at an upward angle, halfway between a hook and an uppercut. It was neither.

It was a slap.

Maybe my hand was cupped just right or maybe it connected at the perfect angle. Whatever it was, my slap cracked off the side of Alexi's head like a starter pistol. The sound echoed through the silent arena. The whole place was holding its breath.

It was all there in the footage. The two times Alexi had been hurt, he was standing up and turning in the same motion, which was a no-no for a guy with his ailment. He covered it well. His whole game revolved around disguising it. The minimal movement. The hooks to anchor you in front of him. The utter lack of kicks. If Alexi went to the mat, he stayed there. Standing up while short on oxygen was a big trigger for his condition.

It was a good thing I had my hands up because Alexi's counter hook came for my chin. It thudded off my forearm, and there I was, in hugging range. Another heartbeat here and I was done. I launched myself into the air, turning my shoulder over as I struck, like I was trying to hurl a baseball into the clouds. My hand smacked Alexi upside the ear as I spun away.

Alexi trained remotely and privately, with a small team of guys who had to know. He did all his cardio on his ass. He didn't drive a car. Then there was his lack of reaction to the announcer, to the bell.

Among other afflictions, Alexi Mirovich was stone deaf.

I used my momentum to fuel an aerial, measuring the distance to avoid collision with a wall. The tumbling routine landed me a solid ten feet away. Alexi closed in, taking the opportunity to shift back to orthodox. He squinted, his jaw tight.

He knew I knew his secret:

The Bull of St. Petersburg had labyrinthitis.

16

FOR YOUR NORMAL, EVERYDAY PERSON LABYRINTHITIS isn't a big deal. Whenever your balance vanishes, you can take a seat and wait it out. Turn down the lights, reduce your stress or fatigue, and in time your vision will return to normal. You won't want to puke, and you'll be able to stand up.

But Alexi was currently trapped under blaring lights, trying to catch an annoying pest who kept smacking him in his ringing ears.

Namely, me.

If I had any chance in hell, it was through triggering Alexi's vertigo. To accomplish that, I had to get the fluid in his ear rolling around all inflamed. So here I was, playing tag for mortal stakes. Was it wrong of me, taking advantage of Alexi's affliction? I probably felt as guilty as Paris did, trembling in the bushes with an arrow for Achilles.

We were back where each of us had entered the pit. Neither of us had a mark on them, but now Alexi knew what I was up to. The two minutes our bout had lasted felt like ten. My strategy was a high-cardio one. If I ran out of gas before triggering an episode I was toast.

Alexi went back to basics, shuffling in to close the gap and waiting for me to lead. If I didn't throw anything meriting a counter, all the better. He'd tie me up and haul me down. If that happened, I wasn't getting back up.

I darted into range then bounded away as Alexi threw a lead hook, high and tight. He'd adjusted his punch, turning his elbow over and ducking his head into his shoulder to guard his ears. It left his body open but Alexi had bigger problems.

I lunged in, again faking from too far out. Alexi read I was going low and launched an uppercut on course to end me. It missed because I went extra low, hitting the mat to pick his ankle. It was a garbage takedown, easy to stuff, but you had to pull your leg out, and Alexi wasn't about to hop around on one foot.

Alexi did the only thing he could and sprawled out flat. I scrambled away like Daffy Duck before he could squash me into the mat. It was a huge waste of energy on my part. All these attacks were. None of them had any effectiveness. No fighter in his right mind would have done any of this.

But now Alexi had to get up.

He put both hands on the mat as he looked toward me. I was too far away to take advantage of him being down and I also wasn't foolish enough to try. You didn't charge a bull. He got both feet under himself and squatted up slowly, extending his fingers to keep four-point contact for as long as possible, a man trying to stand on thin ice.

Alexi didn't want to switch feet, but orthodox was where he felt most stable. I waited until he resumed his measured shuffle to dart in again and kicked out at his front calf with my lead leg. All speed, not going for damage, instead trying to upset his base. He had a choice: get kicked or lift his leg.

He chose to get kicked.

I circled, keeping my distance, faking in and out, occasionally kicking at his lead calf. It didn't always work but it never got me in trouble. The technique was too quick, too noncommittal. My piddly little kicks were too low to grab, too far away to counter with a punch.

My fourth kick was a good one. Alexi's front foot slid into line with his rear, putting him on a tightrope. He dropped his hands to balance and I slapped him upside the ear. I faked another low kick and he bought it, so I slapped him again.

Alexi didn't know what to do. There were no rounds, no coaches. His father had always been there to advise him. The son of a bitch who caused his condition in the first place was his sole confidant.

It was always the father. All mine ever gave me was the dual American-British citizenship that was required to play Jove Brand. Guys who spent their lives fighting didn't do it because they had mommy issues.

Alexi needed to get his hands on me and he needed it bad. It made him desperate. He stalked me down, winging wide punches, looking to either drop or hug me.

I dove into rolling leg scissors. The stupid, showy rolling leg scissors. It was the kind of move an eight-year-old tried. The rare times they worked, you ended up on your back and your opponent on his stomach. Nine times out of ten he would beat you to top position in the resulting scramble.

Except I didn't try to scramble. I popped up immediately and ran away, leaving Alexi on his knees and elbows. I'd employed another technique useless in the overwhelming majority of scenarios. What was the point of a high-risk takedown that did no damage and conferred no advantage?

Alexi got up again, slow and methodical. His mouth was pursed. To the crowd, it looked like he was patiently annoyed. The pressure the guy must have been feeling. If his condition went public his career was over. He'd managed to conceal it, fighting as rarely as possible for the biggest purses and getting it done quick. Sure, this tournament was underground, but the odds makers were watching. And the gangsters. And the blackmailers.

And he was here as voluntarily as I was. Best-case scenario: participating would get him an early release. Worse case was the choice between fighting or dying. Russian prisons were as dangerous as American ones, except you had fewer rights and no one asked questions when you disappeared forever.

I felt it then: fighter's sympathy. It happened when you'd studied your opponent, profiled him, lived in his head. Being a fighter, you already identified with the guy across from you. No one else understood the training, the stress, the dieting, the sacrifice. How you traded your health for a livelihood. There was no respect, no deeper mutual understanding than there was between two guys trying to take each other out.

Alexi set his stance. I waited until his eyes were on me to nod my head a fraction. To those watching above, I was tucking my chin. There were three ways out. The first: I picked him apart, humiliated him, exposed him. Eventually he wouldn't be able to stand without ever taking a solid hit. The second: he tapped out and raised a million questions. Foremost among them: did Alexi Mirovich throw fights?

The third: Alexi took a fall. A hard one.

Alexi blinked, once and slowly. With his head tilted down and his hands up, no one saw it but me. I came forward. He had to work with me for us to pull this off. We had to trust each other. If he was double-crossing, I wouldn't know about it until I woke up.

I shot for a takedown and Alexi dropped to stuff it. When he did, I came off the mat with a flying knee. It caught him square on the jaw. I felt his head snap back as our bodies collided.

Alexi went down face-first with me on top of him. I pushed off him as I stood, hands ready, but he didn't move. For a horrifying second I thought I broke his neck. As I bent close to check his breath, my body blocking his face, Alexi winked at me.

I did my best to look like a guy who couldn't believe his luck, stumbling back, eyes wide in surprise. It would go down as a fluke, the luckiest punch in the history of combat sports. Maybe a month from now it would be revealed Alexi had a 106-degree fever and a preexisting concussion.

The rumor would take years to spread, if it ever did. Only the elite would ever know what happened.

That Ken Allen beat the best guy in the world.

The crowd was dead silent, except the Japanese golf clappers, who tapped appreciation. I went back and pretended to check on Alexi to hide my over-the-top mugging. Medical got there in under ten seconds. I stumbled off toward my unscrewed door.

No one was waiting to greet me. I went for the showers. I was under the water when the shaking started, my body crashing from the immense chemical dump. I propped a forearm on the wall to keep steady, switching arms to soap up.

I toweled off with the oil-stained rag and got dressed. I was no prima donna, but deodorant would have been nice. Even more, I was missing my harness. The weight of it was like a security blanket. Jove Brand, armed to the teeth, didn't falter in the face of danger. Ken Allen sporting an empty holster quaked.

A handler was waiting in the hallway. In a sign of respect, he kept his distance while gesturing toward the helicopter pad. I stopped outside the nightclub, where I got a lot of tight smiles and a few attaboys. I had cost most of this joint a lot of money, but I'd be damned if I was getting on the helicopter until I knew Diana was safe.

Eventually Fedorov had to come to me. The other alternative was having his goons usher me off at gunpoint, which wouldn't look too good in front of the patrons. Still, it took him an hour to give up. An hour in which hundreds of people saw me alive and well. It didn't engender much confidence. When he came, Anatoly was with him. So was Nat, rolling an aluminum case behind her.

"Four hundred sixty-five thousand and three hundred American dollars," Fedorov said. "Plus five hundred thousand for tournament champion."

"No belt?" I asked. The case was lighter than I thought it would be. Eighty pounds, maybe.

Fedorov gave a single closed-mouth chuckle, more acknowledgment than amusement. "The Calabria girl is on her way home, with my men in a follow car to ensure she arrives safely."

I was usually good at spotting a performance but Fedorov was a brick wall. Why had he invited Nat along? To reassure me? If she was just another employee, she should have looked more concerned about being outed.

"Let us speak more at the dacha," Fedorov said with a gesture.

I took a shot in the dark. "Is your daughter coming with us?"

Fedorov's coal eyes glittered as he shook his head in what I interpreted as disbelief.

I took my spot on the helicopter next to the fire extinguisher, making room for Nat, but she stayed behind. This time Fedorov squeezed in next to Anatoly. We all put on our headsets as the rotors fired up.

Maybe my case was light because it was a bomb. I flipped the latches and paused a beat, figuring if it was, Fedorov would stop us from blowing up. There was a lot of money inside but no plastique.

"How do you like traveling like this?" Fedorov asked.

"Beats hanging off the skids." I clicked the case shut and held it in both hands, ready to block gunfire.

Fedorov rocked in amusement. "Ah yes. That was an impressive stunt in *Near Death*, going from motorcycle to helicopter. How many takes?"

"Three. One to get the jump right then a second to realize how much momentum I was bringing with me. You know, we came up with it on the spot."

"*Da?*"

"Yeah. Kit rented the helicopter for two days to get the aerial shots but wrapped up early. He decided to put the extra time to use, so we improvised some scenes. I almost killed my costar with that flying kick from the helicopter to the rooftop. In addition to narrowly avoiding decapitating myself on the rotors and falling thirteen stories."

"Fascinating," Fedorov said. "They should have you record an audio commentary."

"Maybe if I don't get locked up for two murders."

"Relocation is an option. Your skills are wasted here, coddling make-believe warriors. Come work for me. Not only in front of the camera, but also behind. You could name your price."

It wasn't a tempting offer, not even for a second. "Are your casino chips valid in Russian stores?"

Fedorov sighed, his eyes fading into shadow. I wasn't in love with disappointing him but I also didn't look as good in a mankini as I used to.

"I tried, Anatoly," Fedorov said, turning to his silent mountain of an audience. "I try to scare him but he is fearless. I try to tempt him but he does not fall. I try to beat him but he prevails. I try to buy him and he is not for sale. You are a fanatic, Ken Allen."

I braced myself. This whole fire-extinguisher trick was going to be as bad for me as it was for them. I don't even know if it would make a white cloud like in the movies. If I jumped out maybe I'd live through hitting the water. Even then, I'd have to swim to shore and sneak away.

Fedorov looked rueful. It was the first time he had looked anything.

"I do not wish this, Ken Allen, but these murders must stop." He gestured to Anatoly. The second it took me to process Fedorov's words almost cost me my life.

"Wait. What do you mean the murders must stop?" I shook a finger at Fedorov. "You're the killer!"

Fedorov's confusion was slight, but he recovered in less time than I did, reaching over to push down an enormous pistol I didn't even see Anatoly draw.

"I, you say? *Nyet.* It is you who has come to take my life."

We stared at each other as the helicopter hovered over the moonlit ocean, reviewing our interactions over the past two days.

Everything Fedorov had said, every topic he broached was him warning me. All that stuff about the making of *Near Death*, about Bowman Fletcher really being a spy, was him telling me he knew I was there to murder him.

Except I wasn't.

"Why would I want to kill you?"

"This I do not know. Perhaps for your ex-lover, Dina Calabria. Or perhaps you falsely believe I was the one who sabotaged Kit Calabria's plane, eighteen years ago. Or . . ."

Fedorov paused as if I already knew and he wanted me to confirm, but I had no idea what he was talking about.

"Or what?"

"Because you believe you are the secret heir, that your English father was Bowman Fletcher, and if the Calabria family loses the Brand franchise, it comes to you."

"Bowman Fletcher my fa—?" My bark of amusement hurt Fedorov's version of feelings, but it was the craziest thing I had ever heard. And I thought *I* watched too many movies. "I didn't kill Sir Collin Prestor or Layne Lackey. I'm trying to find out who did."

Fedorov wasn't used to being wrong. "But the method in which they were killed. And your clothes, your weapons, your vehicle. The imitation speaks of obsession."

"The killings are the cause, the rest are the effects," I said.

Fedorov took time to calculate while I tried to kick my brain into gear. Anatoly didn't have a problem holding his hand cannon level.

"I have watched *Near Death* enough to know acting is not among your skills," Fedorov decided. "I know I am not the killer, and if you are not either, then who is?"

"That's what I've been trying to figure out."

If Fedorov wanted the murders stopped, then they were against his interests. I remembered the two non-names from the messenger app on Dean's tablet.

"You're trying to make a deal with Dean Calabria for the Brand franchise, aren't you? If he marries Nat, you become family, and he can transfer the rights to you."

Fedorov mumbled in Russian and the helicopter broke its hover. He had never had a problem with eye contact before, but now he was evading my gaze.

I ducked and weaved for his attention as I went on. "The killer must somehow know details of the Brand contract. He thought if he killed Sir Collin before Sir Collin died as Brand on screen, the rights would default."

I wasn't about to tell Fedorov that the killer was working off a false premise, as Dina had already filmed Sir Collin's exit in secret.

Fedorov spoke into his phone in Russian but didn't say a thing in English until we were out of the helicopter. "I will escort you to your motorcycle."

I walked as slowly as I could without it technically being standing. When the carports were in view, Fedorov spoke again. "Uncover the murderer and you will be well compensated, Ken Allen. These killings are troublesome. Niles Endsworth has gone into hiding, convinced he is the next victim. We cannot locate him."

"Because Dean told him about your deal. Niles would have to sign a new contract too. Who else knows? Whoever knows is a target."

"Then there are no other targets."

Handlers were waiting at the White Stag with my Quarreler and everything else I could have used to kill Fedorov. I took my time gearing up and strapping the case full of cash onto the Stag.

"If it's not you, then who stands to profit?" I asked.

"I already told you."

"Bowman Fletcher's secret heir? Come on, you can't really believe that."

"You said it yourself, Ken Allen. Life imitates art. The killer does not have to *be* the heir. The killer only has to believe they are."

17

WHEN CELLULAR RECEPTION CAME BACK, HALF A dozen voice mails were waiting for me. The first was from Missy, checking in to make sure I was alive. The next four were from Ray. The initial message was short: he had the flash drive, call him. In the second, he hoped I was okay. In the third, he said he would send air support but didn't know where to send it. In the last, he apologized for enabling me. I'd never heard him so worked up. The remaining voice mails would have to wait.

Like every other time I had called him, Ray picked up on the first ring.

"You can stop working on the trick coffin," I said.

"Where the hell have you been?"

"What's on the second flash drive?"

"Oh no pal, you first," Ray replied.

It was a long story. By the time I wrapped up, I was back in Missy's beach house. Ray's periodic exclamations let me know he was still on the line.

"No one is going to believe this," he said when I finished.

"I'm not worried about that. Anyway, it's not like I really beat Alexi. I just pressured him into throwing in the towel."

"Why doesn't he get treatment?" Ray asked.

"That would take steroids, and they would pop on drug tests, which would tarnish his legacy. Unless he got an exemption. But exemptions need to be disclosed on his medicals, which would expose his issue and bar him from the ring."

"Fedorov must have thought you were one cool customer," Ray said.

"Russians don't know cool, only cold."

"Were all those hoops worth it?"

A polite knock on the door informed me my food had arrived. I checked the peephole anyway and rolled the cart in with the Quarreler in my other hand.

"Yes. Maybe. I don't know. This whole thing is like you put three balls of yarn in a bag and shook it up. Here's what we got: Dean maybe made a deal with Fedorov to sell the franchise when he inherits, which is in a few days. Fedorov thought I was there to kill him for Dina and stop the deal. Sir Collin's killer is also trying to stop the deal, for reasons unknown. Fedorov has this crazy theory the killer thinks they are Bowman Fletcher's love child, which means if the Brand contract defaults, they inherit a franchise worth a couple of billion dollars."

"Life ain't a movie, Ken, as much as we all wish it was."

"Now that I think about it, Bryce Crisp also brought it up. When I said no one had ever been able to prove they were Fletcher's kid, he corrected me and said no one had *yet*. I have to wonder why he felt the need to add the 'yet.'"

Unable to wait any longer, I plowed into a steaming pile of chicken and mushrooms.

On the other side of the phone, Ray drummed his fingers on a table. Halfway through, I reminded myself to eat slowly and restarted the conversation.

"Alongside that, Missy and Kit might have secretly married in Hong Kong, and Kit maybe left a lost will transferring the franchise to Missy. I don't think the will is a written document. My guess is it's a video. Film was Kit's chosen medium. He used to make all these little movies with Missy."

"Well, you know what they say, Ken, a picture's worth a thousand words."

Ray's comment shook something loose. I about choked on my chicken.

"It was Layne Lackey who broke into Missy's Ashland house last year. He must have been looking for the will."

"What makes you think it was him?"

"He knew the address—he sent her a letter there. And he had a picture in his place only Missy could have had. He must have taken a picture of the picture when he was in there. That's why it had a weird reflection on it. He took the photo through the glass."

Ray took over while I polished off the poultry. "Well, if he was looking for a will, I don't think he found it."

"Spill it. What's on the drive?"

"Give me a minute," Ray said. He took five. "Okay, so, right now we can view the root menus and unsecured files. Turns out

JOVE BRAND IS NEAR DEATH

Layne wrote Jove Brand fan fiction under the name Brice Crispies. It's way gay."

"You're dating yourself, Ray."

"No, I mean Jove Brand likes guys in it. A lot. Layne doesn't leave much to the imagination. It gets monotonous."

"You read it?"

"I was searching for clues," Ray replied. "It was better than his screenplay at least."

"What about the dossiers?"

"Right now I can see the list but no luck viewing the locked files. Without the password, the only way is to brute force it, which could take years if Layne was as long-winded with passwords as he was describing oral."

"Wonderful," I said.

"Any clue on what he might pick as a password?"

I imagined myself back in Layne's apartment, sitting at the desk. Did Layne have a favorite Brand actor? A favorite film? There had been two of the same poster. What movie had it been for?

"What was the name of Layne Lackey's screenplay?" I asked.

"Hold on, let me check," Ray replied. "*Ungentlemanly Warfare.*"

Which, according to Fedorov, was the ministry Bowman Fletcher belonged to. "Try that."

"You sure? We only got three attempts."

"Not guessing because you have no idea is the same as getting it wrong."

"Hold on, I'll tell my guy."

"This guy, you better trust him," I said.

"Don't you worry about that," Ray replied. "*Ungentlemanly Warfare* is no good. Two tries left."

I was sure I was right. Also, I had no other ideas. "The unsecured files—does Layne use proper capitalization or underscores in their names?"

Another pause from Ray. "Every time."

"Capitalize each word and put in an underscore."

Ray grumbled but didn't argue. "Hey, it worked! Everything is accessible now. Files are on the way to your watch."

"Is this watch secure?"

"Ain't nobody cracking that timepiece."

"All right," I said. The breakthrough should have energized me, but it had the opposite effect. It had been a long day. Cracking the flash drive felt like plowing through the tape at the finish line.

Ray told me a bedtime story as I faded out. "That was a good guess about the coffin. I had it rigged to go up in flames. I was gonna shoot the arrow myself."

MY INTERNAL ALARM had been reset for early evening. I was sore everywhere, but my left side really smarted from sleeping on the Quarreler. I sent my clothes out to the laundry and ordered a metric ton of sashimi from the private chef. The final voice mail was a terse request for a call back from Special Investigator Stern.

"You work weekends?" I asked when she picked up. "You need 'you' time."

"I like my job," Stern replied. "It's time to come in, Allen."

"Oh come on. You aren't buying that I'm dense enough to keep Layne Lackey's phone."

Stern's lighter sounded like a flamethrower. She took a drag before she replied. "Who said anything about a phone?"

"What else could the killer have to frame me with? But they don't know the two of us already talked about Layne's phone. After that exchange, why the heck would I keep it?"

"Because I admitted we couldn't track it."

I managed some simple addition in between flapping my jaw. "It was on, wasn't it? You were staking my place out, waiting for me to show up."

"Where are you, Allen? Let's do brunch."

Something in Stern's voice made me thirsty. I drank a glass of water and thought a little. If she could track me through Ray's security, we'd be talking in person.

"You got a warrant for my arrest, didn't you? Sweet-talked some judge."

I was trying to make her mad. It worked.

"I'll see you soon, Allen," Stern said and hung up.

The combination of the water and my imminent incarceration woke me up. The clock was ticking. I used Missy's immersion blender to butter up some coffee and started in on Layne Lackey's files. The watch screen was too small, so I read the files on my phone. I needed a tablet. Bogart would have had a tablet. I started with the file labeled *Omg_Pulitzer_Prize* due to its promising title.

The meat was in that first file. Everything else—all the interviews, the research, the documents—supported its thesis. My respect for Layne Lackey's journalistic skill climbed to record heights, then plummeted to new lows when I discovered why he hadn't gone public with the tale. It took me past midnight to get through it all. Layne knew everything I had figured out on my own and almost everything I never told him.

He'd also figured out who killed Kit Calabria, and he had the flight manifests to prove it. I stared at the screen for a long time.

All the guilt I had extinguished flared back to life, hotter than ever.

I forced myself to stretch and run a full diagnostic on my body. That I had avoided major injury was nothing short of a miracle. I couldn't keep rolling sevens forever. Or maybe I could. The dice had no memory. When I trusted myself to talk, I called Ray.

"Do you know who the killer is?" he asked.

"No, but I know who he isn't. The Black Knight has two targets left and both of them are going to be at Dean's party. Problem is, the cops would arrest me at the gate, if Dina even let me that close."

Ray practically sung his reply. "Sounds like you need a disguise."

"I have one in mind, if you have the time," I said.

"Ken, in three days I could forge you a suit of armor with a matching broadsword."

"I was thinking of something a little more formal."

I SLEPT THE sun away, which didn't bother me any. Dean's party was an evening affair and I wanted to be fresh at that hour. No wonder so many noir movies took place when they did. Detecting was definitely a night job. It took three tries to work up the courage to call Missy.

"Are you going to Dean's party?" I asked after we exchanged greetings.

"How did you know I was invited?" She was slicing instead of chopping this time. Fruit instead of vegetables.

"Call it an educated guess. Are you going?"

"I am. I want to meet Dean. I'm giving him your watch from *Near Death*," Missy said. "It's time to let it go. I've been wearing it for eighteen years and it's only gotten heavier."

"You should know going to the party might be dangerous."

"What did you find out?" Missy asked. All sounds of preparation stopped.

I knew I had to ask her about Kit, but I couldn't do it. I knew I had to tell her about Kit, but I couldn't do that either. "Nothing I can prove, and nothing I'm willing to tell you just yet, because I'm praying I'm wrong. Do you trust me?"

Missy didn't hesitate. "Yes."

"Are answers worth the risk?"

"How much risk?"

"Life-ending," I admitted.

Missy took a long breath. "Yes."

"Then come to Dean's party."

"Okay," Missy said.

"Did you get a plus one?"

"Yes. Do you need it?"

"I have to crash. If I try coming in the conventional way, I'm going to get dragged out in cuffs. I want you to bring Yuen, if he'll come."

"I'd like that. I haven't seen him since he tortured us in *Near Death*."

"That was a long day. Eight hours strapped to a table, listening to him monologue."

A fond chuckle escaped Missy. "I've had worse ones."

"Here's to hoping Dean's birthday doesn't top the list. If I'm right about all this, I'm going to need all the help I can get come Friday."

THE NEXT TWO days crawled by. I kept my workouts light, drew a blank on how to sneak my gear in with me, and tried to decide what to do with a million bucks. At least I could afford Mercie

Goodday now. Seeing as I was finally about to balance the scales between us, I didn't want to owe Missy anything.

None of this had been about me. The killer's frame job was a means to an end. I was a convenient sap, ready-made to take the fall. Except I wasn't about to take the fall for anyone. No more than I was about to let a sucker puncher walk away with the prize purse.

When I got up Friday evening, I pondered eating carbs, in case it was my last meal. I decided that was a defeatist attitude and made an avocado salad instead. I left a little early to enjoy the cruise to Calabria Cove. The White Stag handled like we were made for each other. A perfect fit, like the blazer on my back or the Quarreler in my hand.

Whatever happened, I would always have these days. I had been cold and I had been starved and I had faced imprisonment and death. Still, sleeping wrapped in a sheet on the floor in front of a dying fire beat any hotel I'd ever stayed in. The walnuts pilfered from those centerpieces ranked among the finest meals I'd eaten.

What perfect days. My whole life, I had been the supporting player in someone else's story. For the first time, I was the lead.

Ray updated my GPS destination when I was an hour out from Calabria Cove. His van was parked in a public beach turnoff. I was expecting a deluxe shaggin' wagon with a wizard airbrushed on the side, but got a panel truck like contractors used, plain in every way. The back was already open with a ramp leading to a bike-sized space. Once I was in, the door lowered behind me. I was securing the Stag when Ray peeked out of the entry that led deeper into the truck.

"Did you have to park next to the only other car in the lot?" I asked.

Ray kept his voice low. "I got something to show you I ain't never showed no one."

"I'll die before I talk."

Ray tried to decide if I was telling the truth. I knew he wasn't out to hurt my feelings, but still.

"I have spent the last five years working in the homes of some pretty big names," I said. "Have I ever told you a single story about any of them?"

I could hear Ray's teeth grinding. He beckoned me in with his chin.

The next section of the truck took up the rest of the back. On one side, there was a workbench with sliding racks to hold every tool I could think of and plenty I didn't know existed. Chances were they hadn't until Ray had fabricated them. The underside of the bench was all drawers, to hold the components making magic consumed. A stack of cases sat in a rack next to the cab entrance. A bank of flat screens was mounted on the wall opposite the workbench. A thin row of computers stood underneath the screens. Or were they a server? I didn't know. There was a reason why I had to mail those flash drives. Instead of a workspace, there was a rolling chair with a built-in lap desk. A keyboard was hinged on one arm and a mutant joystick was hinged on the other.

There was a young woman in the chair.

"Ken, this is my daughter, Elaine," Ray said. "Elaine, this is Ken Allen. Elaine is my daughter, Ken."

The first time Ray said it, it was an introduction. The second time was a warning.

Elaine turned her chair toward me. It was more than a battle station. "Pardon me if I don't curtsy."

It was hard to tell her age. I put her in her late twenties. In defiance of casting conventions she kept her hair natural, forming a bouquet of black curls. She had Ray's eyes, cinnamon and sparkling with mischief. She looked like she smiled a lot. Ray put a hand over my face before I lowered my gaze.

"Pay no attention to the woman behind the curtain," he said.

"Aha!" I said. "This is your hacker guy. Your Bluetooth guy too, I bet. I knew you were too old for that stuff."

"I also program his On Demand so he doesn't miss his shows," Elaine said.

"Aha!" I said again. "Are you going to keep your hand there or did you fashion me blinders?"

When Ray moved his hand we were touching noses. "I've managed to keep Elaine away from actors and other unsavory types. She's the best thing I ever made."

"Aw gee, thanks Dad," Elaine said.

The cases were a safe place to look. "Showing me the goods will calm you down."

Elaine wasn't helping any. "Ooh, so forward."

"Quiet, you," Ray said.

Ray put a hand on my shoulder and rotated me towards the cases. The top case was long enough to store a sniper rifle. When he put it down on the workbench, Elaine sounded a digital drum roll. I cracked the case to gape at the tuxedo I'd requested.

Ray ran me through its features. "The tailcoat is the same as your blazer, but this time I used a more flexible weave with the sleeves, so you can punch with full range of motion. The high cut on the jacket should also help. I scalloped the tails, so they won't tangle you up."

I set the jacket aside and took out the rest. The pants were black, like the jacket. Everything else was white, including the tie.

"The vest locks in the back. You won't know it's there, but the buttons are magnetic in case you need to get it off quick. The shirt looks like silk but it's a neoprene-nylon blend. Light, flexible, and wrinkle free."

"Dry clean only?" I asked.

Ray stroked the fabric. "Like it's going to survive long enough to make it to the cleaners. The low cut in the vest bothers me. There's minimal protective layer where you need it most, the center of your chest."

"My pure heart will protect me."

Ray harrumphed. "The pants are the same stuff as the shirt, with a little extra flex in the crotch."

"Because of all the room he needs down there?" Elaine asked.

"So he can throw kicks, little lady," Ray scolded. "Them being high waisted helps too. No need for suspenders, with how I did the band."

"Guess I can throw out my Chuck Norris Action Jeans," I said.

"The gloves are made from the same stuff as the jacket. They will harden up a bit on impact. I layered them as thick as I could without making you look like Mickey Mouse. The bow tie is breakaway so no one can choke you with it."

"It's not a boomerang or anything?"

Ray stopped to rub his nonexistent scruff. "You know . . . hold on." He made a note right on the table with a fat, flat pencil. "Now for the shoes."

The patent leather gleamed, but the delicate laces and low walls looked like trouble. "I'm not going to be able to run in those, much less fight," I said.

"Oh ye of little faith," Ray replied. "They look like oxfords but when you pair them with these socks here, they lock on. Your foot will fall off before these do."

"So how do I get out of them?"

"Uh." Ray bit his finger.

"You cut the laces and wiggle out of the socks." Elaine groaned.

I cocked a thumb toward Elaine. "She's your test subject?"

"I got weak arches," Ray replied. "Anyway, what were you going to do, wear those high-tops?"

"Point taken." I took a look around. The lavatory adjacent the bike space was as roomy as one you'd find on a bus. "There a secret door to the dressing room?"

"Turn your chair around, Elaine," Ray said.

Elaine's sigh was classic *oh come on, Dad*.

I turned my back and stripped down to my shorts, but when Ray handed me a pair of uber-underoos, I peeled those off too. I dressed slowly, feeling out every piece before adding the next layer. When the ensemble was complete, I shadowboxed, chaining my hands in a complex flowing pattern of attack and defense. It felt like I was wearing a seat belt all over.

"Nice moves," Elaine said.

Ray and I turned to see Elaine studying a screen with me on it.

Elaine grinned. "It's my duty to surveil."

I watched myself on the screen, feeling heat flood my cheeks. Ray had measured me perfectly. The tux fit like a glove. The short scene at the end of *Near Death* was all the time I'd spent in the formals Jove Brand was famous for, and even then you only saw me from the back. There's no scene where I'm sophisticated and worldly. Which was good, because I was neither of those things back then. Or now.

"I look—"

"Like Jove Brand," Elaine said. "Now hold still so we can make you look less like him."

Elaine busted open a makeup case complete with lights.

"I have sensitive skin," I protested.

"This is the good stuff."

It didn't feel like she did much but when Elaine rolled back, my cheeks were contoured, my chin had a cleft, and my eyes were hooded.

"Let's hope this gets me in the door," I said.

"I'll see you in there," Ray replied. "Unlike you, I got invited."

"I don't want you mixed up in this, Ray."

"Don't worry, I'm not looking to play Little John, but you can't fit a Quarreler anywhere in that rig and I got a plan." Ray dug into his pocket and came out with keys. "The car next to us is ours. You can't cruise up to the gate on the White Stag."

RAY'S SEDAN APPEARED off the lot, but a nudge on the gas made the front wheels leave the ground. I took it easy up to Calabria Cove, idling into a queue of vans and sensible compacts. I was early, but I had to be. I wasn't posing as a guest but as one of the many Jove Brands who would be in attendance.

When my turn came, I was confronted by a gate guard who could have been pulled from central casting. If Dina was able to get scale, he probably was.

"Another one, huh?" he asked, peering into the backseat. "Pop the trunk."

It took me a suspicious amount of time to find the trunk release. I was slapping myself for not checking the car closer. Hopefully Ray wasn't housing a mini-gun or missile rack in the boot.

The guard closed the trunk and came back to my window. "You look pretty good."

"Much appreciated, old chap," I said in my best English accent.

"Maybe don't talk if you can help it," he suggested, waving me in.

I followed the other cars into the hangar, where the help's jalopies would be safely segregated from the guests' limos. A bunch of guys basically identical to me were milling around, staring at their phones or reading bent-back scripts. A few were noting in the margins. I made my own note to avoid them. Admiring the fleet put my back to everyone.

Most of the vehicles were decommissioned from Brand films and built by Ray. I spotted the jetpack from *Hunter's Moon* and the ultralight from *Flights of Fancy*. I wondered how long it would be before Ray pushed collapsible wings on me. My guess was I would do about as well as the Coyote did chasing the Road Runner.

Two helicopter mechanics were busy at work, servicing the Blackhawk from *Night Errant*. Diana hadn't wasted any time after escaping from Fedorov's dacha. I would have paid good money to see her mother's face when the flight instructor came calling.

A woman I was glad to not recognize walked out of the service tunnel and gestured for everyone to gather. In four-inch heels and a headset, she looked like Dina was doing someone's husband a big favor.

"Okay, my generic Brand servers." She held for laughter that never came. "We are going to ingress and review how you are to expedite and circulate."

The coordinator tapped away in her heels, beckoning us to follow. I wove into the middle of the pack, hiding in plain sight as one of the gaggle of Jove Brands Dina had hired to serve the party guests.

We passed through the poured-concrete tunnel into a large warehouse space where a temporary kitchen was set up. It was stifling, even with the air exchangers roaring. A long line of tables acted as the expediting area. A map of the Cove with a route traced out to indicate where each service went stood on an easel behind its respective table

I set course for the bar. Serving drinks would get me everywhere. Other Brands had the same idea, but I was probably the only one who didn't plan on sneaking a nip. It was more than alcohol being pure sugar. The Chinese kept Johnnie Walker in business. I hit my lifetime limit inside a year, trying to fit in. There was no competition for the coffee and tea services. Hot drinks were considered complimentary and sober people tipped worse. Also, it was a pain-in-the-butt job, with the pouring and fussing with cream and sweetener.

The coordinator instructed us to initiate conversation with the guests, to not pitch, and to not hand out cards. We were permitted Jove Brand impressions. If asked who we were, we were to say Jove Brand. I wondered how she was going to know which clone to toss if a complaint was registered.

The coordinator clopped off to attend some developing problem. On discovering they didn't have reception inside the Cove, my compatriots were forced to chat, except the ones with the scripts. I should have brought one of my own, for use as repellent. Standing alone drew more eyes, so I drifted toward a clump of Brands, two of which were alpha-dogging for attention.

"She didn't say no stunts," one of them said before throwing a trick front-flip. He landed it but lost a shoe, which buzzed over a tray of Gentleman's Relish sandwiches.

"Good thing I can score without a line," the other said, leaning into a flex that threatened his seams.

I was tempted to mention if either of them could do a handstand push-up they had a chance with Dina, but kept my lips zipped.

It wasn't the longest hour of my life but it made the top five. I was sure any moment now someone was going to point and declare me the genuine article. The coordinator tap-danced back in, waving her arms like we had missed some signal. Her manner spoke of a woman freshly eviscerated by the producer of six successful franchise films. She rolled it downhill in an act of trickle-down classonomics.

The other Brands handled their trays with the expertise every aspirant in This Town involuntarily developed. I watched the other hot-drink guy for tips. He swept his silver tray up with a little dip, switching from both hands to one smoothly. I imitated him and to my relief, nothing went flying. Three decades of martial arts training was really paying off. Who needed college?

It was a minute-long walk to the ballroom. Guests were coming out of the elevator and down the secret stair Diana chastised Dean for using. A count of the tables put the party at an intimate gathering of around three hundred.

I got maybe twenty feet before my tray was cleared out. Walking around with an empty tray was sure to get me noticed. I was the only server to run back to the kitchen.

The second time I got twice as far by weaving through the crowd too fast for the guests to easily loot. The third round I ran straight into Diana Calabria. My makeover wouldn't stand up to close scrutiny. I tried to zip past while she was looking the other way, but she snagged me by the arm. I managed to keep my tray from turning into a discus.

"I'm working here," I mumbled through closed lips.

Diana was dressed like she wanted people to take her seriously. She even had her belly button covered. "You're crashing? Didn't Mom send you an invite?"

"I'd rather be a surprise," I said. Best not to mention I was wanted by the law. "Whenever the killer knows I'm in attendance, they take the opportunity to off someone."

"Oh my God, who?" Diana asked.

"I have no idea. Turns out detecting is stumbling from hunch to hunch. Have you seen Missy Cazale or Ray Ford?"

"I don't know the second name."

Such was the fate of a life behind the screen. "Go find Missy and invite her for a cup of tea."

"Okay."

"There are two tea guys," I said.

Diana rolled her eyes. "I'll look for the older one."

I sprinted back to restock in a demonstration of dedication to my craft. How tray guys didn't have one arm way bigger than the other I'd never know, because I definitely had a dominant side. When I got back, Diana was waiting at the entrance to the hallway with Missy and Yuen.

"My, what a lovely tea party," Yuen rasped.

Once upon a time, I almost killed the guy. Now, I was dragging him into two murders. They don't make greeting cards for that level of sorry.

"Thanks for coming," I told him.

Yuen never had my problem with eye contact. "Are you kidding? Being here tonight is the cherry on top of my book deal."

Missy surveyed her tea options. "Anything herbal?"

"All Earl Grey, I'm afraid."

"When in Rome," Missy said, taking a cup. The little wood box she was already holding kept her from being able to get the cup off the saucer, but she didn't want to set it down. After a moment of weighing her options, she put the saucer back and took the cup by itself.

"That Kit's watch?" I asked.

"And your watch too," Missy explained. "I couldn't just leave it with the other gifts."

The watch I wore in *Near Death*. The watch that played videos. "When did Kit give it to you again?"

"Right before he left to deliver the reels," Missy said. "I hope Dean doesn't mind that it's broken."

That's when everything fell into place. The itch in my gray matter vanished with a click. I dropped my tray on the nearest table. "Do not let that watch go. If anyone tries to take it, scream bloody murder."

My intensity threw Missy for a loop.

"Okay, Ken," she said more to calm me down than anything else.

"I have to find Ray Ford," I said. "Diana, if you see Dean, I need to talk to him. Without your mom and before all the pomp and circumstance."

"I'll try to get him away from Mom," Diana said. She didn't sound too confident.

"You have to. If you don't, this party will live in infamy." I looked to Yuen. "I need to speak with Runshaw Shensei."

Yuen didn't look surprised. I wondered if he was really here on my behalf or if he was beholden to the Shensei brothers. He slipped through the crowd with enviable grace. He wasn't new to galas, having worked as a ringer to spark up the dance floor in the past.

"What's going on?" Missy asked.

"Yeah, what's going on?" Diana echoed.

"You wouldn't believe me if I told you." I stalked off to find Ray.

Fortunately, Ray was also looking for me.

His gift box would have fit a bowling ball. From how Ray was holding it, it might have.

"You move like a fancy panther," Ray said when we were close enough to whisper.

"My watch from *Near Death*, if the battery died, would any videos on it be lost?"

Ray looked offended. "No."

"Come on." I dragged him back to Missy.

Missy had met Ray for maybe eight hours eighteen years ago, but she embraced him like he was a long-lost friend. She did the same with anyone who had once known Kit. I took my watch off while they hugged, then swiped Missy's box out of her grip.

I took Ray's gift box from him and shoved Missy's box containing the video watch into his hands. "Make that old watch run." I set my new watch on top of the box. "For parts."

"How'd you know the gift I brought was for you?" he asked.

"It is?"

Ray winked. "It's got everything a growing hero needs."

I noticed Diana trying to get my attention from across the room.

"Don't let anyone touch that watch," I said to Ray. My heart was pounding like I'd gone twelve rounds. Diana and I nearly collided on account of our combined velocity.

"Dean's in his gym, come on," she said.

She led me back through the whorling halls to Dean's man cave. All of the doors were open but his. Thankfully, Diana knew the code. Not fancying the idea of having to hunt up another doorman, I watched her put it in.

"I should do this alone," I said.

Diana nodded as the door squealed open. I did my best to hide my guilt. If I was right about my old watch from *Near Death*, I was going to ruin her life tonight, along with the lives of everyone she loved. Dean was out on a terrace watching the sunset. He didn't look at me when I joined him. He was wearing a captain's jacket but had skipped the hat, so he only looked half ridiculous.

"You come to yell at me?" he asked.

"Is that what you want?"

"Maybe."

"He got to you the same time he put Nat on Diana, didn't he?" I asked. "Fedorov. After your mom rejected his overtures."

"Yeah," Dean said. "Nat's our go-between."

"What's he offering?"

"Four billion," Dean said.

"No percentages?"

"I don't want any part of Jove Brand," Dean replied. He checked his phone. Unlike the staff, Dean had the Wi-Fi password. The glowing screen highlighted his sullen expression.

"This worth marrying Fedorov's daughter?"

Dean recoiled in shock. "How'd you know?"

"Nat told Diana you were going to propose. Diana told me."

Dean kicked at the stone railing. "Go on, tell me I'm a moron."

"I'm here to listen, Dean." I felt a powerful urge to comfort him. I extended a hand toward his shoulder, then withdrew. We weren't that close.

"The franchise is at its peak," Dean said. "Maybe Niles keeps it going, maybe it tanks. Who can say? Every movie is a giant gamble and the stakes only go up. We sell now, throw the money in safe investments, and the world will end before a Calabria ever has to work again."

Dean's lips were moving, but Fedorov's words were coming out. "There's more to life than money."

"The *legacy*." Dean snorted. "Fedorov told me all about the legacy. About *Near Death* and everything that happened during filming."

I stared at him staring at the sea, trying to find the words. "Listen—"

"I saw your fights," Dean interrupted. "On Fedorov's stream."

"Hope you didn't lose too much."

Dean looked at me for the first time. "Lose? I cleaned up. I knew you'd win."

His belief in me caught me off guard.

"It was stupid to sick Chevalier on you," Dean said.

"Yeah." My smooth reply covered my surprise.

It dawned on me then: Chevalier was the fifth contact on Dean's tablet.

"Mom used them during the last production, in France," Dean said. "After all that stuff online about you being arrested, Mom came and told me you wouldn't kill anyone. That you were investigating the murders yourself, not hiding behind lawyers. That you were even coming here to talk to her. I knew right then you'd find out about the deal."

Dean had been on me since minute one, since Missy arranged my meet with Dina.

"I'm not the hero you think I am, kid."

"They've killed people before, you know. Chevalier," Dean countered. "You walked all over them."

I made an educated guess. "They would have killed me, if you hadn't told them not to."

Dean braced against the sea wind. "I don't kill people. I'm not my mom."

I did my best to neither confirm nor deny.

Dean pinched the bridge of his nose to halt the waterworks. "Fedorov told me everything about the blowup between Mom and Uncle Kit. About you and Mom sneaking around."

I didn't know what to say. What could I say? My eyes started to well up. I clenched my jaw to keep it from trembling.

Dean shook his head at the waves. "I'm getting us out of all this. It's a prison with gold bars. I'm not locking my kids in a tower their whole life."

The prepared statement was understandable. Who knows how many times Dean had practiced it in front of the mirror, bracing for the tempest. But Dean was getting louder. The levels above and below us also had terraces. I guided him away from the edge and into the room, before someone eavesdropped on the story of the century.

I pulled Dean's hankie out of his breast pocket and handed it to him. "Don't worry, kid. You're not going to have to do anything."

"What do you mean?" Dean asked.

"Don't make any big announcements tonight. Don't do any deals. If I'm right, you're about to let your hair down for good. Did you tell anyone else?"

"Just Niles," Dean said. "I thought he deserved to know. It's his future too."

Dean walked me to the door, but I didn't want him tagging along for what was coming next.

"Clean up a little and go mingle. There's safety in numbers. If you see Niles, tell him he's in danger. Sir Collin and Layne Lackey also knew about the deal, and now they're dead. And be careful. Let Stavros out. There's still a killer on the loose."

"Who is it?" Dean asked.

"Kid, I honestly have no idea."

18

THE BALLROOM WAS ABUZZ WHEN I GOT BACK, THE
volume rising with the intoxication level. Most of the guests were
used to being the center of attention, so they tried to talk over
everyone else. I was searching for a friendly face when I spotted
Special Investigator Stern.

She had gone over the top with her undercover, in a long gold
gown that imprisoned her chest but left her arms free. It was slit
up both sides, which not only fit the theme but also allowed a full
range of motion. Her updo gleamed like spun copper. She held her
clutch left-handed in the event she had to draw her gun. It must
have been driving her nuts, trying to spot me among a sea of Jove
Brands.

The Jove Brand theme from *For Love or Money* started up in the background, saxophones belting. Stern was between me and Yuen, scanning the room methodically. Yuen thumbed over his shoulder, toward Runshaw Shensei. I pointed at Stern.

Yuen grinned. He always did like being the center of attention.

By the time Stern registered the ambush, Yuen had swept her off her feet. He led, waltzing her away from me. Man, could he dance. It was a tragedy there were no roles for him that didn't involve flying kicks in This Town. The guy oozed charisma.

Their performance was causing a scene, but storming off would trigger a bigger one, so Stern bit her tongue and stared bloody murder. When she tried to get a look around, Yuen went cheek to cheek. When she tried to beg off, Yuen spun her back into his arms. This was all for my benefit and it was still an effort to tear myself away.

Runshaw Shensei was with his wife, who had to have been a vampire, considering they'd been married forty years and she'd looked thirty the entire time. I approached him head-on, moving with deferential posture.

"If you'll indulge me, I am permitted one last question."

Runshaw grunted admission.

The Shensei brothers had provided Kit with everything he'd needed to produce *Near Death*. Equipment, locations, cast, crew. If, while stranded in Hong Kong, Kit needed a different sort of event facilitated, where would he have turned?

"Did you make wedding arrangements for Kit Calabria?"

"Yes."

The last piece of the puzzle fell into place. My insides wanted out. It never hurt so much to be right.

"Thank you," I said with a slight bow. "I hope you enjoy tonight's show."

Missy found me before I found her. She was managing to hold it together. Life had given her plenty of practice.

"Did Ray get the watch working?" I asked.

"He says so. What's going on, Ken?"

"Let's find Dina."

Missy steeled herself. "I haven't seen her."

"When in doubt, go right to the top."

If I was going to do this, I was going to do it as Ken Allen. I took a glass of water from a coworker's tray and a napkin from a table. What water I didn't use to clean off my disguise, I drank. We took the spiral stair to avoid the elevator operator. The Cove was packed in anticipation of a big announcement. They were going to get one. Missy and I emerged through the bull's-eye into the lighthouse family room and made our way up the stone stairs that hugged the outer wall. The next Jove Brand was on his way down.

Niles Endsworth stiffened when he saw us. He had three inches, twenty pounds and fifteen years on me but here he was worried I was about to crush his throat.

"Did you talk to Dean?" I asked him.

Niles stared at me, expressionless. Here's the thing about actors: People think they are funny and interesting. You would be too, if you had a team of writers behind you. But catch one off script sometime. See how clever they were then.

"Stay where people can see you," I told him. "This will all be over soon."

Niles was a brick wall. One blocking the way.

"Pardon me, sir," I said, gesturing for Missy to go ahead of me. Niles stepped off the side of the stairs, treating the twelve-foot drop like he was skipping down a curb.

"That's Gamesman," Niles said to my back.

"His Brand sounds really good," Missy said when we were halfway up the stairs.

I wasn't impressed. "He's doing a Bryce Crisp delivery with Connor Shaw's inflection. I hope for his sake Niles finds his own voice."

"Tough criticism coming from a Razzie nominee."

"That was honorary."

We met Dina on her way down. She was wearing an aggressively glamorous red evening gown with bare feet. I watched her process the two of us together, coming for her. Dina had been up and down those steps since she kindergarten but now she missed one. She recovered before I got the chance to help her.

"We should do this in private," I told her.

Dina turned around before replying. It concealed her expression but her back was ramrod straight.

"Come on up," she said, waving like it had been a long day but she would do us the favor. By the time Dina was back behind her desk, she was even-keeled.

It was time for my spotlight moment. I should have been reveling in the reveal, but the whole thing made me nauseous.

"I know what got Layne Lackey killed," I began.

"Do you?" Dina said. She locked down, elbows on the table, mouth hidden behind her hands.

"Layne was looking into the Jove Brand film rights. Could they be transferred? Could they be sold? It turns out they can and they can't."

"What does that mean?" Missy asked.

"Only a male can inherit, but the inheritor can transfer the rights to any member of the Calabria family. The contract doesn't specify that the family member has to be a blood relative." I watched Missy closely when I said the next part. "Marrying in is kosher."

Missy looked down, took a breath. Every actor had their process for getting into character. When Missy looked back up, she betrayed nothing.

For her part, Dina didn't look surprised, which surprised me plenty.

"Oh my God," I said, addressing her. "You knew about the wedding? Did Kit reach out to you?"

Dina's eyes swelled with the same dark intensity they had our first night together in Hong Kong. "He told me. He mentioned they were starting a family right away."

I struggled to keep my voice even. "You played me. Made me feel guilty so I'd distance myself, in case Kit let me in on the happy secret."

When Missy spoke, her voice was distant. "What do you mean, Dina played you?"

I unwrapped Ray's present. The knotted ribbon appeared complex but fell apart with a good tug. The time had come to confess. "Dina and I had an affair while *Near Death* was filming. After Kit banned her from the set, she went looking for a spy. Being Jove Brand, I was the obvious choice."

Missy looked from me to Dina. Her composure didn't falter. I couldn't tell what she was thinking, which was a mercy I didn't deserve. I raised the lid on Ray's present. "You got everything you wanted out of Jove Brand, didn't you, Dina? Out of me."

Dina stayed the course, mouth clamped shut. Her slightly flaring nostrils were the only sign I was making a dent. I held back the one question I wasn't sure I wanted answered and kept to the thread. "Kit knew the most crucial time was during the delivery of the print. If the only print of *Near Death* was destroyed, the Calabrias would lose the rights forever."

I pulled out a beautiful wood case and set my thumb against the brass panel. The latches popped open. Then I told Missy the secret I'd kept for eighteen years.

"So we hatched a plan. Kit would play decoy and fly with a dummy print. Meanwhile, I would deliver the real print via motorcycle. Our theory being no one would believe a Calabria would trust Jove Brand's fate to anyone else. When Kit took off, it was with a load of empty cans."

Missy held her breath. Dina was squeezing her hands blue.

"I always assumed that our plan worked, and Kit sacrificed himself to save the franchise. But Kit's killer knew about our plan. Because I told her. To grandstand. To make sure she knew it was me who saved the day."

Missy's gaze bored into Dina. Dina stood up and turned toward the ocean. The glass held the sea change at bay. Her reflection was a ghost against the night.

"What choice did I have left? Kit taunted me. Told me they'd be making babies, right away. He wanted me to know there was no chance I would ever get what should have been mine."

Dina was starting to crack. I forced myself to forge ahead.

"You wanted *Near Death's* print delivered, to keep the franchise safe. Once you knew Kit didn't have the real print, his fate was sealed. Those who didn't believe Kit's plane crash was an accident would blame the usual suspects. After all, Kit himself thought the Russians were behind the overdose of Bryce Crisp's intended successor. I latched on to the same theory, partly because I wanted to believe Kit's death wasn't my fault, but mostly because without a male heir, you had nothing to gain."

Dina found my specter in the glass. It was in her eyes. I said it as I thought it.

"Unless you knew an heir was already on the way."

Dina didn't turn from the tide. "I knew it would be a boy. I knew the moment it happened." Her eyes were eighteen years and a continent away. "At the eleventh hour, my dream had come true. It was fate."

I angled myself to watch both the door and Dina, now that I knew what she was capable of. "From his files, Lackey figured all this out too. But when he died, he was chasing a different secret. Did Layne approach you, Dina? Or did you guess?"

"I'm not taking pitches tonight," Dina said.

I opened Ray's box. The multi-tool went into my breast pocket. The Quarreler I kept in my hand. "Layne theorized that Kit, knowing his life was in danger, might have left a will. Lackey wanted to get his hands on it, bad. Bad enough to break into Missy's place to find it."

I turned to Missy. I had more things to watch than I had eyes. "But you took Kit's will wherever you went, every day for eighteen years."

If Dina had a panic button or shotgun tucked away in a drawer, now was the time. I broke the Quarreler open to find a red quiver staring back at me. There were no other options. When I went to take the watch box from her, Missy held on to it. Her voice was calm, controlled.

"What are you doing, Ken?"

"It's time to let go, Missy."

Missy released the box, her hand quaking. Not wanting to put my weapon down, I flipped it open with one hand and freed the watch from its protective foam.

Dina turned to face me. "This is cruel, what you're doing. Think about Dean."

I didn't have a free hand for pointing fingers. "I am. In fact, I'm the only one thinking about Dean."

Having failed at weaponizing guilt, Dina resorted to gaslighting. "This is a trick. Well, it's not going to work. Outside of this room, our words won't mean anything."

I nodded. "You're right, Dina. But pictures are worth a thousand words."

I triggered the watch's concealed play button. The screen slowly glowed to life. On it, Kit looked tired. His dark beard was showing its first white strands. Stress would do that to you. Both Dina and Missy thought they knew what he was going to say. I thought I knew too.

We were all wrong.

"You're in the shower right now, so I'll keep this short." Kit's image was distorted in the fish-eye lens. His voice was a distant specter. "If the Russians take a shot at me, they're taking it tonight, but Ken and I have them beat. I feel sorry for anyone who tries. Ken almost died too many times to count during filming and never even batted an eye. Whatever happened to him as a kid, my dearest Miss Cee, dude needs therapy."

Kit looked over toward the bathroom. The shower was running. I looked over at Missy now. Seeing Kit again tore down the barriers that had held fast her entire adult life. Her expression didn't waver, but silent tears rolled down her face.

It hit me harder than if she had broken down. There was crying and there was crying and then there was Missy Cazale. On the small screen, eighteen years in the past, Kit addressed her for the last time.

"I wanted to say I love you and I wish we had the chance to make all those movies we talked about. I'll never know what you saw in me, but I'm forever thankful you did. Now, time to make it formal."

Kit took a breath and cleared his throat.

"I, Kit Calabria, being of sound mind and body, hereby transfer the rights to Jove Brand to my sister, Dina, who should have had them all along."

Kit laughed, once, surprised at himself. "Guess I'm off script, but it sounds right, now that I've said it. After our call, Dina, I felt so sick. No, what I felt like was Pop. I have to stop thinking about what he wanted and start thinking about what's right. Jove Brand is all yours now, whether you birth a boy or not, so for God's sake stop trying. No one is that Catholic."

Kit turned his head at the sound of the shower stopping. From the bathroom, Past Missy said something the camera didn't pick up.

"I love you both, you gifted chicks," Kit said. He held for a two-count to help the edit, then the screen went black.

The three of us sat there, silent.

I had been 100 percent certain Kit was about to transfer the rights to Missy. Did Missy suspect it too? Did she even know the watch really worked? Maybe it broke before she could find out, or maybe she couldn't bring herself to look. Either way, Missy didn't want to battle Dina over Jove Brand. She didn't want Jove Brand. She wanted Kit. They had their June wedding, but the summer sun never shined on her again.

Missy was gathering but now Dina broke. Everything she had dammed up for eighteen years came rushing out. She wailed and shook and sunk to the ground.

I guess I would have too, if I had killed the brother who loved me for nothing.

"I didn't answer the phone. Why didn't I answer the phone? I. Should. Have. Answered. The. Phone."

I knelt next to Dina while the tide rolled in.

"Fate sent Dean. Fate made sure the rights would be safe."

Fate wasn't responsible for either of those things. That's why I didn't comfort her. That, and having just witnessed Kit being himself for the last, best time.

If I was ever going to get Dina when she was weak, the time was now.

"He was blackmailing you, wasn't he?" I asked. "Layne Lackey. The condo, the car. And he kept turning up the heat. Him, I understand. You did what you had to do. But why Sir Collin? Did Layne tip him somehow?"

"What?" Dina looked up at me in genuine confusion.

I sent some confusion back. "You didn't kill them?"

"It wasn't Fedorov?" Dina asked.

Missy found her feet. Her presence filled the room. She was a giant on the screen, but that was nothing compared to her live. She was done crying.

"You killed me too, Dina."

Looking at Missy was like staring into an eclipse. Dina had to shade her eyes.

"Since Kit died, the only way I could live was to become someone else. You killed me too." Missy's voice was diamond hard. "How could you fathom what you were doing? You've never loved anyone but yourself."

Missy stopped in the doorway. "You're every measure your father's daughter."

Dina swallowed a breath. Missy answered before Dina could ask.

"I won't tell, but not for you." The doorway was somehow big enough to let Missy pass. She didn't look back. "I'll stay quiet because I loved Kit, and love means sacrifice."

I'm not sure how long it took for Missy's spell to break. My brain rebooted to a blank screen. I had solved Missy's mystery and come up empty on mine. Sir Collin and Layne Lackey's deaths had nothing to do with *Near Death*.

Nothing at all.

"Who the hell is the killer?" I went to rub my forehead and smacked myself with the Quarreler.

Dina was anchored in place. "I don't know. But everyone's down there waiting. What am I going to tell them?"

It wasn't that I couldn't prove Dina did it. Proof didn't matter. This wasn't about me or what I thought was right. I knew what Missy wanted, and what Dean didn't want.

In the end, it came down to Kit.

Kit was bigger than vengeance. He wouldn't have wanted his sister dying in prison. He wouldn't have wanted his nephew marrying Fedorov's daughter in some weird dynastic movie deal. Kit gave his life to save Jove Brand. Expose Dina now, and everything he died for would be tarnished.

I handed the watch to Dina. "Let Kit tell them."

Dina turned on her webcam to check the damage. She was in the middle of fixing her face when she almost broke down again. "Oh God. Dean."

"Dean will be fine. Better than fine. He'll be free," I said.

Dina muttered to herself as she revised her presentation. "I can play this, then keep everything else the same. At least I don't have change anything about Niles."

"What about Niles?" I asked.

Talking it out would help Dina get her sea legs back, and it wasn't like I was busy solving two murders or clearing my name.

Dina took a makeup bag out of a drawer. She tried to reapply her mascara, but her hand wouldn't stop shaking.

"Niles's connection to Brand, his grandfather being Bowman Fletcher's editor." Dina started to steady. Talking about what wasn't really on her mind helped her recover. "Then the big coming out. A gay Brand. How's that for diversity?"

"Niles is gay?" I asked.

"And into daddies." Dina smirked. "I told you: Niles was dying to meet all the old Brands, so we introduced him to Bryce Crisp. It was love at first sight. They've been shacked up ever since."

Niles was the younger man at Bryce's place?

Bryce had seen the Jove Brand contract.

That's *Gamesman*, Niles had said to me on the stairs, before sticking the drop like a gymnast. Niles, the action star. Niles, who'd been taking motorcycle lessons. That's when it finally clicked.

"Niles Endsworth is the Black Knight."

"What?" Dina said.

"Niles is the killer. The gloves, the Black Knight outfit, the motorcycle, he cribbed all of it from Bryce."

And it was how both Chevalier and Stern got to Bryce's so quick. Bryce told Niles about our meeting, then Niles dropped a dime to Stern and Dean. He was going to kill Bryce with me placed at the scene. It took me a minute to put it all together. Pacing helped.

"Fedorov told me Fletcher had an affair with his editor's daughter. Niles must think he's Fletcher's son. In his head, if the rights revert, they revert to him."

"No way that's true," Dina said.

"It doesn't have to be true. It only has to be the story Niles believes." Fedorov, of all people, had been right. I imagined Niles, peeking out from Bryce Crisp's kitchen to discover me cosplaying. "Niles believes becoming Jove Brand is his birthright. The idea of anyone else playing the role must blow his top."

Dina's jaw dropped. "He replaced Hamilton Price."

"Was Niles in England when Ham died?"

"They were dating," Dina replied. Her voice fell to a whisper. "And it was his idea, using you on *Beautiful Downtown Burbank*."

I didn't have time to get incensed on my own behalf. I was too busy thinking about someone else. Someone who had confided in Niles. Someone who, Niles thought, was about to steal his inheritance.

"Dean!"

I snatched a fountain pen off Dina's desk before hitting a sprint and took the stairs in bounds. I passed through the fire pit and stopped at the top of the spiral stair, scanning for Dean. No way the guest of honor should be alone, but none of the clusters of party-goers surrounded him. Where was he?

A three-story metal spiral staircase was not designed for fast transit. I forced myself to take it a step at a time. I hurdled the last turn of the spiral and pushed my way through the crowd toward Dean's room, doing my best to conceal the Quarreler behind my thigh. The optical illusion of the whorling hall got me angling so far sideways I almost wiped out. The iris door was sealed but that meant nothing. There was another way into Dean's room, for someone who could do what Niles could.

I punched in the code. The second the opening was big enough, I dove through. I rolled to a crouch, aiming to put a fléchette into Niles Endsworth, but my sights were empty.

I stalked across the room, mindful of being blindsided. None of the shadows were big enough to jump out of, but I pointed the Quarreler at them anyway. Two bodies were waiting for me on the terrace.

19

NILES MUST HAVE GOTTEN TO STAVROS FIRST, BECAUSE
he was purple as a grape and done twitching. But Dean was still
fighting, kicking like he was trying to paddle on dry land.

"I'm here, kid." I dropped the Quarreler and pulled out the
multi-tool. "You aren't going to like this but it's gotta happen."

I unscrewed Dina's pen and dumped out its guts. The rear half
had the better tube. I snapped the knife blade open, tucked the tube
into my left hand and used my forefinger to mark the indentation
under Dean's Adam's apple.

I took a breath and slit Dean's throat.

I cut an opening about the size of my finger tip, pushing firmly.
The sensation of the blade slipping through Dean's neck and into

his airway made me burst into a full sweat. I set down the knife and took the pen tube into my right hand while pinching the cut open with my left.

If I had done everything right, there wouldn't be much blood, but I'd only ever witnessed the procedure the one time. It saved me from killing my friend then. It was going to keep Niles Endsworth from racking up another victim now.

It was the helicopter kick everyone kept bringing up. There had been no time to practice it. The wind gets pretty wicked thirteen stories high. My jacket might as well have been a parachute. But when I jumped out of the helicopter, the wind switched direction and what had been a parachute became a pair of wings. Yuen didn't budge—he trusted me to adjust. But I didn't. Desperate to get the shot and not look like the amateur I was, I panicked, and my foot caught him flush on the throat.

Kit was all over it. He rushed to the rescue with his dad's cigar trimmer in one hand and the pen he used to write the script in the other. I did Kit's dirty work, but he kept my hands clean. Now it was my turn.

Getting the tube in was a nightmare. Screwing it down worked better than pushing. Beads of sweat rained off my face to pool with Dean's tears.

The first drink of air hit Dean's lungs. His back arched as his body sucked in all the oxygen it could get. I didn't have any tape, but I did have a bow tie. I slipped it onto Dean and used the knot to anchor the tube in place.

"Don't worry kid," I said. "Chicks dig scars."

Niles was long gone, but I spotted where he must have dropped. The terraces below were fifteen feet down. The ones after were thirty. Hundreds of feet later those were rocks and ocean. The closest terrace was directly under this one. Whatever technique Niles used to make sure he landed on it I didn't know. I was going to have to catch him the old-fashioned way.

I heard the Quarreler skidding over the edge too late. I spun as it fell toward the waiting waves, caught a glint of metal, and delivered a tight crescent kick that sent a pistol tumbling off to join it.

All I knew was, someone had snuck up behind me. My kick had been delivered on instinct. As it connected, I realized I was attacking a cop. Stern's counter-kick swept out my base leg. I posted an arm to stop myself from face-planting. Stuck in a Twister position, I raised my free hand to ward her off.

"Wait! It's Endsworth!" I yelled.

Against the night sky, the bow tie around Dean's neck all but concealed the tube. Between the timeline and the motive and the details there was too much to cover to convince Stern it wasn't me. First and foremost, I wanted to explain why she didn't pass Niles Endsworth on her way here. Why no one passed him on the stair up to the roof where Sir Collin died. Because he didn't use the stairs.

I said the first five words that came to mind.

"Niles used parkour! To kill!"

Stern's eyes flicked toward the ledge to confirm her gun was gone. There was no concealing a backup piece in that dress. She had dumped her shoes on the way. What Stern saw was the prime suspect and two bodies. I needed her to believe me. Still, it was hard to say out loud.

"Dean's my son."

Stern froze, glanced from Dean to me and back.

"Look at him. Look at his face. I wouldn't kill my own kid."

Stern circled me to get closer to Dean. She saw his fair hair and skin. His features, reminiscent of renaissance sculpture. She had recently watched *Near Death*, with a twenty-one year-old Ken Allen, and now she was looking at Dean Calabria, eighteen years later.

Stern knelt down to make sure Dean stayed stable. "Go, Allen. But I'm right behind you."

I was sprinting across Dean's gym on the quest for medical help when Dina burst through the door.

"Where's Dean?"

I pointed toward the balcony. "He's alive but needs help now."

Dina's expression was a mix of relief, gratitude, and apology. She rushed to the wall intercom and started shouting orders.

Something in me I had been holding down for decades boiled to the surface. My skin was pulsing in time with my heartbeat. My scalp was so hot, I thought my hair might burst into flames.

My whole life, I never wanted to strike anyone in anger. Sure, I had wanted to succeed and I had wanted to win and I had wanted to survive. But never had I wanted to hurt someone for the sake of hurting them.

It wasn't only that Niles had gone after Dean or that Niles was trying to frame me. It was that the bastard wouldn't stand toe-to-toe. He was a bully who ambushed people who couldn't defend themselves in the first place. I wanted to hammer a hole straight through Niles Endsworth's perfect face.

I found the stairs at the entrance to the ballroom and descended a smooth spiral like the inside of a shell. The room at the end of the hall was double the size of Dean's gym above. A suitable space for a museum.

A lot of people became hoarders when their parents died, unwilling or unable to discard anything connected to them. Now imagine someone whose father had made a dozen big-budget movies.

The cavernous space was crammed with everything Jove Brand. Miniatures and models lined aisles and hung from ceilings. Racks and stands and cases displayed everything from prop weapons to typewriters to tea sets. Mannequins stood in costume. The walls were papered in discarded matte paintings, creating portals to places that had only ever existed in the minds of the audience.

I stalked the history of us all, one Jove Brand hunting another. One of the mannequins was naked, with Niles's tux pooled at its feet. He had taken the time to get into character.

Silhouetted against the terrace, Niles was buckling on the para-suit from *Flights of Fancy*. I was too late. There was no closing the distance in time. My Quarreler was gone. My knife was forgotten on the terrace above. The only thing I had to reach Niles was my voice.

"You better run!"

Niles stopped mid-latch. I walked forward confidently, in no rush, standing tall, arms wide like I was trying to scare off a bear.

"We both know you can't take me."

Stern had been right the whole time but she'd suspected the wrong man. Maybe Niles really was Bowman Fletcher's son, or maybe, like so many of us who don't know our fathers, he just needed to believe that his was special. That he was a lost prince questing to claim his kingdom.

Maybe he had planned to kill Sir Collin all along and had invited me to play patsy. Or maybe Niles's tepid audience reception combined with my ovations had ruined his big moment, detonated his inner doomsday device, and sent him spiraling into fantasyland. That's what I was hoping for. That in his head, I had usurped him as Jove Brand.

I was praying I was the villain in Niles Endsworth's story.

"What are you waiting for?" I asked. "Fly away, little pretender. Everyone knows if it were for real, I'm the toughest Brand, hands down."

Every word brought me a step closer.

"Put me in a room with Connor Shaw, Bryce Crisp, and Sir Collin, and I'd wipe the floor with all of them at the same time. Same goes for you, poser."

Niles was twitching. His leg straps hung loose and he was flicking the quick release buckle on his chest over and over, as if he had a nervous tic.

"That's why you've been framing me." I tossed my tuxedo jacket aside, a casual show of confidence that cost me my protection. "Why you ran at Bryce's. Because you can't take me. You know it, I know it, and the world knows it. So float away, Mary Poppins, before I beat you back to reality."

Niles looked toward the terrace, his smart and his crazy doing battle. I nearly had him, but improv was never one of my strengths. I searched for something to tilt him over.

"I have the Quarreler and I have the jacket and I have the Stag. There can only be one Jove Brand, and that's me. Now and forever."

Niles triggered the quick release and charged me. I asked for it, now I was going to get it. He was fifteen years younger than me, at his physical peak, and there was no drug testing to get a SAG card. He had spent his whole life training to be Jove Brand and fulfill his destiny. He had killed anyone who got in the way. Everything—all the work and the pain and the necessary deeds—had led to this moment.

Niles trucked in with full commitment. Usually, charging attacks were easy to avoid, but his flying knee nearly ended me because I was too busy processing what he was wearing.

He was in my Jove Brand wardrobe from *Near Death*, sporting the actual salmon jacket I wore eighteen years ago. Here's a little bit of trivia: I picked it out. What could I say? It was stylish back then. Niles had abandoned the Black Knight for another role: Ken Allen.

Being late on the draw forced me to block the knee. The metric ton of momentum behind it required the use of both arms to soak. Niles hit a beautiful switch in midair, his rear knee coming up to slam my own hands into my face.

Niles launched a back kick the instant he touched down, followed immediately with a question-mark kick I checked way too late. There was a certain sting you felt when a bone broke. My forearm stung that way.

I thought I had an opening but got blasted with a side kick I never saw coming. Niles had been waiting for me. It caught me clean in the ribs and ripped the wind from my lungs. He used the opportunity to put out a picture-perfect hook kick into a round kick designed to tap both my temples.

I slipped the first kick and checked the second with my broken arm. It felt like when the dentist pokes to see if you're numb enough to get to work but you aren't. Niles threw a straight rear hand into a spinning back fist meant to catch me as I circled out. I slipped both by the skin of my teeth. By all rights I should have eaten the attacks, except the sequence of techniques tweaked my muscle memory.

I was yet to throw a single punch back. Fighting could be like tennis. If you controlled the pace and kept sending hard shots in, your opponent was never able to mount their own offense.

Niles had a level of cardio achievable only through obsession. He didn't hesitate at all, firing off a lead hand at my liver into a high backfist into a lead hook. His continuation into a scything back elbow into an uppercut was when I realized how I had miraculously survived the onslaught. There was only one guy I had ever known who employed that specific combination.

Me.

Niles Endsworth wasn't only dressing the part. He was imitating me in *Near Death*, mimicking all my moves, down to crushing throats. Everyone he had killed, he had killed playing Ken Allen.

I was experiencing the hypothetical situation every aging athlete played out in their heads. Could you beat a past version of yourself? Did the experience you'd gained outweigh the vigor of youth? The truth was, unless someone invented a time machine, you'd never know.

I was about to find out.

Niles came off his uppercut with a sweeping gesture intended to force my guard aside for the rear hand knockout. Knowing what was coming helped time his blur of a punch. I rolled an elbow over it, forcing it down. My follow-up back fist connected. There wasn't a lot behind it. Niles was so damn fast I didn't want to strike out swinging for the fences.

I might as well have slapped a statue for all the reaction I got. If Niles was cycling, which with his body-fat percentage you better believe he was, he was going to be nigh impossible to drop. On top of that, he was basking in the extreme self-confidence of being undefeated. When you had never been beaten, you fought without fear.

I swept my left hand to cover the line of attack as I circled out. Niles did the same and our arms crossed like swords, except my blade had a crack in it. I snapped my hand down, testing his guard. Niles soaked it like a tempered spring and a numbing shock ran from my fingertips to my elbow. We circled, wrists crossed, our rear hands loose under our chins. The mirror was reflecting back better than what I was giving it.

I tried to think about all the guys who had cleaned my clock over the last twenty years. What were my weaknesses back then? What lessons had I learned at the end of a fist?

Niles went for a low kick. I yanked his arm to hiccup the kick and checked it with my back foot. Ducking under Niles's follow-up high kick, I spun into a sweep aimed at his knee. Niles's rear leg supported all his weight. If my sweep landed, it was over.

But Niles whirled his kick into a butterfly twist. I used to be able to pull that combination off, way back when. His rear leg brushed my hair as my sweep passed under his airborne body. If you were choreographing a fight, you couldn't have hoped for a cleaner exchange.

Our left legs clashed as we threw low round kicks at the same time. Then our right legs, as we high kicked. I caught the ghost of a wince on Niles's face as our shins collided at full speed. So I had one advantage: a lifetime of taking damage. My nerves were deader, my bones more ragged. I knew how to fight hurt. How to keep going on an empty tank.

If Niles were me, I'd throw a side kick to preserve distance and reset. On that theory, I launched a leg on an intercept course. Our knees clashed like charging rams. I was ready for it, Niles wasn't, and a grunt of pain escaped before he could silence it. When Niles threw a knife hand toward my eyes I met it with my own, the ridge of my hand slamming into the pinkie he fused shooting *Raid the Roof*. The one reminder he had that he was human.

Niles withdrew the crippled digit on instinct. I used the opening to put a right hook into the brick wall of his abdomen. I missed a follow-up uppercut, but in a moment of inspiration I reversed direction and chopped him on the Adam's apple.

It was a short, quick tap, but Niles recoiled like he'd been stabbed.

I put a finger in his face. "You aren't Jove Brand."

Good and pissed off, Niles tried to slap my hand away. I circled under the attempt and chopped the side of his neck. I've hit people harder with pillows, but it made him stagger back.

"You aren't even a second-rate Ken Allen."

Niles absolutely lost it. He issued a blistering series of punches and kicks, jumping and dropping, twisting and spinning. If I hadn't dreamt up all the combinations, if I hadn't relived them every time I tortured myself by looping *Near Death* at a hundred pop culture conventions, I would be dead.

Still, I was plenty busy, slipping and checking, circling and soaking, waiting for my moment. Niles slowed down a hair. When he attempted my patented flying backfist into a midair direction change spin-kick, I clotheslined him across the neck. He went down hard, the back of his skull slamming into the stone floor.

I thought it was over, but Niles kipped up, launching to his feet without using his hands. Right into the chop I had waiting for him. It caught him under the chin and he went back down.

I tried to end it then, but Niles rolled away and vaulted into a back handspring before I was able to bury a knee in his windpipe. That he still had enough gas in his tank to pull off a floor routine was terrifying. His eyes were wild as he tried to comprehend what was happening, madly rewriting his story to fit the changing narrative.

Fighting to keep my breath even, I committed to belief in my character. If ever I needed to deliver an authentic performance, the time was now.

"No, not Jove Brand. Not even close. Just Niles Endsworth. And Niles Endsworth is done. I saved Dean. It's over for you. The end."

Niles looked over my shoulder, then over his own, toward the terrace.

"Freeze!" Stern yelled. "Get your dicks in the dirt, both of you." I smiled at Niles as I took a knee. I'd won by running out the clock. The bastard grinned right back. Except my expression was coy and his was feral. He turned and sprinted toward the terrace.

"I'll shoot!" Stern yelled at his back.

Niles didn't listen. There was no time for the para-suit. He vaulted into the night sky like he expected something to catch him. A giant eagle maybe, or a passing hot-air balloon. But nothing did. His leap hit an apex, then he dropped like a rock.

Stern ran to the terrace to look over the railing. I hobbled after to join her, staring down into the dark, rolling water.

Stern looked at the platinum pistol prop in her hand. "Guess he thought it was real."

"Yes, he did," I replied. "All of it."

We watched the water for a while, searching for any sign.

"You know the rule," I said. "If there's no body, we'll see him in the sequel."

As if on cue, the waves pounded Niles Endsworth's corpse against the cliffs. His body was swept out and back until one of his legs got lodged in the rocks. His head stayed underwater.

I should have been worried about Dean. About there being any evidence at all Niles was the killer. I should have been praying that when Bryce Crisp heard Niles was dead he would come forward with everything he knew. I should have been on the phone with Mercie Goodday, preparing a defense.

But all I could think about was what a movie this would make. I wondered who they would get to play me. Someone who looked the part. Blond hair and blue eyes were a must.

My vote was for Daniel Craig.

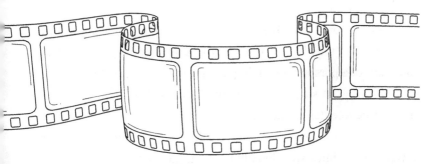

Epilogue

WHAT COULD A MILLION BUCKS BUY YOU IN THIS TOWN? Not much, but it made for a decent down payment. Layne Lackey could have croaked in his condo and it wouldn't have brought the price down, not in a city where so many endings are self-inflicted. But after his sister heard me out, she sold it to me at market value. She even gave me a deal on his collection.

Dean was doing okay. Looking back, he'd had a strong hunch about me but didn't trust his gut enough to voice it, which made him a chip off the old block.

You didn't live in the gym because of your mother. When a young man strapped gloves on, his father's touch tightened the laces.

I wish I could say Missy got her happy ending, but she wasn't in that kind of tale. Hers was a tragedy. Some people get lucky and find their one person. God help them if they lost them. At least she got closure. The suspicions haunting her had been real. She was finally free to enter her next act.

I could have gone back to my old gig, got more money for fewer clients, but I was done being a bit player in someone else's vehicle. So I hung out a shingle and waited for word to spread. Despite how everything turned out—or maybe because of it—Dina helped me with the license, like she said she would. She also issued me special usage rights. On paper, I was a parody. She stopped short of officially endorsing me, which was fine. When everything came out, I figured it would be all the PR I needed.

Instead Stern got a lot of attention she didn't want. She was the only cop on the scene and therefore the hero who had saved Ken Allen, damsel in distress. Now she was a celebrity cop, put on the sort of fluff cases she spent her whole career avoiding. She was not amused. At least she didn't arrest me at the scene. Probably because she wanted me healthy for the rematch.

Seven weeks went by while I lived off the sale of my condo and refused book deals for the story of the Jove Brand murders. It was easy money. I'd be set for life and the main attraction at all the cons. I'd be liked and favorited instead of roasted across all platforms.

If I wanted, I could finally make the story all about me. Have my big redemption moment. But it meant airing the dirty laundry. It meant turning people into characters and making their deaths plot-points. I'd have to make my bones displaying their skeletons.

No way.

I had never talked. And I never would.

Dina took advantage of all the free media to announce a new Jove Brand had been chosen and the old screenplay scrapped. Layne Lackey's lifelong dream was coming true. Calabria Films bought *Ungentlemanly Warfare* from Layne Lackey's estate. It was garbage, but it had a great title. The rest could be fixed in rewrites.

Ray helped renovate my new digs. And by helped I mean he did everything while I played gofer and blended a lot of smoothies. Knowing how he felt about my privacy, I slept in full pajamas, rolled up in a sleeping bag, but I wasn't about to criticize how my guardian angel went about his business.

Among other renovations, he set up a musical cue in place of a bell when the front door opened. It gave me time to hit my mark.

Clutching a locked attaché, Mercie Goodday was dressed for business. "You've got your desk backwards."

Backwards was a matter of perspective. I didn't belong in Tender's seat. The person behind the desk offered the assignments, he didn't accept them.

"Yeah, it's pretty heavy," I said.

"But you have so much free time," Mercie replied. She set the attaché down on the desk and took a seat. "Maybe you should consider lowering your rates."

I didn't take the bait. Missy had taught me otherwise. She probably learned it from Mercie in the first place. I wasn't out to troll the stream. I wanted the big fish.

"I can't speak to your competence, but my clients love your concept, and based on your prior vocation, they attest you can be discreet," Mercie said.

"I'm definitely discreet." I knew better than to claim competence.

Mercie studied me for a while but failed to locate the mess she'd met in a jail cell. She opened up the attaché and took out an NDA. I signed it without being asked, making sure to use the button on my pen which produced ink. All of Ray's housewarming gifts had the potential to burn the place down.

Mercie confirmed my signature before breaking the silence. "I have a client who has been accused of a sexual assault she did not commit. She has an airtight alibi but employing it would end her career."

"What's the alibi?"

"She was big-game hunting."

"Yeah, that'll do it."

"My client wants to employ you to prove her innocence while maintaining her reputation. Operating under me will provide privilege, but time is a factor. We are prepared to compensate you for round-the-clock action and pay any expenses you incur." Mercie sat back and crossed her legs. She was good at it. "What do you say, Mr. Allen?"

When I opened the file and saw who was staring back at me, I let out a whistle. Jove Brand could have kept his composure, but Ken Allen would never be that level of cool.

"That's PI Allen, Miss Goodday. And I say let the games begin."

The End

Acknowledgments

Each and every person who touched this book made it better.

In chronological order:

To my mother, who passed on a love of reading. Look Ma, I did it!

To my wife, who was there every day and has never, ever gotten sick of me agonizing over every last word.

To NaNoWriMoTown and Owen Bondono, for keeping that first draft flowing.

Next comes Rick Marshall, who caught many, many errors no one else ever had to see. Mel Pinsler pointed out character shortcomings and possible plot holes. Rob Reeve performed a detailed editorial pass before it went out into the world.

I owe a tremendous debt to Pitchwars. Special thanks to Gigi Pandian, the best role model a writer could have. Gigi helped me believe in my writing, which is the greatest gift anyone can give a writer.

Tina Chan, Tiffany Liu, and Irene Reed provided insights regarding cultural nuances in the text. Thank you.

To my agent Lucienne Diver, for believing. There is insufficient space here to sing her praises. Thank you, thank you, thank you.

The book owes its razor edge to the expertise of my editor, Helga Schier. I am incredibly fortunate to have her in my corner.

Thanks to the CamCat team. Sue Arroyo, whose love of books shines through, Laura Wooffitt marketing maven, and Maryann Appel, who created an image that crystalized a complicated concept.

As always, any mistakes or shortcomings are mine, and mine alone.

For Further Discussion

1. What drew you to the book? Did the book deliver?

2. Which fictional character is Ken Allen based on? How are they alike? How are they different?

3. In mystery, what do you think is more important, plot or character?

4. What is going on behind in other character's heads during the scenes? For example, what do you think Dean is thinking when he is talking to Ken? What is Dina thinking when Ken Allen shows up asking questions about her dark secret?

5. What hints are laid for future books in the series in this book? Which characters do you want to see again?

6. What do you think is the big secret in Ken Allen's personal life?

7. Which one of Ken's gadgets is your favorite? Why?

8. How relevant are martial arts and the philosophy behind them to Ken's character?

9. Ken Allen's dead pan humor is relevant to the story. Which one is your favorite line? Why?

10. If this were turned into a movie, who should play the main characters?

About the Author

J. A. Crawford wanted to grow up to be a superhero. He studied Criminal Justice at Wayne State University, specializing in criminal procedure and interrogation. Despite what his family thinks, Joe is not a spy.

When he isn't writing, he travels the country investigating disaster sites. Before that, he taught Criminal Justice, Montessori Kindergarten, and several martial arts. Joe is an alum of the Pitchwars program. Joe has too many interests and finds every topic under the sun absolutely fascinating. He especially loves the stories behind the stories.

Joe splits his time between Michigan and California. He is married to his first and biggest fan, who is not allowed to bring home any more pets.

———

Check in on Joe at **www.jacrawford.net**

For more Jove Brand lore, visit
www.jovebrandfan.com

If you enjoyed
Jove Brand Is Near Death **by J. A. Crawford,**
then try this excerpt from
Beneath the Marigolds **by Emily C. Whitson.**

Prologue

knew too much. On that island, on that godforsaken singles' retreat.
I knew too much.

I ruminated on that thought, chewing it carefully, repeatedly, while Magda the makeup artist transformed me into a life-size, porcelain doll of nightmares. Ghastly white face, penciled-in eyebrows, blood-red lips. I'd look beautiful from a distance, she had told me, leaving the other part of the sentence unspoken: *up close, it's frightening.* She tsked as she dabbed my damp forehead for the fourth time, her Russian accent thickening with frustration.

"Vhy you sveating so much?"

I worried my voice would come out haggard, so I shrugged, a little too forcefully. Magda shook her head, her pink bob sashaying amongst the grand, all-white bathroom, as she muttered something foreign under her breath. My eyes danced across the various makeup brushes on the vanity until they landed on one in particular. I shifted my weight in the silk-cushioned chair, toyed with my watch.

"Magda, what do you want out of this retreat?"

No response.

Did she not hear me, or did she choose not to respond? In the silence, I was able to hear Christina's high-heeled footsteps outside the bathroom.

Click, clack. Click, click.

When I first met the host of the singles' retreat, I was in awe of her presence, her unflappable poise. Shoulders back, she walked with a purpose, one foot in front of another, and though she was a couple inches shorter than me, she seemed larger than life. Her icy eyes, which were colored with only the faintest shade of blue, seemed to hold the secrets of the world—secrets she intended to keep. But I had stumbled upon them, just a few short hours before, and I was now afraid her gait represented something more sinister: the march of an executioner.

Click, clack. Click, clack.

Her stride matched the even tick of my watch, and a drop of sweat trickled down my back. Was I being ridiculous? Surely Christina wouldn't hurt me. She had been reasonable with me earlier, hadn't she?

"One meenute," Magda shouted at the retreat's host. She doused my fire-red curls in hairspray one last time before asking me if I was ready to go.

"I just need to use the bathroom," I wheezed through shallow breaths. "I'll be right out."

Magda exaggerated her sigh before shuffling out of the white-marble immurement, closing the doors behind her with a huff. My last remnants of safety and rational thinking left with her.

I shoved the vanity chair underneath the handles of the entrance. I grabbed the makeup brush with the flattest head and made my way to the water closet. I gingerly closed the lid of the toilet and slipped off my heels before tip-toeing on top so I could face the window. After removing the beading, I inserted the head of the makeup brush between the frame and glass. The brush's handle cracked under the pressure, but it was enough to lever the glass out of its mounting. I placed the glass on the ground as gently as I've ever handled any object, trying not to make even the slightest of sounds, before hoisting myself up and through the window. I jumped into the black night, only partially illuminated by the full moon and the artificial lights of the retreat. I allowed my eyes to adjust.

And then, I ran.

The loose branches of the island forest whipped at my cheeks, my limbs, my mouth. The soles of my feet split open from fallen twigs and other debris, but the adrenalin kept the pain at bay. I tripped over something unseen, and my hands broke my fall. Just a few cuts, and a little blood. I couldn't see it, but I could feel it.

I jumped up, forcing myself to keep moving. The near darkness was blinding, so I held my bloody hands up, trying to block my face. The farther I ran, the more similar the trunks of the trees became. How long had I been running? I gauged about a mile. I slowed down to gather my bearings. Behind me, the lights of the mansion brightened the sky, but they were only the size of a flower petal from that distance.

I heard the hum of a moving car come and go. I must have been near the road. I was about to keep moving when I heard the snap of twigs. Footsteps. I stopped breathing. I swiveled to my left and right, but nothing. I exhaled. It was just my imagination. I continued away from the lights. Away from the retreat.

And then someone stepped toward me: Christina. Her face was partially covered in darkness, but her pale eyes stood out like fireflies.

"It doesn't have to be like this," she said. Her expression remained a mystery in the darkness.

I turned behind me, but one of her handlers was blocking that path. Christina took another step forward, and I jerked away, tripping over the gnarled roots of the forest in the process. My head broke the fall this time, and my ears rang from the pain.

Her handler reached for my left hand, and for a moment, I thought he was going to help me stand. Instead, he twisted my ring finger to an unnatural position. As my bone cracked, my screams reverberated through the woods.

It was showtime.

1:Ann

'm an attorney. A corporate attorney, to be precise—not the kind most
often portrayed in books and movies. I don't go to court, and I don't
deal with murderers. I close deals—mergers and acquisitions, mostly—
behind my desk in the quiet of my office. In layman's terms: I help
people buy and sell companies. It's not quite as dramatic as the life of
a trial attorney, but it's safe, it pays well, and now that I'm a partner, I
can dedicate some of my time to matters closer to my heart. But like a
trial attorney—and all good attorneys, really—I spend my day combing
through facts.

As such, here are the facts: Reese Marigold, has been missing for
thirty-one days.

She had been scheduled to arrive in Nashville after a four-week stay
at an exclusive singles' retreat. Flight records indicate she boarded her
plane as scheduled, and several witnesses recall seeing a woman on the

flight who matched Reese's description: mid-thirties, red hair, about five-four. She was hard to miss: she donned a bubblegum-pink jumpsuit, keeping the hood up and sunglasses on throughout the flight. I remember seeing this eccentric outfit as I waited for Reese at the airport, but I knew from the mannerisms and gait it wasn't Reese. The police think I could have been mistaken, though, so they asked a few witnesses about this rose-clad woman. Apparently she was as quiet as she was eye-catching, ignoring anyone who spoke to her.

"Again," I huffed in the interview room at the police station, "that's not Reese. Reese can talk to a wall. She's a social butterfly." I threw my hands up in exasperation, but no one in the room seemed to care.

Once the flight landed in Nashville, video footage from airport security shows "Reese" de-boarding the plane, collecting her single bag, and heading for ground transportation. She did not make any other stops before getting into the back seat of a beat-up 1992 Ford Festiva. The car was tagless and had tinted windows, so it was impossible to track. It wasn't until police received a tip that they discovered the car three days later near the Riverfront Park, burned to a crisp, ashes littering the ground like confetti.

Only the charred remains of a suitcase were inside. Forensic technicians believe the car was wiped clean before it exploded, although it was difficult to know for certain. Reese's wallet and cell phone were found about thirty feet away, concealed in the overgrown grass.

Her cell phone history didn't reveal much. There was a missed call from an ex-boyfriend, Luca Ferrari, made two weeks before the retreat started. Reese's relationship with Luca had ended seven years prior, but since Reese was granted an order of protection after Luca attacked her, he was automatically suspect.

To my relief and disappointment, Luca has a rock-solid alibi. He also lives two-thousand miles away in Los Angeles—has for six years now.

Police interviewed several other men who had relationships with Reese, but each was occupied during the crucial window of opportunity.

There was one noteworthy text. For the entire duration of the singles' retreat, Reese sent only one message to an unregistered number on the last day of her stay. Her radio silence wasn't considered unusual, as the retreat forbids the use of media in an attempt to force participants to focus on "the journey." It said: *I need to get away. Pick me up at the Nashville airport tomorrow at noon.*

The police contacted the phone carrier of the unregistered phone number, but it was determined to be a burner phone. There were no outgoing calls or messages, no history of any kind, except for the single incoming text from Reese. The burner was discovered with her mobile and wallet in the park.

I found all of this disconcerting, especially her silence toward me. The police didn't share my concern, though, as perhaps she was upset that I hadn't attended the retreat with her. She had, after all, been urging me to go. She had even filled out an application for me, earning me a spot on the island along with her. *We could get engaged at the same time,* she had pleaded. For Reese's sake, I pretended to consider. Of course, I didn't go; that wasn't my thing. So Reese went alone. A hopeless romantic, she was always on a mission to find her next man, her miracle, and her latest obsession was this singles' retreat.

So if things didn't go as planned, if she didn't find love, perhaps she was taking out her frustration on me, police supposed. I told them that was ridiculous. In the ten years I've known Reese, I can count on my two hands the number of times I've seen Reese angry. Afraid, yes. Sad, definitely. But petty? Absolutely not. She would never let my worry fester like this over something like not going on a trip with her.

No, something had to have happened on that island. Something terrible.

Right from the start, I knew the retreat seemed too good to be true. Isolated on its own private island, about a ten-minute plane ride from Hawaii, Last Chance was established with the sole intention of helping people find *true love*. A *soulmate*. Give me a break. I begged the police to investigate, but because the island is outside of their jurisdiction, there is only so much they could do without more probable cause.

And besides, they said, Reese wanted to disappear, according to her last text message. She told an employee at the retreat that an associate of hers helped people get out of town. And according to her mom, she ran away countless times in her youth. Before she joined Nashville's most prestigious dance company, she had trouble with drugs and alcohol. Nevermind that she had a turbulent childhood, or that she's been sober for twelve years. Nevermind that she's helped me, and many others, find solace through Alcoholics Anonymous. Nevermind that she was my sponsor in AA for ten years, my closest friend, the only real family I've had since my parents passed. Reese was flighty, shady.

A drunk.

So the investigation dwindled. Life moved on. But not for me. For the past thirty-one days, I have been swimming in the facts of Reese's disappearance. My mind has been laser-focused on her last movements— primarily on the retreat. I haven't eaten, haven't slept. Twice I've awoken to the sound of an ambulance, after passing out from unbearable chest pain, and twice I've been told I had suffered severe panic attacks.

I only began to breathe semi-normally after I sent in my deposit to Last Chance.

I know something happened on that retreat, and I have every intention of finding out what.

CamCat Books

VISIT US ONLINE FOR
MORE BOOKS TO LIVE IN:
CAMCATBOOKS.COM

FOLLOW US

CamCatBooks   @CamCatBooks   @CamCat_Books

CPSIA information can be obtained
at www.ICGtesting.com
Printed in the USA
LVHW091521090921
697436LV00015B/841/J

9 780744 301700